TRUTH CHANGER

Books by Kay L Moody

Truth Seer Trilogy

The Elements of Kamdaria

HER STRENGTH MAY BRING DESTRUCTION.

TRUTH CHANGER

KAY L MOODY

MARTEN
PRESS

Truth Changer
Truth Seer Trilogy Book 3
By Kay L Moody

Published by Marten Press
3731 W 10400 S, Ste 102
South Jordan, UT 84009

www.MartenPress.com

Cover by Shawnda Craig
Edited by Deborah Spencer and Justin Greer

ISBN: 978-1-7324588-4-0

To my children
Thank you for letting me
work on something I love so much.

ONE

"WELCOME BACK."

Carlotta Santini turned to give her most faithful servant a smile. It was a calculated gesture that would help him know he was appreciated—but not too appreciated. He was the only one besides Takara who had ever known her true identity as Judge. She desperately needed him, but she didn't want him to know it.

He did better when he got affirmation. Too much of it made him sloppy.

"Hello, Vikal," Carlotta said to the man. The lime green T on his chest was displayed proudly. He featured it as prominently as the round scar on his forehead. He had received that scar in the catacombs twenty years ago when a flood caused him to hit his head on stone and black out. Vikal was later revived but without the son he had entered the catacombs with.

Carlotta smoothed the wrinkles out of her gray dress pants. Pulsing yellow splotches fell away from Vikal's skin. She knew they represented his eagerness, but the indistinct shapes were nothing more than a nuisance. She used to rely on the colors to know what emotions other's felt. Now, she could read emotions using only voice and body language cues. The less

7

she relied on the colors, the more indistinct their colors and shapes became.

She settled her face into a calm and collected expression, devoid of the relief she felt. Vikal always responded better when he was trying to prove himself.

"Tell me Takara is dead," she said without breaking eye contact.

His head bobbed up and down, the desire to prove himself dripped off his skin in blue-gray drops so heavy, it looked like they were magnetized to the ground. "Yes, we sent a team of taggers with the police just like you ordered. Harrison injected the poison while the police were fighting over whose bubble car to put Takara in. They don't know it was us. I think they suspect, but they also don't care. They're glad she's dead."

"And what about Marco?" she asked as she took a hairbrush from the bag he had brought. "I assume you know where he is."

Vikal cleared his throat, obviously delaying his response as long as possible. "He's with that girl. The one from the catacombs that you thought would save us. We tried to intercept them as they left the Egyptian Council chambers, but we couldn't do it without the Egyptian police suspecting us."

"Why not?"

He swallowed as his eyes found a spot on the ground to stare at. "Unfortunately, we're working *with* the Egyptian Council. We had to in order to stop Takara. It was that girl's idea. I know it's not ideal, but it was the only way."

Carlotta let one of her eyebrows slide up her forehead just enough to make him squirm in place. "Not ideal?"

He reached for the fraying hem of his shirt as he spoke, averting his eyes. "Yes, because now we're on their side and that's ..." His voice trailed off. It took him three excruciating seconds before he understood. In an instant, his eyes lit up and his whole body glowed with realization. "Wait, we *wanted* to be on their side. This is perfect!"

She rolled her eyes at his ignorance and took pleasure in how he squirmed again, tugging harder at the frays in his shirt hem.

She brought the brush to her head and started smoothing the hair that had been matted for months. "We do have one problem. Imara Kalu is now on their side too. Fortunately, I can turn them against her easily. In fact, it's part of my plan."

A rust-colored string of doubt fell away from Vikal. As soon as the emotion escaped him, he shifted his shoulders as if he could shrug the doubt away. "How can you turn them against her? They love her. She and her friends just saved the city. They almost gave her the empty seat on the Egyptian Council, even though she doesn't live in Egypt."

"Really?" Carlotta asked, holding the brush mid-stroke. "Interesting. She will play her part well."

"Her part?"

"Don't worry about that. For now, I need to convince the Egyptian Council to arrest Imara, and then call a global vote to make me judge and ruler of this world."

More strings of doubt snaked their way out of Vikal's skin, but he made fists with his hands as if willing them away. "What do you need? I'll gather the taggers. We know a lot about the Egyptian Council, who they care about, what they love, that sort of thing. We can bribe over half of them. But the other members will be trickier to convince."

Carlotta let out a scoff. "Have you already forgotten my skills? I am the most powerful truth seer this world has ever known. I don't need anything from you."

Vikal's fingers twitched as he stared back at her. He wanted to believe her. He wanted so much to trust implicitly, but the logical part of his mind was clearly making it difficult. He seemed to force a look of hope onto his face, but he couldn't seem to stop himself from asking, "How could you possibly convince them to arrest her?"

She continued brushing through her hair and answered flippantly. He needed to know she only gave an answer as a favor to him. It wasn't something she needed to do. "Blackmail, obviously," she said, brushing through her matted strands. "I'll use my truth seer abilities to find out what each of the Egyptian Council members loves most, and then I'll take it away. I'll have control in less than an hour."

In truth, it would be much more difficult than that. She would need every bit of the information Vikal had gathered, but he didn't need to know that. It would take blackmail, bribery, persuasion, and all her truth seeing abilities. It wouldn't be easy, but as she always did, she would make it *look* easy.

Vikal couldn't hide his doubt anymore. Along with the rust-colored strings now enveloping him, a deep crease appeared between his eyebrows. Tugging on his frayed shirt hem, he said, "We've been trying to get control of the Egyptian Council for years. If you could do it that easily, why didn't we act years ago?"

"Because." She stood up and threw the brush at him, so he'd have to catch it and stop picking at his hem. She lifted her chin into the air. "I can use my truth seer abilities to get what I want out of people when I am with them in person. But I can't get every council member from around the world to vote for me as judge. There are too many of them. For that, we need someone even more persuasive than I am."

Desperation burst from Vikal's skin in a flurry of brown flakes. Carlotta didn't try to hide her disappointment at his lack of belief in her. "How could we find such a person?" he asked.

"That's why Imara has to be arrested," Carlotta said, snatching the brush from his hands. She shook the hair out of her face and swept it behind her shoulders. She made sure to exude the deepest confidence. With each of her tiny movements, Vikal's confidence in her seemed to grow.

Finally, he understood what she needed him to understand. He didn't need to worry about the plan. He only needed to worry about the individual tasks she gave him.

"Oh, and Vikal? One more thing."

"Yes?" he asked, his eyes finally as eager as they had been at the start of the conversation.

"My brother, Marco, must die. If he lives, Imara and the others will use him as a symbol for their movement. They will try to tell his story to show that tagging is unnecessary and harmful. If we are going to have any chance at all, Marco cannot survive this day."

Vikal dropped to one knee. His entire body seemed to shake with the desire to prove his faithfulness. She allowed him to take her hand as he solemnly said, "I swear to you, by the end of this day, either he will be dead, or I will be."

11

TWO

ALIVE.

Imara Kalu shuddered at the word even an hour later.

Carlotta Santini had been many things to Imara: teacher, mentor, Judge. In no part of her brain could she have imagined that alive would be the worst of all.

Imara sat slumped in a chair at headquarters. The other desks and chairs were filled with Abe and his co-workers. *Former* co-workers. She still couldn't believe he had sold his portion of the business. Husani flicked small chips at Keiko's newly cut amber-colored hair, but she ignored him and scowled at the ground. Naki paced through the room, breathing so fast she'd soon be hyperventilating. Siluk ran a hand through his black hair and kept trying to let out a laugh.

As if that would help.

Carlotta Santini was alive, and Imara just *knew* that every victory they had gained was about to be ripped away. Marco seemed to be the only one with no reaction at all. He sat in a corner like a man on death row, resigned to his inevitable fate.

Imara turned back toward the recording that played on the wall hologram. Professor Santini kept saying the same words over and over.

Alive. Alive. Alive.

Edrice kept glancing back at the recording as if glaring at it might make it disappear. As she glanced back this time, she and Imara caught each other's stares. Edrice said nothing, but merely gulped and turned back to her own hologram screen. She had dozens of windows open with security footage and police alerts. It all seemed so useless now. What could Edrice find that they didn't already know?

Imara looked back the recording. The matted hair and sunken eyes of her former mentor haunted her just as they had the first time she saw them. Imara exerted every effort to force some emotion into herself. Any emotion. Mostly she felt cold.

She had spent months carrying the guilt of Professor Santini's death only to find out she had survived the catacombs. Imara had spent so much effort keeping the golden transporter away from Professor Santini. Then, she had finally trusted Abe and let him destroy the ruby transporter crystal.

And it was all for nothing.

Apparently, Professor Santini had had a second transporter crystal all along.

The victories Imara had gained in the past months felt empty. Every pore in her skin tingled with regret. So much for trusting others. So much for stopping Sef. So much for Abe selling his business to be with her. None of it mattered now because Carlotta Santini was alive. One thought danced around inside her, and she clung to it like the last umbrella in the middle of a hurricane.

She didn't know what Professor Santini would try now that she was back. She didn't know how things would change.

But she knew what she wanted to do. What she *needed* to do. The truth burned through her as if her very soul understood it. She kept saying the words in her head, hoping the repetition would help it stick.

Over and over she thought: *I have to keep people from dying.*

"Takara is dead," Edrice said as she fiddled with the brick-red ribbon in her hair. "The Egyptian police aren't saying it was poison, but the security footage shows Takara angry and resisting arrest one moment and dead on the ground the next. There were several taggers nearby, but the police aren't looking into anything at all. Considering how much they wanted Takara dead, I doubt they ever will." She sat in her normal spot at her desk, but the lines around her eyes had deepened. A faint raven black rash of anxiety skittered out around her.

Abe had cleaned Imara's eyes three times in the last ten minutes, which meant she could make out a few emotions with her recovering hila. They would fade soon, but for now, she had some small sense of everyone's feelings.

The plum-colored worms of discomfort wriggling out of Marco Santini's skin matched the expression on his face. He dug his fingernails into his knee as he gulped. With his eyes darting from one end of the room to the other, he said, "Can you take me back home now?"

Abe frowned, indecision weighing his eyebrows down. "We don't know if you'll be safe there. Santini knows where you were living."

Naki danced on her toes. Short fear spikes grew out of her skin as she spoke. "I want to go home too. Professor Santini is focused on the Egyptian Council right now, but who knows how long it will take for her to get whatever it is she wants. She's going to come after us next."

"I think we should all leave. And Naki's right; we should probably do it soon," Imara said.

Keiko stomped her foot so hard that her short amber hair flew over her shoulders. "I'm not leaving Cairo. Santini barely knows my name. Why do you think she cares about us anyway?"

Abe opened his mouth to answer, but no words came out. For a moment, he just stood there gaping. Naki and Siluk spent a moment staring at each other, but now they turned to Imara. As if she had all the answers.

Unfortunately, in this case, Imara did.

"Professor Santini wants to make tagging mainstream. She has big plans for it, and even though I don't know exactly what they are, I know she wanted me for something. No matter what, we can't underestimate her. Professor Santini is smart. Crafty. She knows how to trick people into thinking her lies have shades of truth. The biggest challenge won't be getting to her. The biggest challenge will be convincing everyone that she's wrong. The sooner we get out of here and come up with a plan, the better."

Abe flung a bag over his shoulder. A glint of periwinkle shined out from his copper skin. Imara recognized the emotion as one she had seen in the catacombs, but it had been so long now, she couldn't remember what it represented. Just as she concentrated on it, the periwinkle seemed to fade away.

"We need to stop talking and start moving," Abe said, locking his eyes onto hers. "It's too dangerous to take Marco back to Alaska. We should go to your house in Kenya, but I

15

don't think we should take a regular flight. They'll be able to track us if we do."

Abe must have known Imara would protest this idea. He was suggesting they take his jet, which she was still way too terrified for. He raised his eyebrows in a pointed stare, trying to convince her to listen.

Edrice jumped to her feet and let out a gasp, clapping a hand over her mouth. "They just…" She looked up slightly from her hologram screen until she made eye contact with Imara. The moment their eyes met, Edrice turned her face away and closed her eyes. "I'm so sorry," she said.

Abe's jaw flexed as he gritted his teeth together. "What happened?"

Edrice turned away from both of them and wrung her hands. A spattering of cerulean chunks left her skin, which was only more frustrating. This was a new emotion Imara didn't recognize. She normally loved seeing new emotions, knowing that she was capable of seeing both good and bad now. Except, because it was new, she had no idea what it could possibly mean. Whatever it was, it didn't look good.

Edrice peeked over her shoulder at Imara before looking away quickly. She bit her lip and said, "The police just sent an order for your arrest."

"For my arrest?" Abe with a snarl. "What do they think they're playing at? I didn't break any—"

"Not you." Edrice looked back, and now Imara could place the emotion even though it had faded out of her sight. Regret.

"They're saying you attempted to murder Carlotta Santini in the catacombs. Your airport pass and bubble car privileges are both frozen until further notice."

"Frozen?" Imara managed to choke out through her constricted throat.

"They want to arrest Imara?" Abe said in disbelief. He let out a huff even a bull envy. Kicking a chair to the floor, he said, "She tried to save Santini, not murder her. We have three people in this room that could prove it. After a quick phone call to my dad, we'd have another one."

Reaching for the familiar tuft of hair at the back of her neck, Imara chewed her lip as she thought. Again, her mantra flitted through her mind. *I have to keep people from dying.* Would the taggers go after Marco next? How long could they hide him?

If they arrested her, would Professor Santini try to use her to get to Marco?

Professor Santini had been counting on Imara in the catacombs. She gave her the chance to leave quietly, and Imara hadn't taken it. She knew as surely as the sun rose each morning that whatever Santini wanted with her, it would be better to never find out.

"You know they won't let you plead your case, right?" Siluk said. "The taggers will try to kill you before you make it to the council chambers."

She tugged her hair harder, trying to discover a scenario where he was wrong. Either fear blinded her, or else Siluk was right.

"You need to run," he said. "Let's get you back home and the Kenyan police can defend you since they already know you're trustworthy."

"How?" Somehow, she managed a small laugh as she said it. "How can I run when my airport pass is frozen? Someone could take me as a passenger in a bubble car, but it would still take a week to drive to Nairobi from here. Even on the highest speed setting."

"You don't need an airport pass if we take my jet," Abe said with a wink.

Her gut twisted, and it must have shown on her face because he immediately reached for her hand. "I know you're afraid of heights and can barely survive a plane ride," he said as the warmth of his fingers seeped into her skin. "But I promise I can be a really safe pilot when I need to be."

"Terrified," she said under her breath. "Not afraid, terrified."

He squeezed her hand and the memory of him selling his business just so he could be with her flooded her mind. "I promise you," he said. "I'll keep you safe no matter what the cost."

After a little gulp, she said, "Just promise you'll hold my hand if I get scared."

He let out a chuckle. "I'm for sure going to hold your hand either way, so don't worry about that."

Before she could melt into him, Edrice gasped even louder than she had the first time and then let out an audible gulp. "It's too late," she said in rush of breath. "I was watching the main team, but they sent a backup team. Or... it might be taggers, which is probably worse."

As she spoke, a pound shook the door to headquarters. It sounded like a battering ram.

"I'm sorry," Edrice said. She looked over at Imara and a faint hint of the cerulean regret splattered away from her skin again. "They tricked me."

Siluk glanced down the hall. "Let's just break a window and jump out the back."

"We can't," Husani said. "Impact proof glass."

Before anyone else could speak, the door to headquarters blew open in a shower of sparks.

Imara shoved Marco under a desk and out of sight in the last second before the intruders entered the main office. A swarm of taggers filled the room, not a single Egyptian police officer among them. No wonder Edrice hadn't seen them coming. The taggers meant to get rid of Imara before the police arrived.

To her surprise, none of them came near her. Instead, the two dozen taggers trained their guns on every other person in the room, except Marco, who was still safely hidden. Within seconds, all her friends had multiple guns to their heads, and their arms were twisted firmly behind their backs. All before they had a moment to breathe.

"Come with us or they die," one of the taggers said to Imara. The round scar on his forehead brought back several unpleasant memories, the first being the graduation party when Naki got kidnapped. Something about his stance and the way the other taggers looked to him made her think he had some kind of authority. Maybe he was Professor Santini's right-hand man.

Regardless, her friends were in trouble and the only thing she knew for sure was that she had to keep people from dying. Especially her friends. Abe looked to her and twitched his head as if saying no, but she ignored it. She had no time to find another way.

"Fine," she said before she could change her mind. "I'm coming."

"Imara!" Abe struggled against the two taggers holding him back, ignoring the two guns trained on his forehead.

With a sniff, she turned and avoided all eye contact as she marched out of the room.

"Stop!" he shouted. "We can fight. Don't—"

His voice faded as she walked out the door of headquarters. Nothing he said could change her mind now. She couldn't let him die. Not any of them. If she couldn't save them by turning herself in, then what was she even good for?

The tagger with the round scar on his forehead wore a triumphant smirk as he took hold of her elbow. He nodded to the other taggers and they quietly followed her out of headquarters.

"Imara!" Abe called from inside the main office. She tried to ignore it as she climbed into the bubble car parked outside. Half the taggers piled in after her while the other half filled up a second bubble car.

Appearing at the headquarters' entrance, Naki clutched her braids with a look of anguish. Abe waved his arms through the air as she sat in the bubble car.

But it was too late. The bubble car began its acceleration and soon it hovered down the road too far for Abe to ever catch up. The taggers sneered at her, but she didn't have to try to ignore them. She was too busy thinking of a way out. Eight taggers and one of her. It wouldn't be easy.

Could she escape while they were still in the bubble car? It was probably best if she never made it to wherever they were going. She shifted slightly in her seat until she was right next to the bubble car's hologram screen.

She blinked for a moment as she tried to arrange her face into something that looked sad. Or desperate. Actually, both would probably be better. Once she had her face arranged just right, she let out an exasperated sigh and dropped her head into her hands.

With her head in her lap, she inched herself closer to the bubble car's hologram screen. Turning her head slightly to hide her hands, she used her knuckle to swipe at the hologram screen. For effect, she let out a fake sob. But a quiet one, so it wouldn't seem too suspicious.

What was it Edrice had taught her about this? The bubble car had some automatic protocol that would force it to stop and make the door open. Imara swiped through the screen, searching for the protocol.

She realized she'd been too quiet and let out another sob that was probably just a bit too dramatic. Hopefully the taggers wouldn't notice. For extra effect, she sniffed as she continued to swipe through the different apps on the hologram screen.

There it was.

What would she do once she activated the protocol? She had a stun gun on her that the taggers had failed to take. If the bubble car jerked to a stop like she hoped, she'd probably be able to jump out and get some cover before they could grab her. Then she could stun at least a couple of them before they caught up to her again. She'd just have to order a bubble car as she fought them off.

No.

She couldn't order a bubble car. Her bubble car privileges had been frozen too.

Waiting until she came up with a better plan would have been nice, but she didn't have time for that. She'd just have to wing it.

Taking a deep breath, she shifted her heels into the air so only the balls of her feet touched the floor of the bubble car. Then, she tapped the hologram screen.

Nothing.

The bubble car kept driving through the street for two whole seconds before anything changed. But then. The car jolted to a stop.

Since she had been expecting it, Imara reacted faster than any of the taggers. Leaping from the bubble car, she launched herself toward an alley. She aimed the stun gun over her shoulder as she ran, taking out two of the taggers.

Once in the alley, her stomach dropped. An unforgiving dead end sat in front of her. After a grimace, she pushed her chin into the air. She'd just have to go out guns a-blazing.

She took hold of a wooden barrel stored in the alley and slammed it into one of the taggers as he passed her. She jumped over the barrel and stunned another. Before she could reach the alley opening, a third tagger started shooting.

Not knowing where the bullets came from, she ducked as she ran from the alley. She tore down the street looking for anything that could help. Her feet crunched over a pile of glass shards. She could throw those into the taggers' eyes, but that seemed a little barbaric.

Shooting the stun gun over her shoulder seemed like her only option, but that wouldn't work indefinitely. There wasn't any time for new ideas.

In desperation, she noticed a bubble car coming up the street toward her. Maybe she could flag them down and beg for help. It wasn't a perfect idea, but it was something.

As the car approached, she noticed a familiar face in the window. Copper skin and luscious dark locks. An intensity in his eyes that burned like fire.

Abe.

Relief washed over her. She pushed herself toward the bubble car, barely remembering to dodge bullets.

He didn't stop the bubble car as it approached. He just forced the door open while it hovered over the street. That should have been impossible, but maybe Edrice knew a trick about that too.

With the door open, he reached out for her, and she threw herself into his arms. As he pulled her inside, a gunshot sounded.

The bullet hit her squarely in the calf.

THREE

"YOU HAVE TO STOP SACRIFICING YOURSELF like that," Abe said, almost with a laugh.

The laugh halted, and his body tensed as his eyes found her leg. He dropped to his knees as he shoved Imara onto the seat. Crammed into the upholstery, she realized they weren't alone. Naki and Siluk sat nearby, and apparently Naki was navigating.

"It's…," Abe said with a clear note of panic in his voice. "It's okay, I think."

He slapped the seat behind him in wild movements as if trying to grab something. Pain burned through her calf as she gripped the seat. Each tiny bump of the car shot a wave of agony through her. It felt like someone had shoved a red-hot poker through her calf.

Abe whirled around as he slapped the seat behind him. When he turned and saw an empty seat, he swore and punched the seat. "Of course I didn't bring my bag. Why would I remember my bag when I actually need it?"

He pulled the bottom of his shirt up to his teeth and tore off a piece of it. When he grabbed her leg, a scream burst through her lips. Now it felt like someone had taken a sledge

24

hammer to the red-hot poker in her leg. He pressed the torn shirt piece to her wound and said, "Hold this."

Waves of pain burned through as she obeyed him. He tore another section of cloth off his shirt, and shook his head before wrapping his hand around her calf again. "The bullet is lodged in your leg, but it's in the muscle. That's a good thing. It shouldn't bleed too much if we apply enough pressure. I'll remove the bullet as soon as I get some medical supplies."

"You forgot your medical supplies?" Naki screamed. Her nervous energy rippled through the car, hitting Imara like a splash of cold water to the face. Naki clutched Siluk's shoulder so hard, it made him grimace. Or maybe he was worried about the bullet wound.

Siluk tried to remove himself from her death grip as he said, "Calm down, Naki. I'm sure Abe has medical supplies on his jet."

Naki dug her fingers deeper into Siluk's shoulder and let out a shriek. "We can't wait that long. We have to stop somewhere now. Can't you see her face?"

Though she couldn't see it herself, Imara knew her face had to look bad. Each time a wave of pain shot through her, her face contorted even more. Now her breaths came out in hard and shallow bursts. Even Abe's touch didn't seem to have the pain-killing effect it usually did.

"We can't stop," Siluk practically shouted as he attempted to peel Naki's fingers away from his shoulder. "If we don't get Imara out of Egypt immediately, she'll be dead by the end of the day, and not from that bullet."

Abe tied another strip of cloth over Imara's wound. He looked calm except for the deepening frown on his face. "She'll be fine. This will be good enough until we get to Kenya. It only takes eighteen minutes in my jet, maybe less if I fly fast."

He pressed both his thumbs above the bullet wound into the soft muscle under the back of her knee. He rubbed small circles into the spot. The burning didn't let up, but it seemed to have less bite. His frown deepened further as if sickened by her agony. "It's more important that we get out of here before the taggers or the Egyptian police get to Imara."

After a few more rotations of his thumbs, he sighed and settled into the seat beside her. "I can't do anything about the pain though." He took her hand but didn't meet her eye. "Do you think you can bear it?"

She dug her teeth into her bottom lip before attempting to answer. "I…" She sucked in a breath and gripped Abe's hand as if it was the only thing keeping her head above water in the midst of a whirlpool. "At least it will keep my mind off the flight. I can't be—" She gasped and pressed her face into the familiar comfort of Abe's shoulder. "I can't be scared if I'm focused on the pain."

He pulled her closer, but she sensed tension in his muscles. It didn't take long to see why. Just outside the bubble car, the airport came into view. Police cars lined the streets with blockades in all the roads.

"It's not a problem," Abe assured. "They're only blocking the main airport. I have a private hanger that's accessible from a side road. Husani and Keiko should already be there with Marco. Edrice will stay here to keep us updated on everything that's happening in Egypt."

The bubble car seemed to shudder as they veered away from the police cars, as if it was unwilling to take them down the road they needed to go.

Since the vein nearest her bullet wound felt like it had its own heartbeat, the shuddering bubble car wasn't too much of a bother. The burning bursts of pain shooting through her leg were a much bigger concern.

As a line of private hangers came into view, she saw another bubble car and was foolish enough to let out a sigh of relief. The moment the sigh escaped her lips, three more bubble cars swerved in front of them. Each of the cars was full.

She couldn't make out whether the people were taggers or police, but it didn't matter because another wave of pain made her double over. Naki was shouting again. Shrieking was probably a better description. Abe and Siluk were arguing about something. The bubble car was shuddering again and with each moment, the shudders felt more like jerks.

Just as pain hammered through her calf, the bubble car came to an abrupt halt. She clutched her leg and tried to let out a scream. Before she could find her voice, someone had lifted her from the ground and thrown her over their shoulder. For a moment, she thought it was Naki and couldn't understand how Naki suddenly had the strength to carry her like this. But then she caught a whiff of a musky scent lined with soil and tree bark. A milky scent flittered through the other smells.

Siluk.

"Put me down!"

Siluk only laughed. She tried to jump out of his grip, but his years of subsistence living must have given him stronger muscles than she realized. He held her firmly as he ran, no matter how much she struggled.

Finally, she gave up and tried to look for the others. Naki had run ahead and was almost at the bright blue jet she knew was Abe's. She couldn't find Abe, but the bubble car with Keiko, Husani, and Marco hovered in front of them, heading their way.

When it was close, another bubble car sped in front of it. The new car had its doors forced open. forced its doors open. Keiko and Husani managed to get away, but Marco wasn't so lucky. The tagger with the round scar on his forehead, the same one that had gotten to Imara earlier, wrapped an arm around Marco's neck and squeezed.

Imara struggled even harder now. She pounded Siluk's back, not trying to keep her touch gentle. "They're going to kill him. We rescued him from Takara. We can't let him die now."

Siluk grunted at her hits but managed to keep running. She hit harder and started wiggling to get her body out of his grip. Now Siluk growled. "Would you stop that? I'm supposed to get you to the jet, whether you like it or not. Abe was going to try to steal some medical instrument from one of the police officers."

Ignoring him, Imara continued to wiggle until she was almost certain she would escape Siluk's grip. She couldn't let Marco die. Not now. Just when she freed herself, her feet hit the ground, and a burning hot sledgehammer pounded through her calf. She collapsed to the ground. The air seemed to escape her.

"Did you forget about the bullet in your leg?" Siluk said through his teeth.

She pushed him away and tried to get to her feet. She had to do something. She had to try. She had to keep people from dying. No matter what happened, she wouldn't let Marco die unless she died first. She pushed herself onto her good leg and started hopping toward Marco.

She realized at once that Marco was on the ground. The tagger with the round scar on his forehead wore a triumphant look, and even though she searched, she couldn't see Marco's chest rise and fall with breath.

No.

She couldn't be too late.

Not yet.

"Just go without us," Keiko said through the haze filling Imara's mind. She managed to turn her head just long enough to see Keiko and Husani stuck behind a barricade of plastic boards and sandbags. The barricade had been set up behind Imara and the jet was in front of her. She, Naki, Abe, and Siluk were all in front of the barricade and able to get to the jet. Husani and Keiko were not. They had a bubble car, but no way past the barricade.

Another second later, Imara felt arms around her waist again, but these ones felt much gentler. Abe hoisted her off the ground and bolted toward his jet.

"Did you get the thing you needed?" Siluk asked.

Imara didn't hear Abe's response. She didn't feel his arms anymore either. In fact, she could barely even register her pain. The world seemed to be fading into gray and the only thing she could sense was the name on her lips.

"Marco," she said.

She blinked.

Even though it felt like a split second, when she opened her eyes, she was sitting in a space that looked frighteningly like a cockpit. She heard metallic pings against the jet. Bullets. Her body began convulsing and, somehow, she recognized Abe's voice amidst the other noises that assaulted her.

"It's okay. You're going to be fine. *We're* going to be fine. Once I get us in the air and going the right way, Siluk can take the controls and I'll fix up your wound."

His voice had a calming effect on her right up until the jet started rising off the ground. Her body shook harder. Just as a wave of terror was about to seize her, a fresh pain dug into her calf. Her throat felt raw before she realized she was screaming.

"Just a few more minutes," Abe said. He was attempting to speak calmly, but the panic rising in him came out in every syllable he spoke.

She slammed her eyes shut unable to take both the pain and the sight of the jet rising into the air. Gripping her leg, she tried to rock her body back and forth. She had one brief moment where it seemed like she could take it, but then she remembered Marco's body lying there.

Dead.

Marco Santini was dead. Carlotta Santini was alive.

And it was all her fault.

FOUR

ABE COULD HEAL WOUNDS IN RECORD TIME.
Imara clung to that thought as she gripped her leg. It was more
pleasant than the other thought floating around in her brain.
*Why haven't I passed out yet? I just want to pass out so I don't have to
feel this anymore.*

She squeezed her eyelids shut tighter and tried to force
those thoughts away. Abe would heal her soon enough, but
that didn't take away the pain now. Even if he'd fix it in one
minute flat, she still had to find a way to endure those sixty
seconds.

It ended up taking three minutes.

Her jaw shook from clenching it so tight. Tears slid down
her cheeks, which didn't make any sense. How could she be
crying when her brain was so busy processing the pain? And
how could one tiny little hunk of metal hurt this much?

"Siluk." Abe's voice sounded so far away considering he
sat right next to her. More voices muddled together as Abe
explained the controls. Sometimes the words would jump out
and she'd want to cover her ears. But mostly the words
sounded feathery and cushioned. Near, but out of reach.

Suddenly, the warmth of Abe's hand closed over her own. He helped her out of the cockpit while the world kept hiding behind the black spots in her vision. His arm held her by the waist, and he was telling her to not put her foot down. But the words didn't register until knives seemed to shoot up from her feet and into her shin bone.

The next thing she knew, she was propped up on a pillow of some sort and Abe was digging through a bag of medical supplies. Naki whispered as she dabbed a wet rag across Imara's forehead. Was the rag wet from water or was she sweating that much?

It didn't take long for her senses to return. Apparently, Abe had stolen a packet of nano bots from one of the police cars. That, combined with some painkillers, and the fact that Abe was a healer, meant her bullet wound felt like little more than a scrape after only a few minutes.

She had to admit, having a healer boyfriend *was* pretty convenient.

She breathed in for what felt like the first time, since her chest no longer constricted from pain.

"Is she going to have a scar?" Naki asked as she dabbed the rag across Imara's forehead. Naki fiddled with the tiny black braids in her hair as she looked anxiously at Abe.

"Maybe," Abe said, dropping the rest of the bandages into his bag. "I'll know more in a few days."

He wrapped warm hands around Imara's calf and rubbed just above the wound. He had used ointment with painkiller and given her oral painkillers too, but his hands always made the biggest difference. The gentle pressure of his thumbs seemed to release the pain as well as some of the worry plaguing her mind.

"Could you ask Siluk the distance until Nairobi?" Abe asked Naki. "It should be in that box on the bottom left corner of the control panel."

As soon as she left, Abe stopped staring at Imara's calf and started staring at her eyes instead. Her heart flip flopped the moment they made eye contact.

Something was different now.

She couldn't just see it; she could feel it. In Egypt, there had always been some deep part of him that held back. He gave himself to her, but never all the way. But it was different now. Since he sold his business, the connection between them was blossoming into something it had never been before. Something she had never felt with anyone.

"You know," he said. The olive green in his eyes looked extra bright against the russet brown. Even the maroon specks seemed to dance in his eyes like a laugh. A look just short of a grin settled onto his face. "It wouldn't hurt for you to be the damsel in distress and just let me rescue you for once."

"Marco Santini is dead," she said. A weight seemed to drop inside her.

Abe's shoulders shook, and he flinched. "That's not our fault."

Imara huffed in an attempt to hide the tears that threatened to spill from her eyes. "I tried to save him but Siluk wouldn't let me go. I had to wriggle out of his grip, and even then, he held me back."

"You had a bullet wound. You couldn't have saved Marco even if you had tried. I told Siluk to hold you back."

She pushed her palms into her eyelids as emotions crashed around inside of her. "It's not our fault, it's *my* fault."

"Why?" Abe asked as she sniffed. When she peeked through her eyelids, he almost looked angry.

She turned away from him and answered, "It *is* my fault or else I'd be dead, and he'd be alive. If I can't save people, then what am I good for?"

"Wait," Abe said with less anger in his voice. Now he seemed more concerned. Or maybe it was frustrated. Without her hila, she couldn't tell. "What do you mean—"

"I just want—" She didn't mean to interrupt him, but the words spewed out of her mouth before she could stop them. She continued to turn away from him and wrapped her arms around her stomach. More tears welled in her eyes, but she did her best to hold them back. It wouldn't do any good to cry.

Abe pulled one of her hands away from her stomach until his fingers were interlaced between hers. "What do you want?" he asked in a much gentler voice.

Rubbing her eyes, she said, "I want to keep people from dying. That's all I ask. No more death. Marco, Rajesh, Aida, Headmaster Bello. They've all died for this stupid cause that makes things worse, not better. It's too much. I want to keep people from dying."

He rubbed his thumb across the back of her hand before he answered. When he did, his voice was gentle again. "Okay," he said. "That's what we'll try to do. I don't think we'll always succeed, especially not with Santini back, but we'll try. Our goal is to keep people alive."

Of course he understood. She and Abe were cut from the same cloth. They had the same goals. And in this moment, she couldn't have appreciated that more. She wanted to kiss him, but Naki appeared before she got the chance.

"Siluk says we're getting close." She made a pointed stare at their interlocked hands and then frowned dramatically. But she didn't say anything. It probably helped that Abe had been so determined to keep Imara safe from the taggers and Egyptian police, but Naki would likely still hate him for a while. Plus, she still had to convince her parents that Abe wasn't the flaky, non-committal boyfriend they thought he was. If she managed that, then they might have a shot at making this work.

As Abe led Imara back to the cockpit, he whispered, "It *was* brave of you to try and save Marco, but it's okay to protect yourself too. You know that, right?"

She was saved from having to respond when the door to the cockpit opened. At the sight of the clouds floating past the window, she clutched the back wall of the cockpit. No matter how she told herself not to, her eyes found the ground, which was way too far away. She sucked in a breath and collapsed in a trembling heap.

Abe sat down at the controls. At least she assumed that's what he was doing. She wasn't about to open her eyes to find out. After a few clicks and chimes from the control panel, Naki tried to pat Imara on the shoulder.

Imara shook the hand away and burrowed her head deep into her hands. Even though she couldn't see the ground, she still knew it was there. Down there. Way too far down. Her body started trembling even harder.

"Do something," Naki said.

Imara could easily imagine her sister with a hand on one hip and a glare that was probably directed toward Abe.

"Right, a distraction," Abe said. "Uh…"

Imara buried her face deeper into her hands. None of this was enough to distract her. All she could see in her head was Abe's jet plummeting to the earth in a cloud of smoke. And now she imagined it on fire. *Great.* Just what she needed.

"Uh," Abe said again. "Oh yeah, I think I can permanently heal your hila."

Her head snapped up and her jaw dropped down before she could stop herself. The sight of the way-too-far-away ground made her stomach turn, but for once, it wasn't as pressing as the other thought in her mind.

"Permanently?" she asked. She shut her eyes and buried her face back in her hands, but this time, covering her eyes was enough to keep her anxiety at bay.

"I could be wrong," Abe said. "I don't want to get your hopes up."

Imara bit her lip as she considered her next words. She felt a little guilty for keeping this part to herself, but she didn't know how Abe would react at the time. Finally, she managed to get the words out. "I've already seen some emotions." Now that she said it, she felt silly for being so nervous.

She peeked through her hands to gauge his reaction. If he was surprised, it didn't show. Instead, he just nodded. "Whenever I get the goop out of your eyes, right?"

A grin grew on her face as she covered her eyes again. The ground was still too far away, and Marco was still dead. Plus, she was a fugitive running from the Egyptian Council. But…

He could heal her hila.

She'd never stop feeling guilty over Marco's death, and she'd always be afraid of heights, but at least the fugitive thing didn't seem so important anymore. Abe could heal her hila.

This time, things would be different. She'd look for positive emotions, not just negative ones. She would learn to see emotions and consider many possible interpretations before she assumed the first one that came to her mind.

With the right attitude and judgment, her hila could become the gift it was meant to be. No longer a curse. And if Professor Santini didn't know Imara's hila had been healed, that could give them the advantage they needed to stop her.

She could handle anything now.

"You know that mission when we were trying to get into the warehouse because the code had changed?" Abe asked. "You asked me to get the goop out of your eyes and then you looked at the control panel like you did when you were seeing through illusions in the catacomb. I think the eraserfall severed the connection between your eyes and your brain. Well, not the whole connection obviously, since you can still see. But I think there are some nerves that make you see emotions in color. I'm pretty sure you just see body language and your brain interprets it as the color thingies you see coming off people's skin."

"That's amazing," she said, and without thinking, her eyes flew open. Her head reeled at the sight of the ground, which somehow looked even farther away than before. She clutched the back wall and slammed her eyes shut again. "That's really great, Abe. How much longer?"

"We're almost there. Should I keep distracting you?"

"Keep trying, yes, but…" She peeked through her eyelids and a shudder shook through her arms.

"So, as I was saying," Abe said in a louder voice. "It's all about the goop in your eyes. The goop is residue from the eraserfall, and it keeps the connection severed. I think it works a bit like a virus. If I get rid of some of the goop, it heals your hila temporarily. But then the goop will always grow back because some of it is still there. If I get rid of the goop all at once, then it will be gone completely and won't come back. Your hila should be healed permanently."

Permanently. A word she hadn't dared to hope for in months. Her eyes fluttered open for a moment and she noticed that a cloud almost completely covered the cockpit window. Behind the cloud something big and heavy lingered, but she couldn't tell what it was.

She let out a gasp and Abe turned back to look at her. "Uh," he said. "You better close your eyes."

Her voice squeaked in terror as her eyes slammed shut.

"No, we're safe. I promise we're safe."

She squeezed her eyes so tight, stars erupted from her eyelids.

Every bump of the jet made her stomach reel. She tried to ignore the sensation, but the bumps were getting bigger and her ears were popping. A huge bump rattled through her and her stomach chose that moment to perform a series of somersaults. *How much longer?*

"We're here," Abe said, taking her hand.

For a moment, she couldn't bear to open her eyes in case it was a joke. But Abe wouldn't tease her about something so serious. When she finally forced her eyelids open, she noticed tall concrete buildings with sparkly windows.

Apparently *here* was a tiny back part of the Kenyan airport she had never seen before. The one thing she did recognize was the ground. And they were on it. She let out a heavy sigh.

"I don't think I've ever seen you squirm so much in my life," Abe said with a grin.

She gave him a playful smack on the shoulder and let confidence flow through her as she rolled her shoulders back. Now that they were on the ground, where they were supposed to be, all her terror subsided in an instant. One thing did annoy her, though. Abe was such a skilled pilot, and she'd obviously never be able to enjoy it.

But then again, maybe she would. Abe had helped her change since they first met. He always seemed to know exactly what she needed to overcome her fears and weaknesses. Maybe someday, she could handle a jet ride without breaking her fingers from clutching the armrest too hard.

Before she could wrap her arms around him, Naki appeared at their side, and her glare looked even worse than before.

"What's our plan?" Siluk said when he appeared a moment later.

"I can take you home later today," Abe said.

"No." Siluk wore a look of determination that didn't quite fit him. He was usually relaxed and cool, but now his shoulders were hunched, and a crease had appeared between his eyebrows. "I don't want to go home. Santini is planning something and I want to be around to stop whatever she starts. I messaged Darius, and he wants to help. I bet we can find other people who want to help too."

Abe scratched his eyebrow as he nodded. He wore a simple smile as if he agreed, but something was different about it. Something barely detectable. He seemed... annoyed? Why would he be annoyed? He wanted to stop the taggers more than anyone. The more help they could get, the better. The look of annoyance flitted away, and Abe nodded again, this time more resolutely.

"Fine. We'll have to get this fugitive thing figured out first. We'll just get the Kenyan Council to side with Imara so they can clear things up with the Egyptian Council."

As he ordered a bubble car, Imara said, "It might be difficult to get the Kenyan Council on my side since Safiya got framed for murder."

Abe grimaced.

"She got what? Naki asked, keeping up her steady glare toward Abe.

"It's fine," Imara said. "Maybe she already cleared that up. She's smart. If not, we'll just find a way to exonerate her and then get rid of any taggers left here in Kenya. Once that's done, we'll ask the Kenyan Council to help with my fugitive status. As long as we have Safiya on our side, things should be fine."

FIVE

AFTER AN UNEVENTFUL BUBBLE CAR RIDE, Imara opened the door to her apartment and everyone piled in after her. Naki stayed uncharacteristically quiet while they discussed their plans.

"Maybe we're stressing too much about this," Abe said. "The Egyptian Council stayed uncorrupted even with Sef around. They ignored the taggers for years and wouldn't give them the power they wanted. Just because Santini is back doesn't mean she has complete control."

"Yeah, but Professor Santini must have convinced them to arrest me. Right after I saved them all from Sef, I might add." Imara slouched down onto the ground in the front room. Her anxiety was too high for sitting on the couch.

"That's what scared me too," Siluk said. "How could the Egyptian Council be against the taggers for so long and suddenly now do what they want? What power does Santini have over them?"

Imara rolled her eyes. "She's probably just bribing them or blackmailing them."

Siluk frowned. "Yeah, but with what?"

"Do you want to stay here, Siluk?" Naki twisted two braid strands around her finger as she spoke. Nervous energy came off her. She cleared her throat and seemed to stand a little taller. "It's probably going to take some time to stop Santini or whatever we're going to do. You can sleep here—and Darius too if he wants. The rooms are big enough that we could fit a bunch of people if we have to. As long as they don't mind sleeping on the floor."

Imara blinked at her sister. Why exactly did Naki think *this* was the most important thing to discuss right now?

Naki's unease seemed to melt away, and she flipped her braids back behind her head. "I guess Abe can stay too, if you *have* to." She didn't hide the grimace as she said it. "Imara can move into my bedroom and Abe and Siluk, you two can stay in Imara's room."

Naki made no attempt to hide her ulterior motive of keeping Abe and Imara apart, but it didn't matter. Everything was different now. Abe had sold his business just to be with Imara. He'd get on Naki's good side and their parents'. He'd show Imara real commitment. If he didn't, she'd break up with him without any of Naki's meddling. Still, she had a feeling that least a few of her nights ahead would include Naki listing various reasons she should break up with Abe.

"I'll start moving my things into your room," Imara said. "And I'll find some sleeping bags."

"I'll help," Abe said with a smile.

Naki glared again, but before they could do anything, Abe's ring started buzzing with a phone call. Soon enough, Edrice's face appeared on Abe's hologram screen looking back at them.

"You're not going to like this," she said.

Imara pushed herself to Abe's side as her stomach dropped. "Is it Keiko and Husani?"

"Oh come on," Keiko said, appearing on the hologram screen next to Edrice. "You know I'm tougher than that. It took Husani and me forever to get away, and we had to go into hiding, but we're safe."

A wave of relief washed over Imara as she let out a sigh. It didn't last long when she remembered that not everyone had survived that fight.

"I think you need to come get Keiko out of here, Abe. Santini is looking for her." Husani's eyes dipped as he spoke. The frown tugging at his lips showed more concern than he'd ever exhibited before.

Keiko just rolled her eyes. "I'm fine."

"I think we can all agree on how incredibly *fine* you are," Husani said with a grin. "I'm more concerned with your safety at the moment."

Now Edrice rolled her eyes. "You two are insufferable. Do you even remember why we decided to call them? We have bigger issues to deal with at the moment besides your incessant flirting."

Keiko flinched at those words and looked away. "You're really not going to like it," she said.

While still on the call, Edrice sent some documents that mostly looked like boring notes from an Egyptian Council meeting that ended a few minutes prior. Entire conversations were documented, including three pages on what they were going to eat for lunch that day. A few pages later, the notes started to get more interesting.

"Santini is calling a global vote?" Abe asked.

"That's not all," Edrice said. "She wants to create a new position and has nominated herself for it. If her global vote is passed, she'll become the global judge of the entire world. It's a new position with no rules, so there could potentially be no restrictions on power. And there are no other nominations or candidates or campaigning, just a simple yes or no vote. If she gets the councils from around the world to vote for her, she'd have limitless power."

"That's insane," Abe said. "Nobody is going to go for that. Tell me the other territories have refused the global vote."

"She has the Egyptian Council on her side. They've already convinced several territories to agree to the vote. Italy agreed first. No surprise there since Santini is from Italy. But then, she got Russia to agree, and then India, Bulgaria, and Germany— and that's just in the last few minutes. It's having a snowball effect, and more territories have already agreed. I've considered the politics. It doesn't look good. This global vote is definitely going to happen. I think our only chance is to convince the different councils to vote against Santini when the time comes."

Siluk flopped onto the couch while the crease between his eyes deepened. "So, you're saying Santini is about to take over the world and we only have a minuscule chance of stopping her."

Abe flicked his eyes toward Siluk and showed the tiniest hint of annoyance. But it was gone so fast, Imara was certain she had imagined it. Abe turned back to his hologram screen. "Thanks, Edrice. Let us know if there are any other developments. We're going to try to clear Imara's fugitive status first, and then we'll deal with Santini. And Husani, let me know if things get too dangerous for Keiko, and I'll come pick her up."

As he ended the phone call, the apartment door flew open, and Imara flinched on instinct. She crept for the couch, certain that the Egyptian police had followed her here and were going to take her back to Egypt.

Instead, she was met with a sight that seemed only slightly less terrifying and probably trickier to deal with.

"Where have you been?" Imara's dad said with a booming voice. He found Abe among them a moment later and pierced him with a glare that rivaled Naki's.

Imara's mom had her arms crossed in front of her with lips pressed into a thin line. "We need to talk," she said.

SIX

IMARA'S DAD HAD HER IN A BONE-CRUSHING hug before she could think what to do next. "Oh, my baby girl," he said. "We got a notification about your arrest. We thought you'd be stuck in Egypt forever."

She held onto her dad for a second longer than he did, grateful for the chance to just relax for a moment. When he pulled away, she shook the curls off her forehead with an air of flippancy. "It's going to be fine. I have eyewitnesses that can prove I never attempted to murder Professor Santini. I just have to get the Kenyan Council on my side."

Imara's mom squeezed Imara's shoulder while she bit her lip. "How did you get out of Egypt? You've told us such awful things about the taggers. And now the Egyptian Council is on their side? How did you escape?"

The smile came to her lips easily this time. "That was all thanks to Abe. I couldn't have done it without him."

The expression on both her parents' faces quickly dissolved into sneers. They'd been carefully avoiding Abe's eyes previously, but now they wrinkled their noses with identical expressions of disgust. Imara's stomach twisted in an even tighter knot than before.

46

"Let's go sit down," she said after clearing her throat. She ushered her parents into the front room and made everyone sit. When her parents tried to speak, she interrupted by asking what she could feed them. Drinks and snacks couldn't hurt the situation. She spent the next several minutes batting away any significant conversation while she busied herself getting things together.

A few minutes later, she came into the front room with a plate of snacks. Both her parents still unabashedly sneered at Abe. Abe seemed to have lost his confidence and tugged at his collar. His jaw worked up down as if deciding whether or not he should open his mouth.

The plate of snacks seemed to signal that conversation was now allowed. Imara's mom opened her mouth, but before she could say anything Siluk interrupted.

"Your name is Chalondra, right?" Siluk said to Imara's mom while casually running his fingers through his hair. He turned to her dad next and asked, "And you're Talib?"

The sneer on her mom's face brightened to a glowing smile. "Yes, that's right. How are you, Siluk?"

While a grin spread over Siluk's face, Abe gulped so hard Imara could hear it. She did appreciate that Siluk had gotten the sneers off her parents' faces, but getting them to like Siluk wasn't much of a priority. She didn't know what to think of it.

In the meantime, Abe took her hand as they both watched Siluk charm her parents. Abe flexed his jaw as he watched, a hint of that same annoyance broadcasting itself through every feature on his face.

Trying to reassure him, Imara squeezed his hand and gave him a smile. Just as he smiled back, her dad said, "And what about you, *Abe*? When are you going back to Egypt?"

Abe scratched the back of his neck as he spoke. "I'm uh… I'm going to stay here for a little while."

"He quit his job," Naki said with no small amount of wrath.

Both of her parents' eyes went wide at this piece of news. She could practically hear them forming the word *unemployed* in their heads.

Imara figured it would be best to jump in before that word got thrown around. "He didn't quit," she said. "He sold his portion of the business. He's an entrepreneur."

Her mom raised an eyebrow. "So, you're unemployed now?"

There it was. She wanted to growl at her parents. Abe had given up everything to be with her and now they treated him like this? She wasn't expecting a pleasant reunion, but she had been hoping for a civil one. Abe had avoided her family for months and kept Imara away from them, so it wasn't like they didn't have a reason to hate him. But he wasn't the non-committal person they thought he was. At least not anymore.

She just wished they would be a little more willing to give him a second chance. It would take time to build that trust up again. Too much time.

Abe cleared his throat as he tugged at his shirt collar. "Like Imara said, I sold my portion of the business. So, I have a huge amount in savings. Once things settle down, I want to start a new business. One I can dedicate the rest of my life to. Hopefully I can start it here in Nairobi."

He tried a charming smile, but her parents didn't take the bait.

Her dad actually glowered. He folded his arms over his chest. "You're going to live *here*? In this apartment? You're going to take advantage of the fact that my daughter has a place to live and you don't?"

"Dad!"

He continued as if she had never spoken. "And what do you mean *once things settle down*? That's not a timeline. It could mean anything. A week, a month, a year? How long before you have a reliable income?"

"I can find my own apartment," Abe said.

Her mom let out a cough that sounded suspiciously like a scoff. "And how will you pay for an apartment if you don't even have a job?"

"Mom!" This time she wouldn't let her parents continue without some interference. "He has savings, remember? Abe is brilliant. He owned a business for years."

"But it was a failing business, wasn't it?" her dad asked.

"Uh," Abe said, swiping at the line of sweat glistening at his hair line.

Imara clenched her jaw. Maybe he deserved a tiny bit of criticism, but this was too much. She got to her feet and rolled her shoulders back so she could stand at her highest height. "Enough of this. Abe is a good person, which you'll find out the longer you know him. If you want an example of how amazing he is, how about this? He says he can heal my hila. Did you know Abe is a healer?"

At this, the expression on both of her parents faces changed in an instant. Just as she predicted.

"I thought you were mashimo," Imara's mom said with one eyebrow raised.

"So did I," Abe said. "For almost all my life I thought that. Imara was the only one who believed in me and she's the only reason I know what I am now. I don't know where I'd be without her." He squeezed her hand and took a quick look into her eyes. In that moment, his smile turned, and his expression seemed to set. His confidence seemed to come back in a wave, but more importantly, hope glistened from his eyes. Abe was back.

A smile escaped onto her lips as her heart melted. His gaze always seemed to do that, but this time was special. Maybe everything would be special from now on. When she managed to pull her eyes away, it seemed that his look had melted more than just her own heart. Her parents stared at Abe and the look he was giving her, and it seemed to warm at least some of their iciness.

"So," Abe said, clearing his throat. "Chalondra and Talib, right? It's a pleasure to meet you again. I'm sorry it took so long, but I do hope we see a lot more of each other in the future."

Naki let out a scoff as she rolled her eyes back into her head. "I'll believe it when I see it."

"What are your hilas?" Abe asked, somehow unaffected by Naki's retort. Luckily, Imara's mom loved talking about their family hilas. He was getting on their good sides already.

"I'm a smell taster," Imara's mom said. "It's barely even a hila. Most people taste smells when they eat anyway. But I can taste smells even if they aren't in my mouth. Like flowers and fabric."

"Of course it's a hila," Siluk said with a charming smile. "Smell hilas are the best hilas. Everyone knows that."

Imara's mom snickered before she continued. "Talib is a temperature seer. The best part is how our hilas were passed onto our girls. We didn't pass on our exact hilas, but Naki is a taster like me, and Imara is a seer like Talib."

Naki rolled her eyes again as she reached for some snacks. "You're the only person who thinks that's fresh, Mom."

Abe scooted to the edge of his seat and opened his eyes wide. "I think it's fascinating. And Naki got the temperature thing from you, Talib. I wonder if most truth seers have a seer parent, but maybe not. Truth seers are so rare."

For a moment, the words hung in the air. Imara's dad sat forward. He opened his mouth and then closed it again. After another breath, he finally asked, "Can you really heal her hila?" He looked to the side as if afraid to look when the answer was given. "Or only a little?"

"I don't want to give you false hope." Abe's voice quivered as the words came out. He did a tiny shake of the head and cleared his voice. This time, the words came out stronger. "But yes, I think I can heal it completely. There's this goop in Imara's eyes. If it works the way I think it does, then I can heal her hila permanently. The actual procedure might take a few hours."

Tears glistened in her mom's eyes, which was a very good sign. Her mom wasn't usually very emotional. On the other hand, her dad beamed as silent tears slid down his cheeks. "That's wonderful," he said.

Naki took the opportunity to glare at Abe, but it didn't matter now. He would still have to do a lot to prove his commitment, but Imara knew he would. And her parents were finally willing to give him a second chance.

Abe wrapped an arm around her shoulders. "Tell me more about Imara," he said. "What was she like as a child?"

"Do you know the story of how Imara saved our lives?" her dad asked. Just like always, a twinkle appeared in his eyes as he said it.

Abe turned to her with a chuckle, apparently not noticing how rigid her shoulders had become. "Why am I not surprised a story like that exists?"

"Oh, I love this story," Siluk with a grin. "This is probably my favorite story in the whole world."

Yet again, that annoyance flashed through Abe's eyes. His jaw clenched, but it relaxed a moment later when he turned to her dad with an expectant look. "What happened?"

"No one needs to hear that story." Imara's cheeks grew hot as she spoke. Would Abe's healing abilities let him know that a lump was forming in her throat? She hoped not. She tried to swallow the lump and said, "You tell this story way too much, and it's not even good."

"It happened when Imara was only fifteen," her dad said, completely ignoring every word she had just said.

Abe leaned in toward him, already fascinated by the tale even though literally nothing had happened yet.

She opened her mouth to stop the story, but her mom picked up where her dad left off as if they were reading it from a script. "We were leaving a party, and I was wearing my most expensive jewelry," her mom said.

"All of the sudden, we were attacked!" Her dad raised his voice, making them all jump. He threw his hands into the air for the best possible effect.

Now that the shock of his raised voice had worn off, Imara rolled her eyes. "A man threatened to kill us if we didn't give him my mom's jewelry." She shrugged. "So, I stole his gun, and he ran away. It wasn't a big deal."

"Wasn't a big deal?" her dad said with a gasp. He clapped a hand over his heart.

"It was very heroic," her mom said with a glowing smile. "Imara was only fifteen. She frightened away one of the most notorious murderers Nairobi has ever seen. The police were able to catch him after Imara explained to them what he looked like. She saved our lives and probably many others."

Naki straightened her back, and a look of pride filled her eyes that was even more ridiculous than her parents'. Naki seemed to have forgotten that she was supposed to be mad at Abe. Instead, she spoke solemnly with her finger and thumb stroking one of her tiny braids. "The man said, 'Give me the jewelry or you die.'" A little smile twitched at her lips. "But anytime Imara is faced with a bad choice and a worse one, she likes to find a third option."

Grinning widely, her mom dropped her chin into the palm of her hand. "Before I could even remove the jewelry, Imara hit the man in the gut and stole the gun away from him. He tried to get it back, but she was already calling the police. The man decided to run instead."

Abe turned to her with the same look all of them were giving her now. She hated it more than anything in the world. Attempting, yet again, to swallow the lump in her throat, she waved a hand through the air. "It wasn't a big deal. I saw that he was paying more attention to the jewelry than to me. Then, I could see that his anxiety increased like it does during fight or flight. I realized he would run away if he was threatened anymore. I just used his emotions against him. It was nothing."

Still ignoring her protests, her dad said, "They say hilas are like superpowers, but Imara is the only one I know who comes close to being a superhero."

Abe grinned at that, but Imara stood up and refused to look at any of them. Without a word, she started gathering the dishes. If they wouldn't stop talking, she'd just have to hide out in the kitchen until they were done.

Before she could lift another plate, a loud knock sounded at the door. When she answered it, a young woman stood in front of her with dreadlocks that fell past her shoulders. The young woman's light brown skin complemented her warm brown eyes. She panted and clutched at her side as if she had just finished a marathon.

"Are you Imara?" she asked.

When Imara nodded, the young woman took a deep breath before she spoke again. The way she breathed in gave a sense of foreboding. Her next words only solidified the feeling. "Safiya needs your help."

SEVEN

THE NEXT MORNING, IMARA GOT INTO A
bubble car with the young woman with light brown skin and
dreadlocks. Mali was her name. She worked at the police
station and apparently was a good friend of Safiya's.

"Thanks again for helping," Mali said as her warm brown
eyes glanced around the bubble car.

Imara reached for the hair on the back of her neck. Abe
had cleaned enough goop from her eyes for her to know that
Mali could be trusted. Still, it didn't ease all her fears. "Are you
sure it's a good idea for me to go to the police station? I'm
currently a fugitive of the Egyptian territory. My airport pass
and bubble car privileges have been frozen."

Mali pulled her dreadlocks up to a bun as she rolled her
eyes. "Uh, we're not idiots. We've had people following your
story since the catacombs, and we're already fighting to get you
exonerated. The Egyptian police *conveniently* lost the video
recorded statements they took from everyone that prove your
innocence. Luckily for you, we actually care about our citizens
and we made copies of the records before they got 'lost.' I
promise, no one in our department cares about your fugitive
status."

Letting out a sigh of relief, Imara sat back against the upholstered seat of the bubble car. Knowing the Kenyan police were on her side did help, but she still had the global vote to worry about. And finding Safiya. Maybe she should have let Abe come with her to the police department. That way, he could clear the goop from her eyes when she needed her hila.

She shook her head. Her ears burned with embarrassment when Mali raised an eyebrow at the movement. Imara pinched the tiny hairs at the back of her neck even harder. Having her hila at the police department could be useful, but she didn't want anyone else to know Abe could heal her hila. It might become an advantage against Professor Santini.

A few minutes later, they arrived at the police department. At the front door, Mali used her ring to open it with her electronic police badge. "You remember those videos Safiya showed you a few months ago, right?" Mali asked in a whisper.

Imara nodded, suppressing the urge to roll her eyes. Mali had asked her this same question a dozen times.

Mali nodded as she pulled back on her fingers to stretch them. They were flexible enough that her fingernails the top of her forearm. It didn't look comfortable. "It was those videos where you had to figure out who in the police department was lying. There was a man and a woman."

"Yes, I remember it clearly," Imara said, doing her best to reassure Mali. For the thousandth time.

Mali nodded so hard her bun almost came loose. She slid her arm up her back to tighten the bun, again in a way that didn't look comfortable. "Good," she said. "We think those two people are hiding Safiya, or at least know where she's hidden. I just need you to point them out and hopefully we can get them to confess."

Imara drummed her fingers on the side of her leg. She had felt nervous walking up to the building, but maybe that was just because she was still afraid of getting sent back to Egypt. Still, it didn't seem like a confession would be that easy to obtain.

"Won't they be suspicious that I'm here?" Imara asked. "The man and the woman who lied?"

Mali stepped into the building with a carefree smile. "Nah, I'll just tell everyone you're here to get the Egyptian fugitive thing figured out."

A short wave of relief was immediately accompanied by a thread of anxiety. Mali seemed so confident that all would be fine. Unfortunately, everything hinged on Imara being able to point out the two liars and having them confess and tell where Safiya was. It didn't seem that easy to her.

At another door, Mali casually pressed the door opener, but quickly turned her body around to wave at a fellow police officer. Except…

She didn't actually turn around. Only her torso moved. Her feet stayed firmly forward while her shoulders almost completely turned the opposite direction.

It might have looked comical on a cartoon character, but to see someone move in such an inhuman way in real life was unnerving.

Mali whipped around. When she noticed Imara's face, Mali snorted and said, "I forgot to tell you my hila. I'm a contortionist."

She snorted again as Imara attempted to arrange her face into an expression that wasn't filled with disgust.

Mali shrugged. "It usually freaks people out the first time they see it, but it's the freshest hila for a fight. I'm super flexible, but I can also move into crazy positions wicked fast. And if anyone ever handcuffs me, I can slip right out with barely any effort." She let out a sigh. A tangerine glow of pride came off her skin. "It's the best hila ever."

Imara was so focused on the tangerine glow, and how it was fading fast, that she didn't notice how quickly Mali's face fell.

Mali rubbed a hand over her forearm and averted her eyes. "But I'm sure you're still fresh and all. Without … without a hila, I mean."

A bubble of laughter started up Imara's throat and she had to clench her jaw to keep it down. It wouldn't be long now until she had her hila back. Permanently. Abe was already gathering the supplies he needed to heal her. Once she finished at the police department, Abe would be waiting at her apartment to bring the colors back for good.

Mali sat on a chair across from Imara and immediately got to work. She leaned so close to her hologram screen, she barely had to reach to touch it. Her eyes narrowed in on the screen when another police officer entered the room and headed toward them.

When Imara glanced toward the officer, she pressed her lips into a thin line.

Mali reached up and leaned back as if stretching, except her back bent at an inhuman angle. Just as she finished yawning, she whispered, "Is he one of them?"

Imara did the tiniest nod she could manage.

Mali nodded and went back to her hologram screen, casual as ever. She wound her mouth into a knot and said, "There you go, I just submitted the videos of the eyewitness accounts that prove your innocence. We submitted the text documents yesterday, but they wanted to see the video witness accounts too. I'm honestly surprised they bothered to make video accounts. The Egyptian police are so useless."

"Thank you," Imara said as she shifted in her chair. Mali was doing much better at pretending everything was normal. Imara wondered if Mali actually had submitted the evidence to get her exonerated. From a quick look at her hologram screen, it looked like she did. It was probably easier to act like she was helping Imara when she actually was. Still, Imara shifted in her chair again, trying to seem less anxious than she felt.

Just as she moved into a new position, another police officer swept into the room. The woman had medium brown skin and a shaved head. Her skin shined as if it had just been slathered in lotion. Even though the woman's hair was different than it had been in the video, Imara recognized her at once. This was the woman who had lied in such a strange way.

Imara reached up for the hair on the back of her neck and dipped her head to the side to point to the woman with her head. Just enough for Mali to notice, but hopefully subtle enough that no one else would.

Mali nodded and switched to the messaging app on her phone. A few minutes later, the police chief came in with a crowd of ten police officers behind him.

"Rehema and Faraji," he said. "You're under arrest for conspiracy. If you tell us everything you know about the taggers, we might go easier on you."

Before Imara could blink, someone had her hands behind her back and an elbow around her throat. She recognized the shiny skin of the lying woman, Rehema, as the one around her. Imara pushed against the arms and her stomach sank when she realized the man, Faraji, had Mali around the throat as well.

Imara's head was already spinning with ideas to get them both free. Maybe none of this was her fault, but that wouldn't stop her from trying to save Mali. She'd never just stand by while someone's life was in danger.

Wedging her elbow into Rehema's ribcage, Imara jabbed as hard as she could. Though Rehema grunted, her grip only tightened. Imara felt air leaving her with each breath, but barely any air was getting back in.

Just as she considered another tactic, she managed a glance at the police chief. The panic in his eyes did nothing to encourage her. She lost another breath struggling against the arms around her.

But before Imara could push against her attacker, Rehema gasped. Mali had unbent herself from a highly unnatural position and kicked Faraji, even though he was already on the floor. "Idiot," she said. "Everyone always forgets I'm a contortionist. Nobody could catch me, no matter how hard they try."

Rehema's grip loosened, and Imara stomped hard on her foot. She kept Imara's hands behind her back, but her grip weakened with each second.

The man practically shriveled in a heap on the ground and said, "I'll tell you everything. I hate the taggers, but they gave me mounds of money! How could I refuse?"

The police chief scoffed at that. "Where is Safiya? She's my best officer, and I'm eager to have her back."

Finally, Rehema released the grip she had on Imara. The shiny-skinned woman took a step back, eyeing the police chief and Faraji equally before she acted. Her breaths became shallower the longer she stood there. After a moment, she blew out a restless breath and started crying into her hands.

With her face covered, Imara couldn't immediately tell if the tears were real or not.

"She's …," Rehema said with a sniffle. "Safiya's dead. The taggers killed her."

The woman's shoulders shook each time she sobbed, but the shakes were more drawn out than they should have been. And the rest of her body? It seemed unusually still combined with the awkward sobs. As Rehema sobbed again, Imara knew it was all for show. She detected a whine in the sob that seemed unnatural.

Imara glanced at Mali and shook her head as inconspicuously as possible.

Mali raised an eyebrow and mouthed the word *lie?*

After Imara nodded in confirmation, Mali grinned. "Nice try, Rehema, but that lie won't work this time. We're still getting a power signal from Safiya's ring. Since rings are powered with living DNA and her ring is specific to her exact DNA, her ring can't send a power signal unless she's alive. Now, tell us where she is."

Faraji let out a tiny gasp. He turned to glance at Rehema but seemed to think better of it. With a gulp, he turned his head to the ground.

"But ...," Rehema said, her voice quavering. "She blocked her power signal. I'm sure she did. She didn't trust anyone in the department. How could you know I was lying?"

The police chief raised one eyebrow with a cool glare. "I think a more important question is, what else are you going to tell us about the taggers?"

Rehema stood with her mouth gaping for a moment. Faraji gave her one last look, then plucked himself off the ground and stood tall. "I'll tell you everything."

An hour later, Safiya stood in the middle of the room with her afro bobbing and a wide smile on her lips. Her arms waved through the air as she recounted the epic tale of her escape from her original pursuers and then about her eventual capture.

The moment the story was over, Imara begged Mali to take her back home. Any other time, Imara would have loved to hear more about Safiya's adventures. But Abe had just messaged her to let her know that everything was ready for healing her hila.

She didn't tell Mali why she needed to get home, only that she needed to do it soon. In the bubble car, Mali rubbed a hand over her forearm as she looked out the window. "I'm sorry your airport pass and bubble car privileges are still frozen. I did send the videos to the Egyptian police, but they're being even more difficult than usual. Maybe Safiya can help us figure it out now that she's back."

It took Imara a moment to realize she should respond. She nodded and said, "Thank you." Luckily, Mali seemed to be just as distracted as her. Mali may have been worried about the fugitive status, but Imara only had one thought in her mind.

Getting her hila back."

EIGHT

THE MOMENT IMARA ENTERED HER A apartment, Abe shooed Naki and Siluk out of it. "Why are you sending them away?" she asked as Abe shut the door behind the others.

"I need a sterile environment." His jaw was set as he spoke, his eyes more serious than usual. When they turned the corner into the front room, the word sterile seemed to take on new meaning. Large plastic sheets covered the walls and all the furniture. Impossibly white towels sat folded on the floor by the couch. A little tray lay on a metal box. The tray had cotton swabs, a clear bottle of eye drops, and various metal and wooden tools. She only recognized the tweezers. A chemical smell surrounded them.

She tried to swallow the growing lump in her throat. When that didn't work, she latched onto another thought that was sure to distract her mind.

"Why couldn't Naki and Siluk stay in the kitchen? Or the bedrooms?"

"I already told you," Abe said, sitting down next the tray of tools. "I need it sterile."

She raised an eyebrow. "And they would disrupt cleanliness even in another room?"

He nodded with another serious look.

"Are you sure you didn't send them away just so we could be alone?"

His serious look fell away, and a grin replaced it. He shrugged. "Ask me again when I'm finished. Then you'll be able to tell with your hila."

She grinned at his wink and it all started to sink in. This was really happening. Abe was going to heal her and bring the colors back. This time, she'd see bad and good. She'd have her hila back.

She did worry about seeing only bad emotions like she had before, but the worry didn't sink too deep. She *could* see the good in people. She just had to look for it. Now, she would finally have that chance. It seemed too wonderful to imagine.

Her back sank into the couch as she settled, ready to make this a reality. Abe wiped her face with a papery cloth soaked in cleaner. The smell of it made her nose wrinkle but Abe seemed pleased with the results. His eyes narrowed as he used a cotton swab to dab the outside of her eye.

"I never got the chance to tell you yesterday," he said. "But I loved the story of how you saved your family from that gunman. You really are incredible."

A niggle of anxiety squirmed its way up Imara's back, making her nose wrinkle again. "You only say that because you don't know the rest of the story. They always make it sound like I'm some hero, but that was one of the lowest moments in my life."

Abe shot her a curious look before grabbing the bottle of eye drops. "Close your eyes, then blink when I say."

He dropped three drops into each eye, and then told her to blink. A burning sensation covered her eyeballs, but it strangely wasn't unpleasant.

He stayed silent as he repeated the process, but he seemed to be watching her carefully. This time when the eye drops fell, they felt less hot and even more pleasant. When he set the eyedrops down a moment later, he said quietly. "It still hurts you. Whatever happened that day."

She nodded, wondering if the tears welling in her eyes would interfere with his healing process.

"Tell me what happened," he said, bringing a cotton swab toward her face.

Blinking back the tears, she took a small breath. The words wouldn't be easy to say but having Abe here would help. "We were coming home from a party," she said. "It wasn't just a random party. It was a work party for my mom. She was the lead in this movie made by independent filmmakers in Nairobi. She was amazing. Really, really amazing. That movie was her big break. She was supposed to become one of the biggest stars in Kenya after that."

Imara's head hung as the pain of the past thrummed through her. "At the party, I told everyone how she thought the producer was an idiot. To be fair, he *was* an idiot. She never would have said it to his face or even to other people at the party. But everyone knew I was a truth seer so they treated the words as if my mom had said them herself. The producer humiliated her because of it and vowed she'd never work in the independent film industry ever again. Because of his influence, he had the power to make that happen."

When Abe turned to the tray of tools, she brushed away a single tear falling down her cheek. He replaced the cotton swab with tweezers, and she continued the story. "I ruined my mom's career in one stupid sentence. I thought I was right because I told the truth. I was so sick of everyone lying all the time. Once I realized what I had done, it was too late, and my mom's acting career was over. I'd never seen her more devastated in my life."

Abe remained stoic as he worked. He focused on his tools, his face barely registering that he heard her. But even after his few minutes of working, she started to see what was happening in his head. Cobalt blue drops began falling away from skin. Slow at first until they were pelting off. Sadness. Except, inside of each small drop of cobalt, a puff of cherry red danced. Love.

Inside the catacombs, she had seen a strato feeling for the first time in her life. A feeling with two different emotions combined in one. Now, after only a few minutes of Abe's work, she was seeing a strato feeling again. This one made her heart soar. He was sad because he loved her. He ached for her.

Seeing it gave her the courage to finish the story. The *real* story. The one that didn't make her look like a hero at all. She wanted to hang her head but with Abe working, she couldn't. Instead, she settled on staring at the ceiling.

"When that mugger ran into our family in the alley, he held the gun to my head and said he would kill me if they didn't give him the jewelry." She bit her lip as she drummed her fingers on her thigh. "In that moment, I wished he *would* kill me. I thought it would be better if I wasn't around to ruin my family's lives. Naki and I weren't friends by then, and I had ruined my mom's career. I figured it was only a matter of time before I destroyed my dad's life too."

She tugged at the seam in her pants. "I'd never seen fear coming off people like I did that day. My mom's hands were shaking so hard, she couldn't remove her jewelry. She was already devastated about her acting career. When she had fear piled on top of it, she could barely move. So, my dad tried to help her, and the guy got mad. He threatened to kill all of them. He said he'd take the jewelry once we were dead. He pointed his gun at my dad.

"Something inside me just snapped. When he was threatening to kill me, I thought I deserved to die. But when he threatened the rest of my family, I thought maybe that could be my redemption. I thought maybe my life wasn't worth saving, but if I could save them, then maybe I wasn't so bad after all. Since I already didn't care whether I lived or died, I fought the man with no regard for my life."

Abe had stopped working now. His jaw was clenched so tight, she could see a vein popping out under his chin. Those cobalt blue drops of sadness pelted off his skin even faster, except now, the cherry red puffs of love had grown so that they encased the drops instead of dancing around inside them. Still, they were nothing to the look in his eyes. He stared like he wanted nothing more than to wrap her up and protect her forever. The somersaults in her stomach seemed to desire the same thing.

To have him care so much made her feel the same as she did the day she first met him. It made her feel like there was something good inside her.

Even after all the mistakes she made.

He turned away as he rubbed his eye. She wondered if a tear was coming out of it. After clearing his throat, he went back to work on her eyes. He didn't say anything for a long time. When he finally did, his voice cracked as he began to speak. "Even if you hadn't saved them, you were still worthy of life."

She knew he would say something like that, but hearing it still worked on her in ways she never expected. The pain and weight of her past seemed to bubble to the surface of her skin. When he looked at her again, the pain kept bubbling up until it seeped out of her completely. Not for the first time since she had known him, some of the weight from her past lifted out of her, healing as it went. Could other healers heal emotional wounds as effectively as Abe?

"Thanks," she said as the last of the weight wisped away. "I guess I still think my only redeeming quality is that I'm willing to sacrifice myself for other people. I'll always have that to some extent, but I guess it would be nice if I believed I had other redeeming qualities too."

He chuckled. "You have several. You are brave and selfless when you try to help others, which is fresh. But you're also loyal and smart and a million other things I could list if I wasn't so distracted by your extreme beauty."

A snicker erupted from her lips before he continued.

"I love how brave you are, but I would appreciate if you had a little bit more respect for your own life. I'm allowed to ask that of you since you already asked it of me."

She snickered again and tried to relax as he brought a strange metal tool toward her eye. A new level of concentration took over his face.

It seemed like a good time to stop talking and just let him work.

NINE

AFTER SEVERAL MORE MINUTES, ABE PUT THE eyedrops in her eyes one last time and announced that he was finished. She sat up slowly. A new wave of anxiety skittered through her. "Do you really think it will work?"

He wilted in place. "Can you ... Can you not see the colors?"

"I've been able to see them almost as soon as you started," she said with a grin. "I meant, do you think it will last this time?"

He tucked his fingers under her chin before tilting it up. "Let me see," he said, taking way more time than necessary to gaze into her eyes. "I don't see or feel any more of the eraserfall crystals, but we'll know in a few hours if I actually got them all." He kept staring into her eyes for several more seconds.

When it became painfully obvious that he was looking just for fun and not for any eraserfall-related reason, she dropped her head onto his shoulder.

"Hopefully you'll start seeing more positive emotions now," he said. "Now that you have a different perspective on life or whatever."

She smiled as a puff of red love escaped his skin. Seeing the color was nice, but feeling his fingers wrapped between hers felt even better. She let time pass just enjoying the moment. But now that the reality had started to settle in, they needed to talk. Even though they needed to have this conversation, she still wanted to avoid it.

With a deep breath, she forced the words out. "Remember in the catacombs when I could see that you desired Naki, and you didn't realize I could see it?"

Abe flinched as he started rolling the little tools up in a plastic sheet. "I desired information from her; I didn't desire *her*."

"I know, but that's not my point," Imara said, waving a hand through the air. "The point is, I see things with my hila that are usually hidden. It sort of makes our relationship unfair."

He nodded slowly while a drip of mustard yellow guilt fell away from his skin. Just as he started talking, a new emotion appeared. A thread that she immediately recognized as desire, but in a color she had never seen before. The brownish reddish thread fluttered out mostly around his shoulders. She decided to call the color cinnamon, but she still didn't know what it represented.

Abe rolled his shoulders back as the cinnamon threads kept fluttering. "People don't keep secrets in a healthy relationship anyway. I didn't technically lie about Edrice, but you probably would have figured out our history if you'd had your hila. Maybe it's better if you do see all my emotions. Then I can't keep anything from you again. I don't think it's a big deal."

"Maybe it *is* a big deal," Imara said, helping him roll up the plastic sheet that covered the couch. "You definitely shouldn't try to keep something big like that hidden from me ever again, but I think it's also important that I don't interpret your emotions without understanding them."

Once the plastic sheet was in a tight roll, she dropped it to the ground with a thud. After a tiny swallow and a short mental pep talk, she said, "I've thought about this and I came up with a solution, sort of." She resisted the impulse to grab the hair on the back of her neck, but she had to do something with her fingers. She started picking at her nails instead. "I'm ... I think you'll agree. Well, I hope you'll agree. I mean, I guess I don't know what you'll think, but I'd love to know your opinion."

Abe had been peeling a plastic sheet off the wall but stopped halfway. He took her by the hand and didn't say another word until they were both sitting on the couch, facing each other. "What's your idea?"

This time, when the cinnamon threads fluttered out around his shoulders, she pinpointed the emotion. Desire to improve.

That gave her the strength she needed to continue, a little less anxious this time. "If I see an emotion and I suspect you don't realize I can see it, I'll tell you what emotion I see. But that's it. I just say the emotion and that's the end of the discussion. If you want to talk about it or explain it, you can, but you don't have to. And I'll do my best to not interpret the emotion."

He blinked a few times before he responded. His jaw worked as if considering her words carefully. Finally, he nodded and said, "I think that's a good idea."

Imara let out a long sigh and everything felt right. For a moment, she even forgot about her fugitive status. There was still plenty to do, but for now, she felt like she could take on the world.

When Abe started running his fingers through the curls on top of her head, she felt even better. She grinned at him and said, "I felt bad having an advantage over you, but you sort of have an advantage over me too. In the catacombs, I knew you desired something from Naki, but you knew I had a wound in my past that involved Naki. That's pretty incredible. I don't think most healers sense emotional wounds like that."

"Well…," Abe said, leaning back into the couch. Small mustard yellow drips of guilt fell away from his skin. "I can't sense emotional wounds either. At least not for most people. I can't explain how it happened in the catacombs except that I was in tune with you more than I've ever been in tune with anyone. I had felt wounds in the past, but the feeling was so muted, I barely even noticed it. Then you came along, and you acted like an amplifier or something. It still took me forever to recognize that I was feeling wounds, but around you, I've always felt them deeper than with anyone else."

Those words made a blossom of heat grow in her chest. With a grin, she said, "I think it's mostly weird that you're a feeling healer. Most healers are seers. That's probably the only reason it took you so long to figure it out."

He smiled as he traced the back of her hand with a light touch. "I never would have believed it without you. Even now, I always feel your wounds more intensely." He shrugged as a playful grin appeared on his face. "I've been thinking about this, and I'm pretty sure we're soulmates."

She snorted but cuddled closer to him anyway.

"Oh, I forgot to tell you," he said. "The Kenyan Council is making a bid tomorrow to move the global vote here in Nairobi instead of in Egypt."

Imara raised an eyebrow. They both left the couch and went back to rolling up the plastic sheets. "How did you find that out?"

"I heard people talking about it while I was out getting supplies. It sounds like most people here are suspicious of Santini and the taggers. Do you think the Kenyan Council has a chance of getting the bid?"

Imara used her thumbnail to loosen the adhesive attaching the plastic sheet to the wall. "Probably. Kenya is one of the most well-respected territories in the world. There's this lady on the Kenyan Council named Makena. Whenever she gives a speech, pretty much everyone in the world agrees with it. She has a lot of influence, but she never abuses it. She's the best."

Abe gathered the rolls of plastic sheets into a pile. "That's encouraging."

"I wonder …," Imara said, tapping her fingers against her thigh. "The Kenyan police will probably handle security for the bid, but they might need extra people for an event that big. I wonder if they might hire me for the event. That way, I'll have firsthand knowledge of everything that happens. Plus, if Santini tries anything, I'll be there to deal with it."

"That's a good idea, except I'm going to ask to be hired too. I don't want you to be alone if Santini or the taggers are at the event." He slid his thumb across his jawline as a look of concentration overtook his face. "If they get the bid and move the vote here, that could change everything. They could stop Santini before the vote even happens." He shrugged. "We'll just have to wait and see what happens during the bid."

TEN

TWO WEEKS LATER, IMARA STOOD AGAINST the wall of the Kenyan Council chambers with a stun gun in her hand. She'd never held a stun gun like this before. Abe's were so much lighter. This one seemed not only heavier, but somehow more deadly. But it wasn't. It was just a regular stun gun. The only reason it was so heavy was so it could knock someone out if needed. Hopefully that wouldn't be needed.

She scanned the nearby hallway one last time before leaning against the wall yet again. Abe hadn't been able to convince the Kenyan police to hire him for the event. It didn't surprise her in the slightest since they knew hardly anything about him, but she acted affronted all the same when they found out.

He didn't like the idea of her working the event without him, but they both agreed that the benefits outweighed the risks. She glanced around the council chambers, noting how much bigger they were than the Egyptian Council chambers. Tall windows covered three of the cream walls, each filled with impact proof glass.

Fifteen council members sat around a dark, mahogany table. They sat at the head of the room, quietly whispering to each other, somehow ignoring the commotion around them. Seated in chairs that filled the rest of the room were news reporters, business owners, and various politicians. Each of them had their hologram screens up with a phone call. The event would be broadcast live, but the various other guests would record it and be on phone calls so no one could tamper with the recording afterward.

Imara twitched at a noise. It took her a moment to realize it was only someone coughing. *Stay calm*, she told herself, taking a deep breath. Keiko had messaged her only a few minutes ago to let her know Professor Santini was still in Egypt. But just because Professor Santini was in Cairo didn't mean the taggers were.

With the influence Kenya had on global politics, it would almost be stupid for Professor Santini to not try something at this event. The Kenyan police were good, but that didn't stop Imara from being on guard. She squeezed the stun gun a little tighter as she glanced around the room again.

If anything happened at this event, she'd be ready.

After several more minutes, a bell rang out and the drum of voices fell silent. A man sitting at the mahogany table spoke first. He welcomed everyone in attendance and anyone watching. Then, he explained how they were making a bid to move the vote for a global judge out of Egypt and into Nairobi.

When he finished, he nodded toward a woman that Imara recognized immediately. Makena, the well-respected Kenyan Council member, sat high in her chair. Her cheekbones shined in the light of the room, but even more noticeable were her eyes. She looked out at the room with such fierce determination, Imara felt inspired even before she had uttered a word.

"I want to begin my remarks with a brief political history," Makena said, her cheekbones still glinting in the light. "There are many young citizens listening who aren't old enough to remember the world before we went global. Since that history is significant to this event, I'll start by briefly explaining. It started fifty years ago when Gordon Wrothman patented his airplane technology that made air travel a thousand times faster and cheaper. In less than a year, global travel became easy and affordable for almost every Earth citizen. Technology had allowed us to communicate across the globe, but now we could travel to another continent just as easily as the next city over.

"Another year later, people started to suggest that we needed a global government. Others fought the idea. They insisted a governing body for the entire world would be too powerful. Eventually, it was decided there would be no global body. Instead, countries would become territories and each territory would have its own council with at least seven members.

"To create a new global law, a citizen or a council must call for a global vote, as Carlotta Santini has done. After calling for the vote, the council for each territory must agree or decline the vote. Once thirty percent of all territories agree to the vote, the global vote must then be held.

"When a global vote is held, all members from each of the councils around the world arrive at a specified location. For one week, these council members discuss the vote. At the end of the week, the vote is taken. If the vote gets a yes from at least seventy percent of council members, the law goes into effect.

"As of this morning, forty-five percent of all territories have agreed to the global vote about whether Carlotta Santini should be the global judge. It is too late to stop the vote from taking place, but we can still change the location of the vote.

"As a member of the Kenyan Council, I officially bid that the global vote location be changed from Cairo, Egypt, to Nairobi, Kenya. I will explain my reasons now."

Makena's face went rigid for a moment and Imara saw a raven black rash of anxiety come out from her skin. The rash didn't fade, but the rigidity in her face was replaced by a look of confidence as she continued speaking. "Our method of creating global laws is not perfect. This system of government is incredibly new compared to other governments in the history of the world. We have some things that work well. Having territories run by councils has been very effective everywhere in the world.

"Even with things that work well, we have other things that have yet to be perfected. We don't have a global judge, but we also don't have any kind of governing body to create or enforce global laws. Each territory is responsible for enforcing global laws. If a certain territory isn't enforcing the laws or if it seems corrupted in any other way, the councils from the other territories can disband it and get new council members voted in, but that may not always be enough.

"I believe it would be wise to have a global judge to interpret laws. But I think it is far more important to have some type of global governing body. If we give someone the powers of a judge, without first having a governing body to balance that power, we would essentially give the judge ultimate control over the entire world. She could interpret laws in ways that made it impossible to remove her from that position of power.

"Regardless of whether Carlotta Santini would be a good judge or not, this is the wrong time to vote for a global judge. We first need to put a governing body in place that has checks in place to prevent corruption.

"It is my opinion—and I think any sane person would agree—that now is not the time to elect a global judge."

Makena took in a breath and pushed herself to her feet. Her eyes looked even more fiercely determined than ever. "That was my opinion even before I knew anything about Carlotta Santini as a person. Over the past few days, I have been informed of many things about Santini and her taggers. Things that have made my hair stand on end. I cannot express to you how deeply I am against the taggers. They are a terrorist group obsessed with moral cleansing. Their ideals will breed distrust and a culture of fear. Though I was adamant before, I now vehemently urge everyone to vote no in the coming global vote."

The room seemed to give a collective shudder as Makena sat back down. She laced her fingers together and said with a relaxed voice, "We still have time before the vote takes place, but the Kenyan Council bids to have the vote moved away from Egypt so the taggers won't have any more influence on council members when the time comes."

Makena nodded to indicate the end of her speech. The news reporters' hands flew into the air, ready with a thousand questions.

Imara didn't realize how tight she was gripping her stun gun until she noticed the cramp in her thumb. She had been afraid before, but now she was positively terrified. Makena had all but asked for a war with the taggers.

As moving as Makena's speech was, Imara knew they had another problem. Tagging was definitely wrong, but Professor Santini had a way of making even the most horrible things seem mild. Plus, she knew how to cover her tracks. The biggest problem the Kenyan Council faced was proving to the world just how bad tagging was.

Imara jumped when a door shut down the hall. She narrowed her eyes and crept toward the door with her finger on the stun gun's trigger. As she played through different combat techniques in her head, a teenager rounded the corner. The boy wore a badge marking him as a member of the youth group who had come to the event. Internally scolding herself for being so jumpy, she lowered the stun gun.

As the teenager moved to join his group, Imara reached for the hair on the back of her neck and tugged it as she chewed on her bottom lip. Her eyes darted around the room, watching for anything suspicious. The emotions she saw seemed to fit with the speech. Wine-red spikes of fear. Marigold triangles of courage. There were a few outlying emotions like guilt and excitement, but nothing that gave her cause for worry.

Maybe Professor Santini hadn't planned anything for this event, but that didn't seem likely. Her former teacher always seemed to plan at least twelve steps ahead. But if she had planned something, what was it? Where were the taggers?

The news conference only lasted another ten minutes, and then people started filing out of the room. Nothing seemed out of the ordinary as they moved. Imara never stopped clutching her stun gun as her head filled with all the possibilities. What if a tagger was hiding behind a trashcan? What if a tagger was hiding in the crowd? What if a tagger threw a bomb?

But soon, everyone had left the building, and still nothing out of the ordinary had occurred. Nothing. It was unnerving. Where were the taggers? She had been certain they would do something at this event. But... nothing.

When no one but the Kenyan Council members remained, Imara moved down the hall to the meeting area for the police officers and other security personnel. She found Mali and Safiya in a corner of the room wearing identical grins.

"That went better than I expected," Mali said to Safiya. "New polls predict this stupid judge vote will lose by ninety percent. Even if half of those territories decide to vote for her when the time comes, the vote will still lose. Forty-five, fifty-five isn't enough to get a vote passed."

"Did you have any trouble during the event?" Imara asked, still clutching her stun gun tighter than necessary.

Mali jumped at Imara's voice but relaxed once she realized who it was. Apparently, Mali was jumpy too. Or maybe it was because she sensed the edge of fear in Imara's words.

Safiya's afro bobbed as she took a step toward Imara and placed a hand on her shoulder. "I know you've been in crazy situations the last few months," Safiya said. "But this is how things usually go here in Nairobi. Smooth. Our police department is world renowned."

Imara nodded, trying to settle the acrobatics going on in her stomach. "I know, it's just... I thought they would try something." She looked over her shoulder at another harmless noise.

Safiya squeezed her shoulder and looked like she was about to say something comforting when Mali jumped into the air.

"The location bid went through!" she said, tapping her ring off. "They'll lock the location in a few minutes, but it's basically settled. The vote is going to be in Nairobi."

"Excellent," Safiya said with a smile. "Now they just have to build a building big enough to fit all the council members that will be coming."

Mali grinned. "They already have a place. That lady who has been trying to get her greenhouse built offered the blueprints for her glass dome plans. They'll use the glass dome for the vote and afterward, she'll convert it into a greenhouse."

Imara clutched her stomach as she looked over her shoulder, certain she'd find something out of the ordinary this time.

She didn't.

But the day wasn't over yet.

ELEVEN

IMARA ENTERED HER APARTMENT AN HOUR later and still, nothing strange had happened. She worried, but at least part of her was finally starting to relax. Maybe Safiya was right. Maybe she was expecting something to go wrong because so much *had* gone wrong for her in the last few months. But this was Kenya. Things didn't usually go wrong here.

As she entered the front room, she saw Abe writing a message on his ring. Naki wasn't around, which wasn't a huge surprise since she didn't usually get home from work until later. Siluk was stretched out on the couch looking more than at home. It had been surprisingly comfortable to have Siluk and Abe around all the time, if a little crowded.

Siluk was the first to notice her presence. "Hey Imara," he said. "This is pretty exciting, isn't it?"

Jagged waves of indigo annoyance shot off Abe's skin as he turned around. Even as he walked to her side, the waves of annoyance didn't fade. She tried not to, but her brain was already trying to interpret the emotion. Was he annoyed that she went to the event without him? Was he annoyed that Siluk had volunteered him to pick up Darius from Greece? Or maybe he was annoyed that he had to stop by his apartment in Egypt because he had forgotten a few things.

She pushed the thoughts out of her mind, but it was difficult considering this was yet another instance when Abe showed annoyance. And she'd only noticed it once they were on their way to Kenya. Was it something she did? She tried again to push the interpretation of his emotion out of her mind.

Only once Abe had pulled her close to his body did he react to Siluk's words. He let out a chuckle. "You think it's exciting that Santini is going to lose the vote?"

Siluk laced his fingers behind his head. "Yes. I also think it's exciting that we're finally going to stop Santini for good. If we can convince the council members to vote against her, no one in the world will trust her or the taggers. They'll have to give up on tagging."

Imara rubbed her hand up and down her arm. "I still can't believe they didn't try anything at the event. I kept expecting it, but nothing happened. I know I should be excited about the location bid, but I kept feeling like something would go wrong. It's..."

"Unnerving?" Abe asked.

She nodded. "The same thing happened in the catacombs. We thought the taggers would come back and kill us, we thought the Judge would kill us, but nothing ever happened. Just like now. It's making me nervous."

"Me too," Abe said. He grabbed his bag from the ground and hitched it onto his shoulder. "Are you sure you don't want to come with me, Siluk? I thought you'd want to be there when I pick up Darius."

Siluk buried himself deeper into the couch. "Nah, Naki asked me to stay so I could help her with dinner tonight. It should be done by the time you get back. I'll just see Darius then."

Imara wanted to go with Abe, but since he had to stop in Egypt and her fugitive status still hadn't been cleared, it wasn't really an option.

"Can I talk to you for a minute?" Abe whispered. He glanced at Siluk and tipped his head, pointing it toward the bedrooms.

She nodded and led him back to the room she now shared with Naki. As comfortable as it felt to have the apartment so full, it meant she didn't get much time alone with Abe. In fact, Siluk or Naki seemed to magically appear anytime they found themselves alone. It wasn't magic at all, of course. It was just Naki being suspicious of Abe. She must have asked Siluk to help keep them apart.

Once in the room, Abe set his bag on the desk. While unzipping it, he licked his lips several times. After opening it, he wiped his palms on his pants before pulling anything from the bag. Finally, he reached in and started pulling something out, but stopped before she could see it. He swallowed and said, "Don't get mad."

That brought an ominous weight to the room, but Abe was too focused on the bag to notice her concern. He reached in and pulled the item out so slowly she finally had to lean forward to see what it was.

A mirror.

"Abe, no," she said, taking a step back.

"I know you're still scared of them."

She shook her head and raised her hands up to her chest. "I can't. Especially not now, I can see the colors again. I can't look."

He pulled the mirror out completely and set it on the desk. The pewter mirror had a long handle under the oval reflective surface. Small opal circles were embedded into the handle. It would have looked beautiful if she weren't so terrified of seeing her face inside it.

"You avoided mirrors even after the eraserfall when you couldn't see the colors. It's no different now than it ever has been."

She cringed but didn't turn away from him. Instead, she sat down on the edge of Naki's bed. She and Naki had been taking turns sleeping on the bed and on the floor. Last night, Naki had slept on the floor, which meant the bed was neatly tidied, and the floor was still covered in blankets and pillows.

Abe sat down next to her, taking his time with the words. "You said when you look in the mirror, all you see is the worst parts of your personality."

A sting heralding tears shot through the inside of her nose. She sniffed as she nodded, trying to suppress them. "The very worst," she said. "It's not just recent things either. It's everything I've ever felt. Maybe I'm better now, but you know my past isn't pretty. I can't face it." She cringed and averted her eyes. "I can't."

Goosebumps prickled up on her skin, despite the warmth in the room. Everything started to feel cold inside her until Abe wrapped his hand around hers. The heat from his skin seemed to spread through her, settling the goosebumps.

"You used to see the worst in everybody, not just the worst in yourself," he said. "But don't you see positive emotions all the time now? Maybe you only saw the worst in yourself because you *thought* the worst of yourself. I think it's time you started to see how much good you have too."

She cringed, but his face became set. He stared at her with unrelenting determination. It made her stomach flop and her heart race. But it also made her want to do what he asked.

"I want you to look in the mirror and find one good thing about yourself. Just one. We'll keep practicing until you don't fear mirrors, but for now, just look for one positive emotion."

She shook her head, trying to convince herself this didn't have to be done. Even as her head moved side to side, the truth settled inside her. Abe was right. He wanted her to be happy, and that meant facing her past. It made her cringe, but maybe with Abe here it wouldn't be so bad.

He grabbed the mirror and turned it so the reflective side faced away from her. Putting his arm around her, he squeezed her shoulder. "I'll be right here the whole time. You can sit closer to me if it helps."

She shook her head, but not to protest. She had already accepted that this was happening. Abe would never stop pestering her until he healed this wound, and she trusted that he could. When she shook her head now, it merely meant *not yet*.

She took in a deep breath and did snuggle closer to him. After taking in one last breath, she let it out slowly and finally nodded.

He lifted the mirror and turned it until her reflection blinked back at her. On instinct, she flinched. She hadn't looked in a mirror properly for six years. Not since she ruined her mom's career.

After less than a second of looking, she had to turn away. Her eyes fell on Abe and the turquoise blue swirls of hope spun around him brighter than ever. As always—maybe even a little *more* now—he believed in her without a trace of doubt. She loved that, but it meant he expected difficult things from her.

But he was right. She was different now. She could do this.

With another deep breath, she turned back to the mirror. A red orange whip of selfishness writhed in an angry twist. Marco died because she had been so focused on the pain of her bullet wound that she couldn't save him. It sounded irrational in her mind, but the longer she looked, the faster the red orange writhed. Fear. The wine-colored spikes grew out so far, she couldn't see the ends of them. Professor Santini would win, and she couldn't stop her.

Blood red flames began burning around her.

Anger.

Why was she doing this again?

She closed her eyes for a break and started listing positive emotions in her mind. Happiness, excitement, love, protective worry.

Come on. She'd been practicing this. She was getting better at finding the good in others. If she could do it with them, why couldn't she do it for herself?

Abe squeezed her hand. What would he say about her? He would call her brave. Selfless. Beautiful.

She opened her eyes again, desperately trying to see herself the way Abe did. Her dark brown skin *was* blemish free. And the soft curls tumbling over her forehead *did* complement the shaved hair on the sides and back of her head. The golden flecks in her black irises were nice. But none of those things were emotions.

She stared harder at the negative emotions until her eyes watered. The anger burned the brightest, though it was nearly eclipsed by the sheer number of fear spikes. What would happen if Professor Santini won? She shook the thought out of her mind and looked again.

The anger only grew. The blood red flames seemed to grow out of control until they raged so far away from her skin that they overtook the smoky swirls of turquoise hope coming off Abe.

When the flames of anger licked away Abe's hope swirls, she had to look away. She buried her face in his shoulder and shook her head.

"I can't," she whispered. "I tried, but I can't."

She expected him to nag, but instead she felt Abe drop the mirror onto the bed. He pulled her close until his arms enveloped her. The thought of her anger flames devouring his hope swirls was enough to make her nauseous. When he held her tighter, the image became a little easier to bear.

She breathed in his spicy, sweet scent and said, "You know, I like having you and Siluk around all the time."

A jagged indigo wave of annoyance rushed out of Abe as he flinched. He quickly covered the look up with a smile, but more annoyance waved out from his skin. Was he annoyed that she had failed with the mirror?

No. She forced herself to stop. She saw an emotion and immediately tried to interpret it. She promised she wouldn't do that anymore. Things had to be different now. She promised Abe if something like this happened, she would tell him.

"What is it?" he asked, running his fingers through the shaved hair on the back of her head.

She swallowed. "I saw an emotion."

"Oh," he said as his nose wrinkled.

"I won't interpret it." She pushed the words out, desperate for him to trust things would be different now. "I saw annoyance. You've had it a couple times in the last few days, but just now was the strongest I've ever seen it. Even before you healed my hila, I noticed you were getting annoyed. I promised I would tell you if I saw something, but I meant it when I said you don't have to explain."

His jaw flexed as he dropped his hand into his lap. "I probably should explain."

"No," she said, shaking her head insistently. "You don't have to. I don't want you to feel obligated just because I can see it."

He dug his knuckles into his leg, swallowing every few seconds. "No, I think I should say something. I've been avoiding it, but it's time."

Her heart sank at those words. She didn't want him to feel obligated. But then again, maybe he wanted to talk about it because it was irritating him enough, not because she could see it. When he took a deep breath, her heart raced, afraid of what he would say.

"It's Siluk."

"Did he say something to you?" she asked, cocking her head to the side. "Did you fight with him about something?"

"No, it's nothing like that," He dug his knuckles into his leg and let the words out in a rush. "He cares about you and it bothers me."

She stared at him for three full seconds trying to make sure she heard him right. And then she laughed. "He doesn't care about me."

Abe cocked one eyebrow up as he glanced over her carefully. "Yes, he does."

She waved a hand through the air casually. "I just mean Siluk is friendly. He cares about everyone. I'm no different to him than any other person on the planet."

"Seriously?"

She laughed again.

Abe started rubbing circles into his temples. "He definitely cares about you. In the catacombs, when he used explosives to bring down that rock wall, the only thing Siluk noticed was you. He pushed you to other side before the rocks fell so you would be separated from the Judge."

Imara rolled her eyes. "He saved Naki too. That means nothing. He probably just realized he could help us, so he did."

Abe folded his arms over his chest and narrowed his eyes until they were nothing more than tiny slits. "What about when you got kidnapped by Takara? I asked him to help and he agreed with no questions asked. He left within the hour. He risked his life to help you."

Imara shifted in her seat but still wasn't comfortable. He left within the hour? Without any provocation? She always assumed Abe had begged him to come or offered him money or something. She swallowed, suddenly feeling even more uncomfortable than she had a minute ago. "Yeah, but he went into the catacombs with us to find Darius. He risked his life then."

Abe let out a scoff. "Yeah, for his very best friend. If he did that for his best friend, what does that make you?"

She blinked back at him, unable to think of a retort.

Abe looked away. Something about his face seemed like he was disappointed that she couldn't argue against that. "When you got shot in the leg in Egypt, he was just as worried as I was."

Imara rubbed her arm as she tried to think of the words. That didn't help and soon she was chewing on her lip, hoping it would jog her brain. Finally, she said, "Siluk and I have a complicated history. We were really good friends at hila school until I realized how often he lied. I got bitter. The change was gradual at first, but by the end, I was pretty awful to him. He knew I hated his lies, but he always acted like we were still friends. But that's partly just how he is. He's very friendly."

With a frown, Abe said, "I'm pretty sure he had a severe crush on you at one point."

She wanted to laugh as soon as he said it, but the noise wouldn't come. The more she thought about it, the more his words made sense. How had she never noticed this before? Siluk always seemed to be around, especially during personal moments. He always talked to her like she would tell him anything.

Still, no matter how much sense it made, nothing changed the way she felt about Siluk. Luckily, that was something Abe would be glad to hear. She took his hand and gazed into his eyes until the jagged waves of annoyance had faded completely. "You might be right about Siluk Even if you're wrong, he and

I definitely have history. But…" she said with a shrug. "You have history too."

"Yeah," Abe said, hanging his head.

She squeezed his hand again and smiled. "I'm not interested in Siluk. At. All. I don't think I ever could be. His lies hurt me badly."

Abe nodded and the torrent of his emotions seemed to settle. "You're right. About the whole history thing. We both know my history almost ruined everything. Or maybe that was my stupidity. Either way, I'm glad we talked about this." With a tiny grin, he said, "Is it bad that I'm glad he hurt you enough that you'd never be interested in him? Because I am relieved to hear you say that."

She snickered in return. "Well, I'm relieved that Edrice made an unethical deal with a cartel leader, so I guess we're even."

Abe started to smile back but seemed to think better of it and reached for her instead. He slid his hand around the back of her neck, pulling her face to his until their foreheads touched. Her heart leapt in her chest as she tasted his breath. Even after months, each kiss felt like seeing fireworks for the first time. The last few days had been so crazy; she couldn't even remember the last time they kissed. He seemed to be thinking the same thing because he leaned forward, ready to make this one count.

Just as his lips grazed hers, the bedroom door opened burst open, and Siluk waved his hologram screen at them.

"Darius has a question about your jet," Siluk said, adjusting his screen so Abe could see it. Jagged waves of indigo annoyance crashed out from Abe's skin as he glared at Siluk.

Siluk only shrugged with a small chuckle. "Did I interrupt something?"

Abe rolled his eyes and he got to his feet. He spoke to Darius on Siluk's hologram screen while he walked out of the room. When he reached the door, he turned back and said to Imara, "I think you should practice every day." He glanced at the mirror, and she nodded back at him. With a smile he said, "I just have to pick up Darius and make a quick stop in Egypt. We should be back before dinner tonight."

She nodded again as he disappeared through the door. She moved the pewter mirror to a drawer in the desk and wished Abe was already back.

TWELVE

IMARA SAT IN A CHAIR AT THE POLICE STATION
a few hours later. She'd spent so much time here lately; it was
starting to feel like she lived here. Unfortunately, Mali and
Safiya were still getting nowhere with her fugitive status in
Egypt. But she was getting to know the other police officers.
In fact, she started to wonder if she should apply for a job.

It used to be her dream job, after all. And she'd gotten it
once before. They would probably hire her on the spot if she
suggested it. But she'd changed so much in the last few
months. She wasn't sure what she wanted now, except to keep
people from dying.

Mali and Safiya sat across from Imara. Safiya's hands
moved through the air as she recounted another story about
her kidnapping. Imara's eyes grew wider with every word.

"And then," Safiya said. "Just when I expected Mali to call,
I answered a call from your boyfriend instead. He starts telling
me how you got kidnapped right when Faraji started shooting
bullets at me."

"He called you in the middle of a firefight?" Imara asked
with a chuckle.

"Technically he called me right before it started. I only
answered because I thought it was Mali. He actually tried to get

97

me to help rescue you even after he saw me barely get away. It was stupid of him, but still sweet. He was really worried for you when I said I couldn't help."

Imara blushed and had to shake her head to clear her mind of the kiss that had taken place only a few hours earlier. He'd be home soon. That thought did nothing to keep Abe out of her head.

"Still no luck with the Egyptian Council," Mali said as she scrolled through her hologram screen. The maroon mounds of frustration coming off her piled up. When she opened her mouth again, a new emotion erupted. Tumbling golden squares of justice all around the maroon mounds. "They shouldn't be able to do this. It's not right."

Imara frowned. Her chances of being cleared were withering away by the minute.

"It's not," Safiya agreed. "But it won't last forever. Once Santini gets voted down, she'll lose whatever influence she has on the Egyptian Council. After the vote, we can get the fugitive status cleared in a few hours."

Mali scowled but apparently didn't have anything to say back.

"Come on, Imara," Safiya said. "I'll take you back to your apartment."

As the two of them walked out of the building, Imara pinched the hem of her shirt. "I'm sorry I can't take myself home."

Safiya waved a hand through the air. "It's nothing. I've had my bubble car privileges frozen too, remember? I'm one of the only people who understands how frustrating this is for you."

Imara nodded with a smile as the tension building in her stomach settled. It felt good to have someone on her side. It was such a simple thing, but one she had lived without for a long time.

Once in the bubble car, Safiya's ring buzzed with a notification and she started tapping away at her hologram screen. Imara decided to use her distraction to check on Abe.

He answered her call a few seconds later wearing a smile that sent a cascade of butterflies through her. "I'm just about to leave Cairo," he said. "Darius had a ton of stuff he's bringing, so my jet is pretty full. Husani is trying to convince me to take Keiko, but I'm not sure I have room. I might have to come back for her later. Did you get the fugitive thing worked out?"

The butterflies inside her swooped to a halt. "No. Safiya thinks we might have to wait until after the global vote. Apparently, Professor Santini has too much power over the Egyptian Council right now."

Abe grimaced. "That's disappointing."

"Imara." Safiya had closed her hologram screen and gave her an expectant look.

"I have to go," Imara said to Abe.

He nodded. "I'm leaving soon. I should be back in less than thirty minutes."

She ended the call with a wide smile, hoping Safiya wouldn't notice how red the tips of her ears were.

Safiya chuckled under her breath. "They need me at the glass dome to check on a security feature. Do you mind coming with me? It can't wait."

"I don't mind at all. What's wrong with the glass dome? Is construction going too slowly? Am I allowed to ask?"

"Construction is right on schedule," Safiya said. "But they just noticed something problematic about the blueprints. The air vent system is set up where it's easy to cut off air to all the bedrooms while keeping air flowing through the rest of the building. The lady in charge says it's important to have it that way for when she converts it to a greenhouse, but obviously it poses a security risk. We don't want to make it easy for anyone to cut off air and kill all of the council members in their sleep."

Imara nodded and quickly wrote a message telling Abe that she was going to the glass dome with Safiya, but that she wouldn't be there long.

A few minutes later, they arrived at the glass dome and Imara's heart nearly stopped at the sight. It was so much bigger than she expected. It had to house hundreds of council members, but it was still bigger than she ever imagined.

The dome reached far into the air, coming the highest in the very middle. The triangular blue tinted glass panes were held in place with thick steel beams.

"I didn't realize it was so close to being finished," Imara said.

"The inside doesn't look as pretty, but it's coming along nicely."

They entered a rectangular door that was set into the glass at an angle. When she saw the inside, her heart nearly stopped again. The natural light filtering through the blue-tinted windows cast a heavenly glow on the white walls. The paint must have had some type of reflective substance inside because the walls glinted in the light as she walked past them.

They rounded a corner and entered a curved corridor. They followed it until they reached a large room with no furniture and unpainted walls. An eerie light hung in the room as if from a speckled light strand.

Safiya narrowed her eyes and tapped her ring with a suspicious glare. "The construction team is supposed to be here. Maybe they took a break because they knew I'd be checking security, but it shouldn't be empty. The police chief is supposed—"

Before she could finish, Imara felt something bludgeoning her from behind. She twirled around to fight even though there were stars in her eyes. She whipped her arms out, trying to hit something. Anything. Instead, a shooting pain knocked her in the back of the neck. Her eyes slammed shut and she fell.

THIRTEEN

IMARA FELT LIKE THE WORLD HAD ONLY BEEN dark for half a second. As she blinked the stars out of her vision, she noticed her surroundings were different. The eerie light had been replaced by bright flood lights that almost blinded her. As her eyes adjusted, the same room as before came into focus. But this time, it wasn't empty.

A crowd of people stood in a circle with their eyes on the ground. They were all looking at something, but she couldn't see what. Long, black lines kept blocking her view.

The people in the room soon fell to the back of her mind as she realized what those lines were. Iron bars surrounded her in a huge black cage with a rounded top. She scowled and looked for a way to break through the bars.

When a scream rang through the room, Imara reacted without a thought. She lunged at her cage, reaching for what looked like the door. Hopefully the cage would be weakest in that spot. Even better, hopefully the lock on the door would be decorative and she wouldn't have to break out at all.

She kept hoping right up until her fingers grazed the iron bars. The moment she made contact with the cage, an electric shock sent her flying onto her back.

The air got knocked out of her when she landed. It took several seconds to catch her breath. When she finally got a gulp of air, she realized the screaming that prompted her to action in the first place hadn't stopped. She jumped back to her feet and peered through the bars of her cage. This time, she kept her hands a safe distance from the electrified iron. After the shock, her eyes had to adjust to the light yet again. Her stomach wound in knots as the scene came into focus.

The first person she recognized put a shiver through her spine. The tagger with the round scar on his forehead stood at the head of the circle with a sinister smile. He held a long, thin device with a fork-like prong on the end of it. He touched it to someone's shoulder and the screams rang out again.

Safiya's screams.

The man pulled the long device away from her shoulder and the screaming stopped abruptly.

"Now are you ready to talk?" Professor Santini's voice sounded as calm and soothing as ever, but it held a bite Imara wouldn't soon forget. "Your contacts app doesn't seem to have contact information for any of your fellow police officers, but I know you have the information on your ring somewhere. Tell me where to find it and this will stop."

Now that her eyes had adjusted, Imara could see Safiya in a heap in the middle of the circle of taggers. Rather than answer Professor Santini's question, Safiya spat at the ground.

Professor Santini responded with a snarl, and Safiya actually smiled back at her. She lifted her chin, making her hair bounce. "You don't know me very well," Safiya said in an even tone. "So, let me tell you about myself. I don't bend to torture.

You aren't the first person who has tried to find my police contacts. Let me assure you, they are well hidden."

A jagged indigo wave of annoyance fluttered away from Professor Santini's skin, but her outward appearance remained calm and collected. She turned away from Safiya as if the conversation were no longer worth her time. "Never mind. I know from experience how effective torture can be. But it's not the only effective method, it's just the fastest." She glanced back at Safiya while a smile tugged at her lips. "I'm a truth seer. I'll scroll through your files and apps. I can assure you that your emotions will betray the information I need."

A weight dropped in Imara that seemed to turn her arms to lead. She wanted to believe it was a bluff, but in her heart, she knew Professor Santini could do exactly what she claimed. Why she wanted Safiya's police contacts remained a mystery, but whatever it was wouldn't be good. Imara had to do something.

She glanced around the cage, hoping to detect a weakness. The cage sat tight to the ground all along the bottom. The rounded top had thicker iron bars, making it seem even more impenetrable than the rest of the cage.

Now that she looked closer, the lock on the door hung open. That would have been helpful if the cage weren't electrified. Since she was the only thing in the cage, it didn't seem probable that she'd find something to push the door open that wouldn't also electrocute her.

With no immediate solution, she began to assess the rest of the room. A few of the taggers had left since she last looked at the circle of them. Professor Santini stood with the scarred tagger on her right. Two other taggers stood with them, towering over Safiya's body.

Four against two. Both she and Safiya had training in hand-to-hand combat. It seemed likely that the taggers didn't have similar training since she had escaped them so easily in Egypt. Even with Safiya injured, she felt certain they could get away long enough to call backup.

They might be in trouble if Professor Santini had a noise gun like she had in the catacombs. But Imara suspected the gun had been unique and was now gone forever. That meant her only problem was the cage.

She looked back at it with a frown. Electric. What did she know about electric fences? If she could give the electricity a place to go, that would help. Unfortunately, the only thing that could do that was her body. It would be pretty pointless since she'd be dead long before the electricity stopped.

"That was easier than I thought," Professor Santini said with a chuckle. Imara glanced over at Safiya. Wine-colored fear jutted out her skin in angular motions. Even with her face perfectly even, she had still given everything away.

Professor Santini tapped away at Safiya's hologram screen wearing a confident smile. A moment later, she clapped her hands together in delight. "Oh look. Just as I suspected, they've all allowed location sharing with you. With the help of our new enforcers, we should have them rounded up within the hour."

Professor Santini turned to the tagger with the round scar on his forehead, which only confirmed Imara's suspicion that he was second in charge. "Vikal, I just sent you the list. Take your team and the new enforcers and let me know when you have all the police."

Vikal nodded abruptly. When he marched out of the room, the other two taggers trailed after him as if he were their master.

Imara opened her mouth to shout when it occurred to her that the cage might not be electrified at all. It might have been a forcefield. Could her voice be heard through a forcefield?

"What are you going to do to the police?" Imara shouted.

Professor Santini turned, seeming to hear Imara with no trouble. "Ah," Professor Santini said, wearing a gentle smile. "I'm glad you're awake. I worried Vikal hit you too hard."

"What are you going to do to them?" Imara asked, ignoring the invitation to small talk. It seemed her voice could penetrate the iron cage, but that didn't rule out a forcefield entirely. Most forcefields blocked out sound, but this one could have just been higher tech than most.

"I'm not going to hurt them," Professor Santini said, glancing at a nearby wall hologram. "Despite what you think, I am not a villain. I want what is best. Unfortunately, our world is still young, and people don't usually know what's best for them."

At this, Professor Santini looked down at Safiya. Imara hadn't noticed before, but she saw now that Safiya's wrists were wrapped in chains.

"You have the blueprints for this building on your ring, don't you?" Professor Santini asked.

Safiya's face remained passive, but a fresh wave of fear spikes jutted out of her skin.

With a chuckle, Professor Santini said, "That's a yes or you wouldn't be so afraid. I have the original blueprints, but unfortunately, the construction team made a few modifications. I need the newest blueprints to make sure they haven't altered my air vents."

"*Your* air vents?" Safiya asked.

Professor Santini chuckled again. "Yes, *my* air vents. Do you have any idea how long I've been planning this? You may think you won a great victory by getting the vote moved to Nairobi, but that was part of my plan from the beginning. The air vents are another integral part of my plan, so tell me where I can find the latest blueprints."

"No." Even sitting in a heap on the ground, Safiya looked resolute. The two of them stared each other down before Safiya opened her mouth again. "I'll never tell—"

Professor Santini pressed a finger over Safiya's lips as if she were nothing more than a child. "I don't need you to tell me, remember?"

For a moment, Safiya looked ready to bite Professor Santini's finger off. Her eyes narrowed with a glare and suddenly, she squeezed her eyes shut. "If I can't see my hologram screen, then I can't give anything away with my emotions."

Professor Santini's mouth twisted as a jagged indigo wave of annoyance skittered off her. She regained her composure a moment later and looked at Safiya with a face as calm as a clear, blue sky. And then she slapped Safiya. Hard.

"Professor Santini!" Imara shouted. She couldn't stand here anymore. She had to do something. Anything. Maybe she could create a distraction.

"Come, come, Imara. I'm not a professor anymore and you aren't my student. I think it's time you call me by my name and drop the *professor*. I prefer Carlotta, but I'd settle for Santini."

Imara clenched her hands into fists. How could Professor Santini stand there discussing her name when her taggers were in the middle of trying to capture the Kenyan police? And how could she slap someone without a trace of guilt dropping away from her skin?

She tapped her chin and then executed a curt nod. "Yes, you should call me Carlotta. I think you've earned it."

Imara grimaced. To think she had earned anything from her former teacher did nothing but fill her with a sense of dread. Still, as much as it pained her to admit, Professor Santini had a point. Carlotta had a point.

An icy chill threaded through her veins. Not Carlotta. She *couldn't* call her Carlotta. It would have to be Santini.

"Now, back to you," Santini said to Safiya. "Please open your eyes. I'd prefer not to force them open."

Safiya squeezed her eyes shut even tighter.

Santini let out a sigh that sounded inappropriately calm. As if her favorite pastry weren't available at the market. Nothing but an inconvenience.

Santini swiped through Safiya's hologram screen, apparently deciding to see what she could find on her own first. Imara's head started spinning wildly. She had to get out of here. She had to save Safiya. And she *had* to do it soon. If everything had already gone according to Santini's plans, then they needed to do something unexpected.

Imara considered her cage again. She couldn't just grab the bars, as she'd already learned. Maybe something else could trigger the electricity. Maybe her belt? It might not be enough to channel the electricity but that wasn't going to stop her from trying.

She pulled the belt off slowly so as not to attract Santini's attention. She took in a short breath and threw the belt at the iron bars. When it hit the cage, a blue light appeared for a split second, surrounding the entire thing. Definitely a forcefield then.

She ripped her golden necklace away from her neck and threw it next. Nothing new happened and she had even fewer ideas than before.

She missed Abe.

After fighting against Sef for years, he always knew about these kinds of things. She blinked as the thought went through her.

Abe.

She could call him. Why hadn't she thought of it yet? In Takara's mansion, she hadn't been able to contact anyone because her hands were tied up or she'd been with Takara. Being inside a cage made her feel as trapped as she had been at Takara's mansion. But this time, she had access to her ring.

She turned her body away as she tapped her ring so Santini wouldn't see the hologram screen. Once she found her messaging app, she typed out the quickest message she could to Abe.

At glass dome. Taggers here. Send help.

She pressed send and tried to ease her beating heart.

Not even a second later, a chime came from Santini's ring. She tapped it with mild interest before glancing back at Imara. "Your messages won't send while you're inside that cage. The forcefield around you blocks all messages in or out."

Imara clenched her teeth, barely managing to keep a frustrated hiss from coming out. Another plan thwarted. Her only hope was getting out of this cage, and she still had no idea how to do that.

Unless...

Abe knew she should have been home by now. They had both allowed location sharing so he could find her if he looked. Even if the forcefield blocked her location, he knew she was at the glass dome. And he could see her power signal. How long would it take for him to get worried?

FOURTEEN

IMARA WRUNG HER HANDS INTO KNOTS AS Santini worked. She scrolled through Safiya's hologram and forced Safiya's eyes open when she needed them. She'd already found the blueprints. She kept looking. Even Safiya didn't seem to understand what she was trying to find now.

Imara kicked the iron cage, hoping something had changed. Of course it hadn't. Even with a light tap, her foot reeled back and caused an electric pain to travel up her calf. Just like every other time she tried kicking the cage.

What could she do now? She'd already tried everything she could think of, plus a few things she'd done without thinking. None of it seemed to do any good.

Santini produced a syringe filled with a pear green liquid. She bent down and whispered into Safiya's ear so Imara couldn't hear.

Shivers shook through her as she watched. Where had her mentor gone? Santini wasn't just talking to Safiya now, she was toying with her. She injected the liquid inside Safiya and the police officer screamed out in pain.

Imara stomped her foot and screamed, "Stop it!" The shivers inside her grew into shudders.

Santini glanced back at her with the smallest hint of interest. "I wouldn't do this to you, my dear. You have no need to worry."

"How can you do this to anyone?" Her stomach churned and bubbled the longer Safiya screamed. "When did you become this person? When did you decide that torture was the best way to get information?"

An angry grimace twitched at Santini's nose. "Takara tortured me endlessly for four months. Do you know what I learned?" She wiped the grimace away and replaced it with a saccharine smile. "Torture is very effective. Some things are worth it for the greater good."

Imara slammed a fist against her cage and barely flinched as the electric shock sent her onto her back. Safiya's screams rang through the room.

"Stop it!" Imara yelled again, tears pooling in her eyes. "I'll tell you what you need to know, just stop hurting her."

"You don't have the information I need," Santini said with a chuckle.

Safiya's eyes rolled back in her head while she tried to catch her breath. She looked dead for a few moments, but then she turned to Imara. The face looked so beyond what Imara had seen the first time Safiya called her for her interview, when she still attended Nazari Academy of Hila.

Safiya's afro hung limp from the sweat lining her forehead. Her muscles drooped, especially around her eyes. She glanced at Imara with no amount of the confidence or bravery she usually wore. Now, her face showed nothing but pain and desperation. Her voice sounded twisted. "Help me," she said. She stared at her through the iron cage until her eyes bored holes straight into Imara's heart. The next word she whispered too softly to hear, but Imara could see her mouth *please*.

As if it weren't hurt enough, Imara's heart seemed to break in two. She took off her shoe and threw it as hard as she could at the forcefield surrounding her. It did nothing. She tried her other shoe. Still nothing.

She grabbed her necklace off the floor and tried to get the forcefield to react to it, but it wouldn't.

She rammed her shoulder into the cage, hoping by some miracle, a weakness would appear. Nothing changed.

She did it again, but this time she met the forcefield with her elbow first. Maybe a smaller contact point would help.

It didn't.

She tried over and over until her body felt like it had been cooked from the inside out from all the electric shocks. As she got to her feet a final time, her body shook and tingled each time she took a step. But she had to get out.

If she didn't, she was certain Safiya would die.

She couldn't let that happen. She had to *keep* people from dying. She couldn't add another person to the list.

As desperation took over, a new idea formed in her mind. She'd grab the bars and not let go. Maybe the electricity would kill her, but Santini might try to stop her from killing herself. Hopefully.

It wasn't much of an idea, but what else could she do?

Meanwhile, Safiya looked even worse than before. Her head lolled to one side and the faint breath coming out of her nose came out so infrequently, it almost seemed like it wasn't coming out at all. That was a thought Imara was unwilling to accept.

She marched to the edge of her cage with a resolution like she had never known. No matter how much her body shook with fear, she was going to do this.

She snatched the bars, determined to not let go. But the cage seemed to have been designed to prevent this exact situation.

After a few seconds of holding the bars, a different kind of electric shock jolted through it. It felt more like a squeezing pinch, and it forced her to release her grip. Less than a second later, she was back on the floor, as helpless as ever.

She didn't have the courage to face Safiya again. Somehow, she knew Safiya only had minutes left. Instead, she curled herself into a ball and wept silent tears. She hugged her knees closer to her chest as wave after wave of anguish crashed over her. She'd tried, hadn't she? She did everything she could.

And it wasn't enough.

Now she turned to the only hope she had left. *Okay, Abe,* she said to herself. *Just this once, I'll be the damsel in distress. Just this once I'll let you rescue me instead of rescuing myself.*

She sniffed as more tears streamed down her cheeks. *And please hurry. I can't save Safiya without you.*

"I'm ready for you now, Imara." Santini's voice held the same soothing lilt it always did, but now that lilt made Imara want to gouge her eyes out. When she heard that voice, all she could see was Safiya's head lolling to the side, her eyes emptying of life.

"Come on now," Santini said, teasing. "What would Abe think of you if he saw you in this state?"

An anger gripped her, giving her the energy to pull her weakened body off the ground. "He knows I'm here." She let the words out slowly so they would have time to sink in. "He knows I should be home by now. And I know he'll do everything he can to help if he thinks I'm in danger."

Santini cocked her head to the side with a patronizing look that brought on another bout of nausea. She clicked her tongue. "You keep forgetting that I've been planning this for years. Being held hostage by Takara was not part of my plans, but I'm not afraid of Abraxas."

"He'll come looking for me. I know he will!" Imara shouted.

"No," Santini said, tapping her ring. "He won't."

She scrolled through her hologram screen until a video started playing. The moment the video started, Imara's broken heart dropped out of her chest all the way down to her toes.

A jet flew through the air. A jet she recognized at once.

Her teeth clenched together as she watched. She prayed that nothing would happen, but she knew something would. Why else would Santini show her this video?

A small ball of fire appeared under the jet. It looked so tiny, it didn't seem capable of much damage. The moment it hit the underside of the jet, everything burst into flames.

She let out a gasp. Her stomach clenched with anxiety.

The jet lost altitude so fast, she had to clasp a hand over her mouth to keep another gasp from escaping. Moments later, it crashed into the ground and massive flames overtook the screen completely.

Her chin quivered as she turned away.

"You should have joined me when you had the chance."

The words set Imara's teeth on edge. She reached for the hair on the back of her neck to keep some level of sanity. At least the sobbing had stopped. Only because her body was too weak to cry, but still. It was something.

"He might have survived," she said, trying to believe it. If anyone could, it was him. He had to.

Santini shrugged. "Maybe he did; it doesn't matter. It looks like he landed in Lodwar, which is a three-hour drive by bubble car, but it's a seven-day walk on foot."

With a grin, Santini tapped through her hologram screen until more videos filled the screen. This time they were news reports. The headlines read *Airports Down Worldwide. Bubble Cars and Planes are Down and No One Knows Why. No Airplanes, No Cars, No Food?*

"What did you do?" Imara whispered.

"I did what had to be done," Santini said, no trace of guilt anywhere around her. As she spoke, Vikal entered the room. "Just like I'm going to do now."

Rather than wait to find out what Santini was talking about, she glanced at the door Vikal had just entered. He left it open.

If she found a way out of the cage, she could escape through that door. She would hoist Safiya over her shoulder and use whatever adrenaline she had left. She just had to get out of the cage.

Her attention reverted to Santini when she noticed another syringe in her hand. Santini injected the clear liquid into the seemingly lifeless Safiya

"This one will kill her," Santini said—as simply as if she were discussing the weather.

Imara froze in place, unable to process the words. She held her breath, telling herself she must have heard wrong.

"She's in great pain right now. Her brain isn't likely to recover from the other drug I gave her. I'm not killing her to be cruel. I'm merely putting her out of her misery."

Imara's lip curled in disgust while ice seemed to spread through her limbs, the truth just beginning to grip her. "You mean you're murdering her. First, you tortured her so badly that her brain can't recover, and now you're going to murder her."

Santini shrugged, still as nonchalant as ever. "I don't see it that way, which I think you know."

Imara glanced at Safiya, holding her breath as she watched. Searching for some sign of life. Begging her eyes to see it. But even the emotions around Safiya had disappeared. Ice seemed to spread through her as a cold chill gripped her.

While Santini tapped away at her hologram screen, Imara asked, "Are you going to kill me too?"

Santini let out a patronizing laugh that was starting to get old. "I told you from the beginning that I need you. I didn't think I would have to force you, but your role is still crucial."

"Why?"

A smile passed over Santini's lips different from any of the others. This time, she didn't try to suppress any of the evil lurking inside. Grass green threads of desire whipped out from her skin. They grew so long, they seemed to disappear beyond the walls of the room. Imara recognized what those threads meant.

Power.

As if she needed a reminder, she saw again just how intensely Santini hungered for control.

"I have an important job for you. You are going to write and give a speech to the council members that will convince them to vote me in as judge."

Imara nearly punched the iron cage before she remembered the shock she'd get. Instead she spoke slowly, through her teeth. "I would never."

Santini's eyes narrowed, taking on a determination that didn't waver. "Never say never, darling."

Imara swallowed, trying to suppress the fear bubbling under her skin. *Never*, she said in her head. *Never, never, never.* Especially not after everything Santini had just done. Especially after Safiya's torture and murder.

No matter how sure Santini seemed, Imara still had control over her own actions. She'd never write a speech like that. Santini couldn't make her.

"Why can't *you* write the speech?" Imara asked. "Your taggers follow you like you're a goddess. If you could convince them about tagging, why can't you convince everyone?"

Santini clicked her tongue, making Imara feel like a lost, little child. "Most of the taggers were in the flood in the catacombs or they had a loved one who died in it. We share common ground. I tend to do better with people one on one. You seem to have a gift for speeches. And, I'll admit, I know Egyptians much better than I know Kenyans."

"That doesn't make any sense," Imara said, rolling her eyes. "People are people, it doesn't matter where they're from. Human nature is the same everywhere."

"Yes," Santini said, tapping her toe. The first outward sign of annoyance she'd shown so far. "I realize you see people differently than I do, which is probably why you are better at speeches than I am. Where I see culture, you see people. I realized a long time ago your gift is stronger than mine. Now I intend to use it to my advantage."

Imara let out a huff through her nostrils as she folded her arms over her chest. "I won't help you," she said. "Not ever."

"Check your ring."

The sudden change in subject took Imara off guard. She shook her head, trying to think where the request had come from. Her thoughts only led her to Safiya's lifeless body and the agony festering in her heart.

"Just check it," Santini said, more forcefully this time.

Imara tapped her ring only to be greeted by her regular hologram screen with absolutely nothing special. She inspected the screen while Santini stared at her, but nothing on it seemed out of the ordinary. Until she noticed her name.

Surprise slammed her in the gut like a sucker punch. There at the top of her hologram screen sat her name. Except now a tag had been added to the end of it.

Imara Zawadi Kalu, hero

The tag burned through her mind like the flames that engulfed Abe's jet.

Santini seemed pleased by her reaction. "Vikal just informed me that the police have been rounded up and are now heavily guarded in a secret location. It wasn't difficult to capture them all considering we had their exact location and the element of surprise."

"Actually …," Vikal said in a voice barely above a whisper.

Santini turned to him with a face completely calm, except for the one eyebrow twitching. Despite her temperate appearance, Imara could see jagged indigo waves of annoyance flowing off her skin.

Vikal gulped and cleared his throat before speaking again, a raven black rash of anxiety growing around him. "One officer escaped." He hung his head. "And blocked her location from us."

Santini's face remained like stone, but blood red flames of anger burned around her. She managed a strained smile and said, "Never mind. What can one officer do? Anyway, I wanted to assure you, Imara, that they aren't dead. I'm not barbaric, despite what you may think. I just needed to get rid of them until the vote is over. They'll be fed and taken care of, but they'll also be out of the way."

"What are you going to do now?" Imara asked. She didn't expect Santini to reveal all her secret plans, but even the tiniest things might be helpful to know.

"Now we start tagging. Since you destroyed my golden transporter, I only have crude tagging devices left. Each device can apply a specific tag. A few of my most trusted taggers will go out with one device and a list of people who deserve that tag. By the end of the day, at least one hundred people will be tagged. By the end of the week, it should be thousands. I expect the citizens will notice the tags soon. And then they can punish the people who have hidden their crimes for too long."

Imara's jaw clenched at the thought.

Santini reached through the cage and Imara started. "Yes," Santini said. "I can reach through the forcefield while you cannot. My taggers and I have a code in our rings that allows us to pass through the forcefield. No code; no passage. And no communication. This forcefield is probably my favorite invention to date, but you still haven't seen the best thing about it."

This time, Imara didn't ask to hear more. She was sick of the games.

Ignoring her silence, Santini leaned closer. "The forcefield can expand. Soon, it will surround the entire city of Nairobi. With my army of taggers and no police to stop us, I'll have complete control. No one can come in or out of the city and no one can send communication of any kind through the forcefield. And I won't lower it until after I win the vote."

Imara was going to run. She decided it right then and there. If Santini planned to expand the forcefield, that meant it wouldn't be keeping her inside the cage. The moment it started to expand, she'd ram into the little door and break through it with her shoulder. She'd run as hard as she could, and she wouldn't look back. She wasn't about to let Santini make a puppet out of her.

They eyed each other carefully for a few moments. At last, Santini gave one last glance at Imara before she tapped a button on her hologram screen. Before Santini could even take a breath, Imara had pushed out of her cage and bolted for the door.

FIFTEEN

WHEN IMARA ESCAPED THE GLASS DOME, SHE took in a deep breath. Her legs seemed stiffer than usual, but she attributed it to the grief still rocking through her. Though the electrocution from the iron cage probably didn't help either.

Once outside the glass dome, something in the air felt different right away. Maybe it was the fact that bubble cars were stopped randomly in the streets. Maybe it was because a buzz of electricity hovered somewhere above. The forcefield had now expanded around the entire city.

No one knew about the police being captured, at least not yet. But even that would most likely be common knowledge soon enough.

She walked past a market where business owners shouted about their wares, but without the gusto they usually had. It unnerved her to no end.

As she glanced down the street, she considered her options. Without a bubble car, her apartment would take almost an hour's walk away. Naki's work was close by. She'd better go there first. She just had to keep moving or else the thought of Safiya's limp curls and lifeless eyes would cripple her for days.

Walking would be good. It would give her time to make sense of everything that had happened. She realized now why Santini had a video of Abe's jet specifically. When Santini broke car and plane travel all around the world, it probably did nothing for private jets like Abe's. She must have targeted his specifically and got video of it to show Imara. There was a chance he survived, but was it really possible with so many flames?

That thought was too much to process, so she thrust it away. Abe was a healer. It didn't matter how much smoke and fire engulfed the jet, the video had been suspiciously devoid of debris. If it was just a fire, he had a chance. He could treat burns easily, even his own burns. And he always had medical supplies with him. He'd be okay. He had to be.

She turned down a familiar street and ran right into Mali. It seemed surprising, but not shocking—until she remembered all the police officers had been captured. All except one.

Imara's mouth dropped open. Mali recovered from the shock much faster. She gripped Imara by the shoulders and got so close her breath warmed Imara's nose.

"Where's Safiya?" Mali asked.

Imara stood as still as a statue. She gulped but couldn't find any words.

"Someone tracked me," Mali said with a glare. "I only got away because of my hila. I can't contact anyone. I think someone targeted the police officers."

Imara gulped again. She had to avert her eyes and the only response she could muster was a tiny nod.

"Do you know what's going on?"

Imara nodded again while a tingle swam through her arms and legs. It was probably a lingering effect of the electrocution, but the images of Safiya popping through her mind didn't help.

"Hey! Are you listening to me? Where is Safiya?"

"She's dead," Imara choked out, only then realizing she was sobbing. "The taggers captured all the police but you. They're in some holding facility, but I don't know where. Airplane and bubble car travel have been broken everywhere around the globe. And, there's this forcefield around the city." It felt strange to speak. Her mouth bit over the words, choking through each one with more effort than it should have taken. "She claimed no messages can get in or out and that people can't travel through it. Maybe we should check to be sure, though. And they're tagging. People are going to get hurt. I have to stop this. I have to keep people from dying."

Mali gripped Imara around the elbow and forced her down the street. "You're in shock," she said. "Is there a safe place we can go that's nearby?"

Imara opened and closed her mouth several times before she realized no words were coming out. Finally, she pointed. Naki's work was only a few minutes from here. Maybe she should message Naki first to make sure she hadn't gone home already. The idea passed through her mind, but her fingers didn't move.

She felt numb. Nothing about the world seemed real. She remembered when she first left the glass dome. Everything felt different. But maybe it wasn't anything with the world at all. Maybe it was her.

Mali tugged her again, forcing her feet to move.

A woman working at one of the market stalls started yelling from behind them. "What is this?" the woman shouted. "Your name says *thief* at the end. What did you do?"

A man replied with remorse in his voice. "That was years ago. I went to jail, and I went to therapy. I'm not that person anymore."

The woman scoffed. "No one can alter names except the government. The Kenyan Council must have changed your name. If they made it public like this, they must have had a reason."

The man shouted back and the sound of it caused Imara's stomach to churn. It had already started. That man had been tagged. People were already turning against him. Distrust and fear would soon be constant companions of everyone in Nairobi.

"Come *on*," Mali said, pulling Imara forward. "I can help you once we get somewhere safe, but right now you have to keep moving." Mali looked over her shoulder before pushing them down an unexpected alleyway.

She led them through a maze of back alleys that were unfamiliar to Imara even though she had lived her whole life in Nairobi. Imara lost track of time and could only replay Safiya's death in her mind. Over and over. Another person dead. There had to be something Imara could have done. She should have been able to save her. There had to be something she missed. If she had only tried a little harder, Safiya might be alive.

Eventually, Mali led them to a familiar street. "Which way?" she asked.

Imara pointed to a building at the end of the road. Naki's work. When they entered the building, her sister was at her side in a moment.

"Is it true?" Naki asked. "Are the planes really down? I tried messaging Darius, but he wouldn't answer. I even tried messaging Abe." Her demeanor changed and periwinkle glints came off her skin. Protective worry. The emotion came alongside the question: "What's wrong?"

Before she could think to answer, Imara collapsed to the ground.

"Do you have any blankets here?" Mali asked.

Time didn't seem to pass. Instead a blanket seemed to appear out of nowhere and Naki was helping her sit up. Without thinking, Imara pulled her knees to her chest and rested her head between them.

"I messaged Siluk," Naki said in a higher pitch than normal. Her panicked voice. "He's still at the apartment. He tried to leave but there was some kind of riot and the street got blocked. He thinks someone got tagged."

Naki may have been using her panicked voice, but she was attempting to remain calm. That attempt shattered a moment later. Imara heard her clap her palms against her cheeks and let out a gasp. "How will we get home if there's a riot? We'll have to live here. Or move in with Mom and Dad! I can't lose my apartment."

"I'll take care of the riot if I can ask a favor," Mali said.

Imara looked up to see Naki bobbing her head up and down. She threw her arms around Mali in a hug. But then she took a step back. "Wait. What kind of favor?"

"I need a place to stay for a few days. The police tracked me with location sharing. I blocked my location, but I think they might have my address."

"Oh," Naki said, letting out a sigh of relief. "Of course you can stay with us. We have so many people at our apartment, one more won't make a difference. You can even sleep on the couch if you want."

Imara pushed herself to her feet, but Naki pushed her back down almost as fast. "You're supposed to be resting," she said through her teeth.

Imara shook her sister's hand off her shoulder. With Safiya dead, her goal had only grown. She couldn't let another person get hurt. Not a single one. "Refuge," Imara said. "We have to provide refuge for the tagged. We have to keep them safe. They can stay at our apartment too."

Naki swallowed while her shoulders trembled. Even without the wine-colored fear spikes, she looked scared. "The tagged? But how can we trust them? They're strangers."

Imara frowned at her sister. She didn't expect opposition from her, but it shouldn't have been too surprising. Naki never was very brave. Maybe it was time for that to change.

"My messages to the other police departments aren't going through," Mali said. "I thought maybe people weren't answering because airplane and car travel are broken, but it's just the people outside of Nairobi. Everyone inside answers right away."

Imara shook her head. "I told you. There's a forcefield around the city. It blocks all messages and keeps people inside."

"That's what you were saying?" Mali asked as her eyebrows trailed up her forehead. "I couldn't understand you at all. Your speech was garbled."

"Really?" Imara asked. It had felt strange when she was speaking. And Mali said she was in shock. How could she have spoken without realizing her speech was garbled?

A moment later, Naki helped her to her feet. Her head swayed once she stood, but grabbing the wall helped with her balance.

Soon, they were heading back to the apartment. She didn't remember making those plans. One minute she was insisting they provide refuge and the next, they were walking down a street at least a few minutes' walk from Naki's work.

SIXTEEN

IMARA CLUTCHED HER STOMACH AS SHE trudged down the street. All she could see in her head was Safiya's body. The guilt seized her muscles; everything felt like ice. Another person dead and she'd done nothing to stop it. No matter how she fought and tried, it was all for nothing. Her brain could barely process it.

Every few seconds, Mali would force Imara's feet forward because she would forget to walk. Her thoughts were a jumbled mess of grief and panic. Safiya dead. Marco dead. Abe… maybe dead. That thought never stuck around long. She'd always force it back to the hidden recesses of her mind with the other things that were too painful to process.

The only other thing Imara was aware of was Naki's panic. Charcoal balls bounced off Naki at regular intervals. She kept spewing words out as if that might help. Mali kept telling Naki to calm down, but it only made Naki talk faster and in a higher pitch.

When they finally arrived at the apartment, Siluk was more panicked than Naki. His hair hung disheveled and his eyes were rimmed with red. "All the planes are down in the entire world. Some of them crashed!" He began pacing across the floor while wringing his hands. "What if Abe's jet went down while he and Darius were on their way back here? What if something happened to them?"

Without any warning at all, bile shot its way up Imara's throat. She gagged and ran to the nearest trash can. The contents of her stomach lined the can as she gagged again. And again. At some point she noticed a blanket had been put around her shoulders.

It took several minutes before she could stand without throwing up. The moment she got to her feet, Siluk met her eyes. "Is Darius dead?" he asked.

She looked away. She had to. How could she look him in the eye while delivering such news? "I don't know."

Siluk grimaced, clearly wanting more of an answer than that. She wanted one too. He stayed calm for a moment, but then his face contorted, and tears seemed to well in his red rimmed eyes. He let out a cough and his calm returned, even if the emotions surrounding him didn't. Cobalt blue drops of sadness pelting off his skin like knives. Mounds upon mounds of maroon frustration. Charcoal balls of panic bouncing so fast, they blurred. She was careful not to look at them too closely. Siluk knew her hila had been healed, but Mali didn't, and Imara wanted to keep that advantage over everyone she could.

"What happened?" Siluk asked, his voice even huskier than before.

Imara grabbed her stomach, ready to lose more food. Tingles spread through her arms and legs, making her feet unsteady. Before she could lose her balance, Siluk put a hand on her shoulder, grounding her. He gave her a simple look of sympathy, which helped more than she expected. Considering his best friend had most likely died, he was handling things pretty well.

"Just tell me what happened," he said. "I can take it."

Naki flashed her teeth at him as she shoved him away. "Maybe you can, but she can't. Darius wasn't the only one in that jet, you know. And anyway, they probably survived. Don't you think they survived, Imara?"

Imara chewed her bottom lip until she tasted blood on her tongue. She didn't dare answer the question directly. Instead, she said, "Abe is a healer."

Naki nodded emphatically. "Exactly. How do you know the jet went down? What did you see?"

"Santini showed me a video," Imara said.

"Santini?" Naki asked as she clapped a hand over her mouth, her breathing even faster than before.

"She's here?" Siluk asked. His voice remained steady, but the charcoal balls of panic blurred even faster around him. And his eyebrows started twitching.

Imara recounted the story with as few details as possible. It was hard enough to relive the moment herself, and with so many charcoal balls of panic in the room, she didn't think Naki could handle all of the truth. So, Imara left out as much as she could, especially glossing over the number of times she'd been electrocuted.

When she got to the part about Abe's jet crashing, her throat choked up. It was easier to replay the scene now that she was imagining a possible survival scenario, but it still wasn't pleasant. "Santini showed me a video. Abe's jet was flying through the air and everything looked fine. But then an orange ball of fire came toward it. As soon as it touched the jet, smoke and fire covered everything. The jet lost altitude. As soon as it touched the ground, it burst into flames."

"But did you see any debris?" Naki asked.

Imara looked at her sister with the happiest face she could manage under the circumstances. "No, I only saw smoke and fire."

Naki's head bounced up and down, wearing a reassuring smile. "That's what I thought. The jet probably had heat proof metal on the outside. Just because the jet lost altitude doesn't mean anyone inside got hurt."

"The flames were pretty high." Her voice sounded so much tinier than usual. She'd been afraid to think it before, but with Naki reassuring her, the words were easier to say.

Naki laughed and waved a hand through the air. "Abe is a healer. Even if it got hot inside the jet, I'm sure he had some remedy for it. How long did the video last after the jet crashed? Did you ever see any movement, like the door opening?"

"No," Imara said, a smidgeon of hope returning. "Santini stopped the video almost as soon as the jet hit the ground. They could have escaped the jet and I wouldn't have known. I never saw anything but the crash."

Naki nodded with that same reassuring smile. She wrapped her hands around Imara's and said, "Exactly, I'm sure he's alive. He has to be."

Siluk grabbed Naki's arm and glared at her. "Don't give her false hope. The sooner we accept the truth, the sooner we can deal with it."

Naki's face went limp when she looked into Siluk's eyes. After gulping, she said, "He can't be dead."

"He is. They both are. We have to accept that." Somehow dark circles had appeared under Siluk's eyes during the course of the conversation.

Naki sniffed and turned away from them. "But I was just starting to like him again. I thought he was the world's biggest jerk and he'd never do anything for Imara. But he actually came to Kenya. He's been at her side and helping her. He was doing everything he should have been doing. And now he's—"

"Dead," Siluk finished.

Imara heard the word, but it didn't feel so heavy anymore. Now that she'd been given the tiniest sliver of hope, her senses seemed to be returning. Her brain started working, clearing out the fog that had been inside her since the glass dome.

Heat seemed to blossom inside her heart and it quickly spread through her entire body. "I have his power signal. We allowed it the other day just in case. As long as he's alive and wearing his ring, I'll see a signal."

Mali entered the room from the hallway with both of her eyebrows raised. "If we can't have communication in or out of the city, what makes you think you'll receive a power signal?"

"Power signals work on a different network than messages," Imara said. "And were you in the bedroom just now?"

"I was checking the windows for security. One of them was unlocked, by the way. So, you're welcome."

"Oh," Imara said, "Thank you. Anyway, I bet Santini didn't think to block the power signal network since hardly anyone uses it, and it doesn't give location or anything useful. It just tells you if the ring is attached to the user."

She found the power app on her ring and held her breath as she tapped on it. She wanted to close her eyes as soon as she tapped. But before she could, she saw four signals blinking back at her, each signal labeled with a first name. Chalondra, Talib, Naki, and—her heart leapt inside her—Abraxas.

"There," she said as a wave of excitement rushed through her.

Naki heaved a sigh of relief.

Siluk glared again. "Rings still have power for hours after a person dies. It takes twelve hours for the power to die completely, sometimes more depending on the person. As long as the ring didn't get completely destroyed, which let's admit, is basically impossible, his ring would still have power right now."

Naki wilted like a dehydrated flower.

A weight seemed to crush Imara's chest. But even as it crushed her, the hope inside her never stopped swirling. "You're right. We won't know for sure until tomorrow." She admitted it unwillingly because somehow, she knew Abe wasn't dead. She could feel it. He couldn't have died without her feeling *something*. Didn't he say they were soulmates? A soulmate would know if the other died.

Mali cleared her throat. "I'm sorry about your friends, or whoever they are, but unfortunately, we have bigger problems to deal with. Riots are popping up everywhere in the city. They're all fighting against the tagged. People have already guessed that something happened to the police. There are other people running around that call themselves enforcers, but they're provoking the riots. We have two major problems.

We need to stop these riots and we need to stop Santini's vote from going through."

Imara scoffed. "Well, the second one should be easy. The glass dome isn't even finished yet, so none of the council members are even in Nairobi."

Mali hung her head in response. "They are here. The last one arrived this morning. We had them arrive early in case something like this happened, but apparently, Santini had more spies in our department than just Faraji and Rehema."

"Oh dear," Naki said. "This is bad. This is very, very bad, isn't it?"

Imara ripped a few hairs from the back of her neck before she realized how hard she was tugging it. The sliver of hope she had a moment earlier seemed to be crushed by images of violence against the tagged.

"Imara can stop the riots." Siluk said, lowering himself onto the couch. "She can do it just by talking to people. If she tells the people to calm down, they'll calm down and stop hurting the tagged."

Mali clenched her jaw. "The tags are inflammatory. They incite action. Just talking won't stop the riots, no matter how persuasive anyone is."

Naki bit the edge of her lip as she raised a finger as if to get attention. But then, she dropped her hand and looked away. Mali was already opening her mouth, but Imara saw amethyst rings dancing off Naki's skin. She'd seen the emotion only once before, so it took a moment to place it.

Anticipation.

Before Mali could speak, Imara asked her sister, "What were you going to say?"

The amethyst rings danced around Naki, but they were soon joined by wine-colored fear spikes. When she spoke, it was in a tiny voice that didn't seem brave enough for the words coming out. "Don't you think it's more important to stop the vote? I know the riots are bad, but they're only a short-term problem. Shouldn't we care more about the future of the world?"

Siluk laughed, which made Naki cower back. "How are we supposed to stop the vote when the city in chaos? If we can stop the riots, the council members are more likely to listen to us about the taggers anyway."

"We *have* to help the tagged," Imara said. "If we don't, no one will."

"We can't waste time helping the tagged. We have to stop the vote," Mali said.

"Refuge," Imara said. The word came more easily to her than it had earlier. Probably because she wasn't in shock now and her brain was moving at its usual speed.

Mali cocked an eyebrow up. "You said that earlier, and it still doesn't make any sense."

"We can find a place for the tagged to hide until all this blows over. Why don't I worry about stopping the riots, and you worry about stopping the vote?"

"I'm going with Imara," Siluk said while rubbing his eyes.

Naki shifted on her feet looking from Imara to Mali.

"Go with Mali," Imara said. "She might need you."

Naki looked like she wanted to respond, but Imara marched toward the door before anyone could say anything else. She didn't want to talk anymore, maybe not ever. She needed a distraction. Anything to keep her from thinking about all the horrible things that had happened.

Things like a jet bursting into flames.

She shoved all her emotions down with a gulp. She had to find a refuge for the tagged. And she had to stay busy enough that she didn't have time to think.

SEVENTEEN

MARCHING THROUGH THE CITY ALONE seemed like a perfectly reasonable idea when Imara left the apartment. Now that she was out here, it didn't feel as smart. She heard someone's footsteps behind her, but she ignored them. No matter what, she had to keep moving. If she stopped to think, the image of Safiya would fill her mind again.

All she could do now was work. Protect the tagged. Keep people from dying.

The streets seemed dark even though the street lamps had turned on just like they always did at twilight. Maybe she should have asked someone to come with her.

She didn't realize Siluk was following her until she froze in front of a building and he ran right into her. She recognized his footsteps must have been the ones following her. It shouldn't have been such a shock. He *did* say he was going to go with her. But she'd been so lost in her own thoughts she didn't even realize he was there until that moment.

"Why'd you stop?" he asked.

She felt her eyebrows fly up her forehead, but she didn't have time to answer. Placing a finger over her lips, she crouched down behind a column in front of the building.

When Siluk didn't follow right away, she pulled him behind her.

Just as he got behind her, a small crowd of people came around the corner. Several people in the crowd had clenched fists. A few even had their fists raised. In the middle of the group stood an older gentleman with deep smile lines. He glanced around from person to person, looking anxious to defend himself.

A woman with fists raised said, "What do you mean you aren't a bad person? You're a molester!"

A bitter taste filled Imara's mouth as she glanced back at Siluk. Ripples of mint green distrust grew out from his skin. He seemed to be thinking the same thing she was. They wanted to help the tagged but a molester? Maybe they should leave him to the mob and find another tagged individual to help.

"I recognize that woman," Siluk whispered.

"The one shouting?"

Siluk nodded. "She was in the riot by our apartment earlier. I think she's one of the enforcers."

Imara's heart sank once the weight of Siluk's words had settled. The mint green ripples of distrust surrounding Siluk had nothing to do with the tagged man, but the woman. She should have known better than to interpret the emotion right away.

"Do you see the way he looks at me?" the shouting woman asked while pointing at the man. "His eyes are traveling all over my body. He *is* a molester. You can tell."

Imara hadn't noticed any such movement in the man's eyes. In fact, he now seemed horrified by the mere suggestion. Imara's head fell to her chest as she let out a sigh. "The enforcers are making people hate the tagged. They're inciting distrust," she whispered to Siluk.

He nodded.

"How can we save them all?" she asked. A chill seemed to surround her.

"We can't. You know we can't." He shrugged. "But we can save a few of them. That's the best we can do."

That wasn't nearly good enough, but maybe Siluk was right. Saving some was better than saving none.

The woman in the crowd lowered her fists, but her frown only deepened. Without warning, she reeled her purse backward, ready to strike the man. Before she could stop herself, Imara jumped out from behind the column and yelled, "Stop!"

All eyes were on her at once. A few of them glared, but she just planted her feet shoulder width apart and tried to look as authoritative as possible. Siluk appeared at her side and also attempted an authoritative look. It turned out a little too friendly, but at least he was trying.

Wanting to get the first word in, Imara said, "Don't hurt that man. I'm here to take him… somewhere." She ended with a nod to hide her blunder.

The woman hung her purse back on her shoulder while giving Imara a sideways glance. "Are you with the police? I thought they were missing. There have been reports—"

"I *am* with the police," Imara said firmly. If the woman was an enforcer, then she'd know Imara was lying. But hopefully the other people in the crowd would believe her. She cleared her voice, then muttered, "Sort of."

The woman narrowed her eyes. "Tap your ring. I want to see your name."

Imara complied without thinking. Once her name shone out from her hologram screen, Imara realized the woman wanted to see if Imara had a tag. Only now did she remember her name did have a tag now. Whether the mob would approve was a whole other question. She glanced at her name and frowned when she saw *Imara Zawadi Kalu, hero*.

The man who had been tagged as a molester took one look at the name and ran.

Imara blinked before she realized what had happened. A moment later, she took off after him. Once out of earshot of the mob, she said, "Wait! I want to help you."

The man seemed surprisingly spry for his age. Imara was a much faster runner after her training in Cairo, but the man still had longer legs than her. Siluk appeared at her side, apparently able to handle this speed much better than her. His subsistence living lifestyle probably had something to do with that.

"You have a tag? Why didn't you tell me?" He spoke as easily as if they were strolling down the road, not racing.

"I forgot," she said, her words coming out in a breathless rush. "Santini did it right after she showed me the video of Abe's jet." Her voice caught on the words and her feet faltered. She couldn't think about that now. She couldn't think about that ever.

Shoving all her emotions to the back of her mind, she said, "Can you catch up to that man and tackle him?"

Siluk increased his speed as he nodded and soon had the man pinned to the ground.

She clutched at a stitch in her side as she caught up to them. "We want—" She stopped to suck in a breath. "We're trying... to... we want to help you," she said at last. She dug her fingers into the stitch, hoping it would help.

Why hadn't she gotten stitches in her side in Cairo? Her heart sank when she realized the only possible reason. Abe had always been nearby when she ran in Cairo. Maybe he had touched a pressure point and took her pain away without realizing it.

She shook her head as she took in another breath. She had to stop thinking about him. His power signal still showed, which meant he might still be alive. And besides, now that she thought of it, another idea popped into her mind. Nairobi had a much higher elevation than Cairo. The stitch might have nothing to do with Abe at all. She could still run.

"We want to help you," Imara said with more force now that she had gotten her breath. "Are you really a good person? Molester is a pretty serious tag."

The man grimaced and turned away from her. As he did, blood red flames of anger burned out from his skin, but inside each flame, a wine-colored fear spike jutted out. The more fear he felt, the more anger she felt.

Santini did this on purpose. She tagged Imara as a hero so anyone with a negative tag wouldn't trust her. How could she ever regain that trust?

"I didn't want this tag either," Imara said quietly.

The man scoffed and turned away from her. She thought he'd take off running again, but Siluk grabbed his elbow and held him in place.

"What did *you* do?" the man asked.

She laughed sadly. "I put my trust in the wrong person. For years, I didn't trust anyone except the one person who deserved it the least. Unfortunately, she craves power more than I ever realized."

The man's fear spikes only grew as he glared back at her. Siluk gripped him tighter and said, "What did you do? Why did you get tagged as a molester?"

The man looked ready to shout when Imara noticed something coming off his skin. Something she had never seen before.

"Wait," she said. "Nobody move."

Siluk opened his mouth, but she just raised a hand in front of him. "Don't talk either. I have to concentrate."

She stared at the emotion coming off the man's skin. She recognized the white-hot strings of pain, but they moved in way she'd never seen. They didn't whip away from any body part or toward any person. Instead, they seemed to whip backward. Not behind the man, but just back. As if calling to the past.

After staring at the strings of pain, she met the man's eyes. He seemed concerned by her sudden interest in his skin, but even more intrigued. "What's your hila?" he asked.

"It happened a long time ago, didn't it?" she said, ignoring his question. "The time that you molested."

The man grimaced and stared at the ground. He seemed to realize he would have to explain eventually, so it might as well be now. "It happened over fifty years ago. I was just a kid. Technically I was eighteen, but the only reason it mattered is because my girlfriend wasn't. We were a month apart in age. It wasn't the first time we had done it. And it *was* consensual. But her parents hated me. So they found a way to make sure I got caught during the one month where I was an adult and she wasn't."

After his short explanation, the last bits of distrust Imara had been holding onto began to fade.

He shrugged while the white-hot strings continued to whip around him. "My girlfriend told the Kenyan Council everything. She took responsibility for it and they decided I wasn't guilty. Her parents disagreed, but nobody else did. I know I shouldn't have done it, but I was only eighteen. And now I have this tag on my name, and nobody is ever going to trust me ever again."

"We can give you…" Siluk glanced over at Imara with a smile and said, "Refuge."

As she nodded, she realized taking all the tagged back to her apartment probably wasn't the best idea. Not because the tagged weren't trustworthy, but because they would run out of room fast and wouldn't be able to help as many people as she wanted.

Before she even had a chance to worry, an idea jumped into her mind. "Follow me," she said, already marching down the road.

She didn't wait to see if the man followed her. Or Siluk. She just had to keep moving. Keep pushing forward. Keep forgetting the emotions that were threatening to spill over and drown her.

When they got close to their destination, they stopped to buy some food and blankets from a market. Enough to last a few days. Finally, they entered a place Imara had only been once before. Safiya's hideout. It was still a mess, but at least the taggers had never found it.

The floor was still littered with food packages, but the walls were empty of the pictures that used to be hanging. A thick layer of dust covered one wall. She used her finger to write a single word in the dust.

Refuge.

Siluk and the man spread the food out and started organizing it. Imara set to work setting up a bed for the man. When she finished, she snuck to a corner of the room and turned away from the others to check her power app.

Four dots still blinked back at her from the screen. She knew it was in her head, but Abe's dot seemed to shine brighter than any of them. "Not dead," she whispered to herself.

EIGHTEEN

ABE STARED AT HIS CONTROLS AS HE FLEW HIS jet over Africa. The controls didn't indicate anything was wrong, but he couldn't shake the feeling that something was off.

"Can you stop whistling for a second?" he asked.

Darius rolled his eyes. Instead of whistling, he switched to tapping the dashboard in front of him. "How much longer until we get there? All this plane travel makes me antsy."

Abe had the strong desire to flick Darius, but instead chose to do a quick, in-flight diagnostic instead. "We've only been flying for twelve minutes. It used to take hours to go this distance."

Darius tapped the dashboard harder. "Yeah, and I would have complained about it back then too."

"Keiko," Abe said suddenly.

He felt bad interrupting her while she was on a phone call with Husani, but he needed her hacking skills.

She popped her head into the cockpit. "I know you think it's safer for me in Nairobi, but I'm still going to help you guys do stuff once we get there. You have to stop treating me like a child."

Abe waved a hand through the air. "That's not what I was going to say. Look at this diagnostic. Does anything look weird to you?"

"Oh," Keiko said with a victorious grin. She glanced over to her hologram screen, which showed Husani grinning even harder than her. She swept up to the dashboard and said to Husani, "See, we're not even in Kenya and they already need my help."

Husani snickered. "That's my girl, showing everybody up without even trying."

Keiko tapped a few controls on the dashboard before she shrugged. "I don't know what the readings for the air outside are supposed to be like, so I don't know if I can help you there."

"They're all in the acceptable range," Abe said. "They just seem too uniform, if you know what I mean."

"Did you know this jet is not pure steel," Darius said with a hand cupped over his ear. "It actually has a lot of impurities, and I'm guessing whoever sold it to you failed to disclose that."

Keiko rolled her eyes, "And you're basing that information on what exactly?"

Darius sat up in his chair with a look that suggested he'd been waiting for this moment. "I have elemental hearing." He pointed his nose a little higher in the air. "I'll be hila wasomi by the end of next summer."

Keiko groaned. "Did we really have to take this guy? I've known him for less than an hour and I'm already about to lose my mind."

Husani snickered from the hologram screen.

Abe ignored them all. "See, right here. Don't these readings look too perfect to you? They're all within range, but there's usually more variance. You don't think there's a program or something messing with the readings, do you?"

Keiko started to shrug until the controls showed a little blip. Abe was ready to dismiss her and send her back to the cab, but when Keiko saw that blip, she lunged forward and put her hands on the controls.

"What is it?" he asked.

Rather than answer, Keiko's fingers flew across the controls even faster than before. A harried look fell over her face.

"Keiko, what is it?" Abe asked again.

"Don't bother her while she's working," Husani said. "She needs to concentrate."

Abe narrowed his eyes at him. "When did you get so mouthy?"

Husani laughed through the hologram screen. "You aren't my boss anymore. I can say whatever I want."

Abe tried to look annoyed, but he had a laugh under his breath, and he knew they both heard it.

"You used to be his boss?" Darius said with one eyebrow cocked up. "How old are you?"

Before Abe could answer, the controls started beeping. The readings for the conditions outside were now off the charts, and not in a good way.

He gulped and turned on auto-pilot. "Everybody to the back," he said. Keiko followed his order without question, but Darius had that look in his eye. He was about to ask a thousand questions, none of which they had time for.

Abe grabbed him by the shoulder and forced him to his feet. "Now!" he said. He still had to push Darius through the cockpit door to get him to comply.

Once in the cab, Darius pouted. "What's going on?"

"Shut up," Keiko yelled at him. Then she turned to Abe. "I marked where we were in the sky before we left the cockpit and I got a copy of the autopilot route. If Husani knows exactly what time we get hit, we can use the exact time it takes to fall plus the autopilot map to figure out our location when we crash."

"When we *what*?" Darius asked. "Crash? Did you say *crash*?"

Abe nodded. "Get ready to time us, Husani. There's going to be a huge fire, but I don't think there will be much of an explosion."

"What is going on?" Darius shouted.

"Do you have anything to help with the heat? Do you think we'll get burned?" Keiko asked.

Abe was already pulling the parachuting suits out of a cupboard. They wouldn't use the parachutes, but the suits had several layers of protection that would help in the heat. Plus, they could use their temperature-controlled underclothes. Hopefully that would be enough.

Wait.

Parachutes.

Should they use the parachutes? Maybe it would be better to parachute out of the jet before the fire ball hit. They wouldn't know exactly where they landed, but they might have a better chance of survival. That is, unless they fell into a fire ball on their way down.

"Will somebody please tell me what is going on?"

The jet shook and Darius fell to the ground.

"That was it, Husani," Keiko said. "Start timing now."

Husani nodded at her from the hologram screen. Every trace of playfulness had been wiped from his face. Now he wore a look that was purely concern. Abe had never seen Husani making a face that looked so … noble? It suited him.

"Put this on," Abe said, shoving the parachute suit at Darius. "And set your temperature-controlled underclothes as cold as they can go."

The temperature-controlled underclothes wouldn't allow temperatures that could cause hypothermia, which seemed smart. But right now, it would have been nice if they could lower the temperature even a few degrees more.

He felt a jolt in his stomach as the jet lost altitude. It took great effort to put the parachute suit on without falling over. And in the end, he did fall over once.

"Are we going to survive this, Abe?" Keiko asked. Her face was solemn, full of acceptance. He should have left her in Cairo. She was supposed to be safer this way and instead, he brought her into a jet that was about to crash to the ground. She looked at him expectantly.

He gulped and turned away. He couldn't lie to her at a time like this. The best he could do was avoid the question.

NINETEEN

IT HAD BEEN ALMOST A WEEK SINCE SANTINI took over the city of Nairobi. Imara wiped disinfectant over a fresh scratch on Naki's forearm. "I'm sorry," Imara said when her sister winced. "I know I'm not very gentle. I just wish Abe were here. We've had so many injuries, and he could fix them up in the blink of an eye. But all you have is me, and I'm not very good at this sort of thing."

Naki winced again but tried to hide it. With a tiny smile, she said, "It's okay. Can you still see his power signal?"

Imara bit her lip as she placed a bandage over her sister's scratch. She hadn't checked since the first day. Every time she tried, fear gripped her too hard and she'd go out to find more of the tagged to distract herself. If he had died in the explosion, his power signal would be gone by now.

A noise sounded through the apartment, and they both jumped before they realized it was just the plumbing. Everything made them jump these days.

Naki grabbed Imara by the hand. It felt nice to have support from her sister. Support they'd both been missing for so long. They didn't always agree, but they were finally reclaiming the relationship they should have had for years.

"What if he's alive?" Naki asked. "I know you're scared that you won't see his power signal, but you've spent all this time stressing about it—and what if you don't have to be worried anyway? What if he's alive?"

Imara nodded and managed to tap her ring, but she couldn't bring herself to check the power signals. She felt the same as she had all along. He couldn't be dead. She would have felt it if he died. She wasn't intuitive like other people were, but she had heard stories. Somehow, people knew when their loved one had passed. But maybe they only knew because of environmental clues. And maybe she didn't have enough clues to know for sure.

She stared at her hologram screen while every muscle in her body seemed to be twitching. Waiting. Fearing. Finally, Naki reached across her and tapped the screen herself.

Imara took in a sharp breath and slammed her eyes shut, too terrified to look. Just before her eyes closed fully, she counted four dots on the screen. In a flash, her eyes flew back open.

Yes.

Four dots.

Naki, Talib, Chalondra, and the last one, Abraxas.

She took in a breath and her whole ribcage seemed to expand more than it had in a week.

Naki squeezed her hand. With a smile, she said, "Now that we have that out the way, Mali and I have an idea."

Imara sat up while a burst of hope bubbled inside her. She could see the dot blinking in her mind now, which made everything worth fighting for again. She just had to keep people from dying like she promised him she would. Once they stopped the vote, she and Abe would be reunited.

"Mali snuck into the glass dome last night. She pretended to be a tagger and luckily none of them recognized her. The council members are all safe, but they aren't allowed to leave the glass dome. They are getting the Nairobi news though. Mali thinks we can draw them out…"

Imara nodded, but she couldn't show more relief even if she wanted to. She was listening to Naki's words, she really was. But her brain was so focused on Abe's dot that all she could really imagine was kissing him once this was all over. She would make it a good one, obviously, but what kind of kiss would be perfect? Would it be a run and jump into his arms kind of kiss? A crying with joy kind of kiss? A desperate and hard kiss?

"Imara," Naki said, a light scolding trimmed the edge of her voice.

Imara sat up straighter and nodded. "I was listening. You said Mali thinks we can draw the council members out by cutting off their food supply."

Naki gave her a long sideways glance. She looked off to the side for a moment and started twirling one of her tiny braids around her finger. "Do *you* think it's a good idea?"

Emerald green ropes of apprehension slithered away from Naki in droves. Seeing them managed to pull Imara's mind away from Abe. Mostly, anyway. She'd never sever that connection completely, even if she wanted to.

"You think it's a bad idea?" Imara asked.

Naki rubbed her arm with a little shrug. "I don't know. Mali is a police officer. She has more experience about this kind of thing. Or maybe I should just say she has experience in general since everyone knows *I* don't know anything about this stuff. But you sort of had to worry about these things in Egypt. What do you think?" She asked the same question again, but something about the way she said it made it seem like she was prodding for a specific answer.

"Why are you so afraid to have an opinion about this?" Imara asked. "You have an opinion about everything. A strong opinion."

Naki frowned. "Not about everything, just about things that don't matter. Can I have a green trash can in my room? No, because I detest green. It stifles my creativity. Whoever invented green trash cans is a fool and never should have been allowed near a factory. See? Pointless."

Imara stared for a moment watching the emotions around her sister. She didn't want to assume the worst about the emotions or interpret them incorrectly, but Naki was saying more than with just her words. As Imara watched the emerald ropes of apprehension, she noticed tiny wine-colored fear spikes growing out from them. Fear spikes had been a constant in Nairobi since Santini got there, but Imara realized these ones might not only be because of Santini. Maybe Naki feared she wasn't good enough. Testing that hypothesis, Imara said, "You're smarter than you think, Naki. And you have good ideas."

Naki covered her stomach with her arms as she turned away. "But I don't have experience like Mali and you. I'm sure

Mali is right. I was going to go along with the plan anyway, I just wanted to see if you thought the same thing."

Imara gathered the small pile of medical supplies and dropped them into the canvas bag that had become their home. She rolled her eyes hard enough that Naki couldn't miss it. "I don't know if you momentarily forgot that I'm a truth seer, but I know you have a ton of apprehension about this plan. You don't have to tell me why, but I would like to know. Maybe you're right."

The emerald ropes of apprehension around Naki were suddenly bathed in a tangerine glow of pride. "You're really interested in what I think?" she asked.

Imara rolled her eyes again, but she made sure to do it with a smile on her face. "Would you just tell me what you think? You're being ridiculous."

Naki snickered. "Okay fine, I'm worried it puts the council members at too much risk. Santini is treating them well right now, but if we cut off their food supply, that might change. I think this plan will hurt the council members more than the taggers. I don't think it will solve anything."

Imara's stomach lurched. In her deepest heart, she wanted to say that Naki was wrong. She wanted to know with complete certainty that Santini would do everything she could to care for the council members. If cutting off the food supply forced the taggers out, Mali would be able to fight them, and Naki could help the council members escape.

But Naki was probably right. If they cut off the food supply, maybe Santini would ration the food they had, making sure she and her taggers got first dibs. They only had another week until the vote. That wasn't enough time to truly affect food supply and force action in their favor.

If only they had more time.

"You're right," Imara said finally.

Before Naki could respond, Siluk rushed into the apartment from outside. "There's another riot," he said. "There are three tagged and a huge mob. We've got to hurry."

Imara started after Siluk, dropping the canvas bag of medical supplies in the process.

"Wait," Naki said.

When Imara looked back, she saw the same disappointment in her sister's face that it showed every time Imara bailed on her while she worked was working in Egypt. The look stopped her in her tracks.

"What's wrong?" she asked. "Are you still injured?"

Naki wrapped her arms around herself. "No, I just have to leave soon, and I was hoping you'd come with me this time. I wish I didn't have to go alone."

"But you're meeting Mali, aren't you?"

Naki nodded as she averted her eyes. A smattering of emotions came off her skin, but none of them helped to pinpoint what was bothering her exactly. Naki was never brave when it came to danger. Maybe that was it. She could command any social situation and make anyone love her in three seconds flat, but she hated danger.

Imara knew this, had always known this, but for a moment, she wondered if there was a specific reason why. "Hey," Imara said with a reassuring smile. "You came to Egypt and shot those guys with the stun gun. You can't say you aren't brave anymore because that was very brave."

Naki waved the words away. "I know, I know. I can do this. I'll be strong. I'll try to be like you." She finished with a little smile. "Just be careful at the riot."

A flood of guilt swept over Imara as she remembered all the times she had left Naki behind to go to Egypt. Desperate to not repeat her past mistakes, Imara said, "Why don't you come with us? We'll find Mali after we save the tagged."

TWENTY

THEY NEVER MADE IT TO THE RIOT. IMARA
turned a corner with Naki and Siluk behind her when a huge
explosion knocked them onto their backs. Imara's ears were
ringing as she got to her feet. Before she could orient herself,
Mali appeared around a corner with a dozen taggers on her
trail.

"RUN!" Mali said.

Imara turned to follow the order, but Mali started
screaming a second later. Facing her again, Imara saw half of
the taggers grabbing Mali from all different angles. She twisted
and contorted her body, getting out of each grip as soon as it
found her. But as soon as she freed herself from one grip,
another hand had her a moment later.

Without a word to each other, Imara, Naki, and Siluk all
lunged forward at the same time. They each had a different
weapon of choice.

Imara used her fists, while Siluk attacked with his feet in
several impressive kicks. Naki seemed to think her fingernails
would be the best method of attack. They weren't as effective,
but the sheer hysteria in her eyes seemed to be enough to
frighten a few of the taggers back.

The taggers all ignored the attacks, except to deflect the blows. They still seemed mostly intent on capturing Mali. Luckily, her hila made that impossible.

One second later, a man with a round scar on his forehead emerged around a corner. Vikal. Imara took a moment to cover her face. She buried it in the stomach of the nearest tagger. Vikal would recognize her and she didn't want Santini to know where she was.

"The tall one with braids," Vikal said. Imara could only assume he meant Naki. "She's the weakest."

Even with her head down, Imara could sense a change in the fight. The taggers shifted focus to Naki and had her pinned down far too fast. Naki started shrieking.

Imara lunged toward another tagger, careful to head for the one farthest away from Vikal. She hid her face from him but managed to see Vikal pointing toward Siluk.

"Try going for his shoulder. He probably injured it recently."

Shoving her elbow into the nearest tagger, Imara tried not to worry so much. Vikal was right. Siluk had injured his shoulder recently. How had he found their weaknesses so quickly?

The answer came to her as a hand wrapped around her mouth. It must have been his hila. She bit down on the hand and slammed her heel into the top of the tagger's foot.

She used a hand to shield her face from Vikal in order to search through the chaos for Mali. Just as she spotted Mali's loose dreadlocks, a hiss sounded through the air.

The sound seemed familiar, but Imara couldn't figure out why until a thick seaweed green fog billowed into the air around them. Her eyes flew to the gun in Vikal's hand, and she immediately recognized it as the fog gun Santini had used in the catacombs. Probably not the exact same one, but one with the same design.

"Cover your mouths!" Mali shouted. "It probably has sedative or poison in it."

Imara nearly tripped over her sister, who was getting back to her feet. She noticed a small eyeroll before Naki said, "It's just fog. I can taste it." After a tiny shake of the head, she said, "If the fog had anything else in it, the taggers would be covering their mouths."

They weren't. Imara hadn't even noticed until Naki pointed it out.

As the fog filled the air, Imara could see fewer and fewer people. Just before the fog enveloped them, Naki's mouth dropped open and her eyes lit up. Wisps of peach pink curiosity danced away from her skin. Each wisp had canary yellow bubbles of excitement fizzing inside.

Naki had an idea.

Before Imara could consider that thought, a hover cart crashed into her chest, forcing her to the ground in a heap. Before she could get up, she heard the hover cart knock into something else, and soon Naki was on top of her with her arms flailing. After a third hit, Siluk landed next to them.

Imara jumped to her feet with her arms out, trying to find the hover cart amidst the fog. The hover cart crashed into her again. She struggled against it. A moment later, she realized the she, Naki, and Siluk were all pinned against a wall with the hover cart keeping them down.

"It's caught on something over here," Siluk said. "I'll try to get us free."

Mali grunted on the other side of the cart as if she had just been shoved to the ground. "There's a hook in the wall a few centimeters from the ground. That's probably what it's stuck to."

Mali grunted again and though she couldn't see it, Imara was pretty sure Mali had just received a heavy punch to the stomach.

"We have to get out of here soon. I think more taggers are coming." As soon as Mali finished speaking, she started screaming. Imara could hear more grunts, but through the fog, she couldn't see anything.

"Almost got it," Siluk said.

"As soon as you get us free," Naki whispered to the two of them, "I'll find the fog gun. I'll use my hila to figure out where the fog is coming from and then I'll steal the gun or break it."

Imara nodded before she remembered no one could see her head anyway. Siluk could focus on the cart and Naki could focus on the gun. Imara would focus on Mali.

She tucked her feet up against the cart and pushed against it. Siluk got it free a second later and with the force of her feet, it went flying.

Imara ran through the fog, completely directionless at first. Then she heard a grunt and recognized it as Mali's. Just as Imara pinpointed which direction to run, Naki shouted "Got it!" A moment later, something hit the ground with a loud crack. And then a smash.

At least Naki had been successful.

Imara heard another of Mali's grunts and lunged forward. She grabbed hold of someone and heard a sigh of relief.

Imara slammed a fist into the side of someone else coming up from her side. Just as she raised her fist again, the blurry outline of people started clearing as the fog drifted away. The thick seaweed green fog thinned out much faster than it had in the catacombs. Probably because they were outside.

Imara swung another fist at a nearby tagger. Mali shoved a knee into a tagger's stomach with a satisfied smile. They quickly moved back to back and started punching as many taggers as they could reach.

A tagger grabbed hold of Mali's wrist and almost pulled her down until a foul smell filled the air. The tagger doubled over—and Siluk appeared with a satisfied smile.

The fog had almost completely cleared now, which left Imara searching for Vikal. She didn't see his face anywhere, but that meant he didn't see her either.

Naki dug her nails into a tagger's forearm, and Imara dared to breathe a sigh of relief. They could do this. All they had to do now was run.

Mali started first and the rest of them all moved to follow her. But the moment Imara turned to run, something hit her across the back of head.

She collapsed, landing on her hands and knees as all air seemed to escape her lungs. When she looked up, she saw that a tagger with huge muscles held Mali around the waist.

A woman shouted, "Right arm," just before Mali reached her right arm behind herself to wriggle out of his grip. Mali grimaced.

"Left leg," the same woman shouted.

She shouted almost a full second before Mali moved her left leg impossibly high. But with the warning, the tagger holding her was able to keep her within his grip.

Now Mali glared.

"Upper back," the woman shouted.

Mali let out an exasperated scream before she said, "How do you know what I'm going to do before I do it?"

Of course they all knew the answer without anyone having to say it. The woman must have had predictive reflexes. Imara couldn't help being impressed by the hila. Even after years at Nazari Academy of Hila, she'd never met anyone with predictive reflexes.

As incredible as it was, she didn't have time to be impressed. She jumped to her feet just as another hit slammed her in the back of her neck.

This time, she fell onto her stomach and had to cough several times before she could breathe again. When she looked up, she had stars in her eyes. Precious seconds passed by while she opened and closed her eyes, waiting for her vision to return.

Mali now had three taggers holding her and the woman kept shouting things out before Mali could move. Vikal stepped toward them with a syringe filled with an orchid-colored liquid. He injected it into Mali before Imara could even scream.

A moment later, Mali went limp, and a tagger threw her over his shoulder. They all disappeared around a corner and Imara kept blinking as she forced herself to her feet.

She wasn't dead. She couldn't be dead.

Santini had injected a clear liquid into Safiya. The one they just injected into Mali was orchid. It was different. Hopefully it was only meant to knock her out.

She began pulling herself off the ground in order to run, but a glint of metal caught her eye. When she turned, she saw a knife stuck deep in Siluk's thigh. Her eyes went wide. She ran toward him.

Before she even reached him, Siluk was already shooing her away. "Go help Naki," he said. "I can take care of this myself."

She wanted to protest but changed her mind when she realized Naki was curled into a ball on the ground. Whimpering.

Imara knelt at her sister's side and helped Naki to her feet. A long scrape mangled the side of Naki's face from her ear to her neck. There didn't seem to be much blood, but it wasn't pretty. They'd need to clean it soon to keep infection away. Once Naki was on her feet and most of her whimpering had stopped, they both hobbled over to Siluk.

He was standing now, and the knife lay on the ground with all traces of blood wiped clean. Siluk tightened a strip of cloth around the wound in his leg, his face wincing with each tiny movement. When he attempted to put his foot down, he quickly lifted his foot and let out a grunt.

"We can help you," Imara said. She stood next to Siluk on the same side as his bad leg. When Imara pointed to Siluk's other side, Naki nodded and took her place there. They both wrapped their arms around his waist while he used their shoulders for support.

They started walking without a word.

Mali was gone.

Imara had been so sure they would get away, but the taggers had outsmarted them in the end. What were they supposed to do now?

"We have to stop the vote," Naki said quietly, apparently having a similar internal discussion.

Imara swallowed, feeling anxiety bubbling inside her. "We have to keep helping the tagged. They'll get hurt if we don't help them. They could die."

Naki let out a huff. "The vote is more important."

"We can't stop the vote," Siluk said in a surprisingly harsh voice. Maybe it was because of his leg. But maybe it wasn't. Blood red flames of anger began burning around him. "We have no chance. All we can do is help the victims. Provide refuge. This is the way the world is going to be now: it's time to accept that."

Imara's jaw dropped as she turned to look at Siluk. He seemed reluctant to make eye contact.

"Is that what you think, Imara?" Naki asked. "Do you want the vote to go through?"

"Of course not, but without Mali…" Imara looked away as a lump grew in her throat. "I don't know if we can do anything. It might be too late."

Naki glared at her while her nostrils flared. "We have to try! Mali's idea might work."

Imara nodded, a glint of hope growing inside her. "Maybe. Maybe we can sneak into the glass dome and figure out a way to help the council members escape. They know they're prisoners, right? We just have to get them out, and I think we can stop the vote."

165

"Just?" Siluk said with a snarl. "Just have to get them out? That's like saying, we just have to climb Mt. Everest by tomorrow morning. You make it sound like one step, but it's thousands of steps. We don't have enough time."

"We just have to hope—"

Siluk scoffed before Imara could finish her sentence. "Hope?" he said. "We just need *hope*? Don't you get it? It's Abe's fault that you're thinking like this. We have no chance of stopping this vote. Look at the signs. The only reason you think we have a chance is because Abe came along and turned you into a stupid, hopeful person. You used to be reasonable."

Imara nearly smacked him in the face regardless of the gaping hole in his leg. She clenched her teeth so hard, she worried they might crack. "Don't blame this on Abe," she said through her teeth.

"He's dead, Imara. You have to accept it. You have to move on."

She blinked back at him, and suddenly his outburst made sense. It was grief. He had turned to anger, while she had turned to doubt. But her doubt was gone now, and she realized he didn't know why.

She forced her muscles to relax as she took in a breath. "I checked the power signals again. Just a few minutes ago. I didn't check before because I was too scared, but I finally checked and his signal's still there. They're alive."

A smoky swirl of turquoise hope danced off Siluk's skin, but wine-colored fear spikes immediately skewered through it. "Show me."

166

She opened the app and pointed. "There…" But as she looked at the power signals her heart dropped in her chest until it fell down, down, down.

Down into her toes until it left her completely. She saw Naki, Chalondra, Talib blinking back, but the last signal was gone.

No more Abraxas.

TWENTY-ONE

THEY WANDERED BACK TO THE APARTMENT
in silence. Imara's head pounded with each step. It didn't make
any sense. She saw Abe's signal. It was there when she checked
it with Naki. How could it be gone now? It had been a week
since the crash. How could it be there one minute and gone a
few minutes later?

He couldn't be dead. She hadn't felt anything. She would
have felt it if he died. Wouldn't she?

Naki forced Imara to eat when they got back, but Imara
had no memory of the food. She didn't remember anything
except a chill that had settled in her bones. And lots of silence.
She had a vague awareness of Naki helping Siluk with his knife
wound, but even that couldn't break her out of the trance that
had enveloped her.

When the sky got darker, Naki helped her into their room
and forced Imara to take the bed even though it wasn't her
night.

Even under the blankets, Imara shivered.

"Take this," Naki said, holding out her hand.

With great effort, Imara turned her head enough to see a
small pill sitting in Naki's palm. She stared at it, thinking she

should have some reaction to it. Instead, she felt nothing but complete indifference.

"It's a sleeping pill," Naki said, dropping the pill into Imara's hand. She forced a cup of water into her other hand, and Imara took the pill without question.

Was this her life now? She'd turn to a pill without question? A pill for sleeping. A pill for feeling.

No.

Even a pill couldn't help her feel now. The emotions had dropped out of her and she didn't think they would ever come back.

ഉଷ୍ଠ୍ୟ

When Imara woke, the room was still dark. She climbed out of bed, stepped over Naki, and slipped into the hallway. Dawn hadn't broken yet, which meant it was too early to be awake. But she couldn't go back to sleep now.

Instead, she wandered into the kitchen where a small light shined. Not from a light bulb. Siluk stood in the corner, using the light from his hologram screen to make a drink. He didn't react when she came into the room, even though she was pretty sure he heard her. When he turned around a moment later, he had two mugs. He held one out to her.

The heat inside the mug warmed her hands. That was the first thing she'd felt in hours. She sipped slowly. When she took in deep breaths, her emotion bubbled and tried to force itself out. But if she took small sips, with tiny breaths, she'd be fine.

She could live like this for the rest of her life. She had to. It wasn't like she had much of a choice.

Siluk held his mug, but he didn't drink. He just stood there, staring at a spot on the back wall of the kitchen. He looked as numb as she felt.

They stood in silence for probably ten minutes. It felt like an hour, but time in general seemed too long now.

"Darius taught me how to make this," Siluk finally said, raising his mug. "It's just an herbal tea, but he had a whole method, and he got angry with me when I didn't do it right. He said, 'People used plants as remedies centuries ago. They're way more effective than people would have you believe. If anyone tries to tell you that manufactured tea is better, then don't trust them. About anything.'"

A smile cracked onto her face without warning. Darius was always getting angry about one thing or another, but he did have a passion for history. One as amusing as it was educational.

"I bought the herbs as soon as you told me about the jet crash. They had to dry and I forgot about them until last night."

Imara's heart started beating faster, but she took a tiny breath and urged herself to calm down. She couldn't deal with this much grief. Not now. Not ever. All she could do was shove it away.

Once the feelings were tucked neatly into the back of her mind, she said, "So many people have died. Headmaster Bello, Aida, all the prisoners Takara killed, that woman on the Egyptian Council." Imara looked away and lowered her voice. "I didn't even know her name."

"And that guy who got shot outside the Egyptian Council chambers."

Imara nodded. "Rajesh," she said, tucking the feelings down farther. She pushed and prodded, but they resisted. They pushed back up on her and wouldn't behave. They snaked around her efforts, slipping through the cracks until one tiny well of tears formed in her eye. "Marco and Safiya," she said in a whisper.

And then Siluk wrapped his callused hand around her arm. "Are you okay?"

A tear splashed onto her cheek while her emotions kept fighting to surface. "I'm really, really not."

He pulled her into a hug, and the one tear had suddenly turned into a rainstorm. Water gushed from her eyes onto Siluk's shoulder, but they were nothing to the torrent of emotions in her heart.

She was vaguely aware that Siluk held her head tight against his chest. It sort of felt nice, but it sort of felt awful. She didn't want to be in his arms. She wanted Abe.

And now those arms were gone forever.

"I'm not okay either," Siluk said.

She could hear that he was crying too. She'd been too consumed with grief to notice before. But now, she forced herself to think about the other life that had been lost in that crash. Darius.

Two whole people were just gone.

Gone and never coming back.

What would she say to Mr. Nazari?

How could she see light again? How could she have hope? Nothing would be the same after this. All she wanted to do was curl into a ball and sob. And sob.

For the rest of her life.

TWENTY-TWO

FOR THE NEXT FIVE DAYS, IMARA CRIED herself to sleep every night. It didn't seem so bad anymore. She could put on a happy enough face during the day and seem like she was fine. Some days, she even tricked herself.

But once night came, and she was tucked safely under her blankets, the tears fell fast and heavy. She had learned to cry silently. She learned to close her mouth though the sobs, but then open her mouth to breathe without being heard.

The hardest part was keeping her body still through the sobs. When it was her night to sleep on the floor, it didn't matter. But when she was sleeping in the bed and she sobbed hard, the bed would shake.

The first night, Naki tried to help. After that, Imara learned to let out her sobs in controlled bursts so her body would stay still.

But during the day, she was fine.

During the day, she forced her emotions down where they belonged, and she actually got things done. They'd scoured the blueprints for the glass dome and come up with a plan to help the council members escape. Their last struggle was figuring out how to get past the taggers who stood as guards.

She and Siluk came back to the apartment late one night. Imara's shoulder was decorated with a long cut from her shoulder to her elbow. A tagger had used a switchblade on her, and it was all they could do to get away.

Once inside, Siluk gave her a clean towel and said, "I'm leaving to get some herbs Darius told me about. He says it can help cuts heal better."

Imara clenched her jaw. *Heal.* He wasn't supposed to say words like that. Not now when she was so fragile. The pain in her arm was deep, but she didn't feel it. But pain from hearing the word *heal.* She could feel that.

When Siluk left the apartment, she flopped onto the couch and curled her body into the fetal position. She held the towel to her arm but never checked to see if it covered the wound or not. She just couldn't bring herself to care.

Even after Siluk's slip up of saying *heal,* she had convinced her emotions to retreat into the box where she kept them. Hopefully she could keep them locked away until she was in bed for the night and Naki was asleep.

While Imara was caught up in her thoughts, Naki came in through the front door. She disappeared down a hall and apparently didn't realize Imara was on the couch until she re-emerged with a jacket a few minutes later.

Her eyes widened, and she rushed to Imara's side, snatching away the towel. "What happened?"

"We got caught in a riot, so we decided to help the tagged. On our way back to the refuge, a tagger caught up to us and cut me with a switchblade."

"Cut you?" Naki let out a huff. "You shouldn't have worried about the tagged. We're supposed to be worrying about the vote now."

"Can't I worry about both?"

"Clearly not." Naki flicked her braids behind her shoulder. "It was Siluk's idea, wasn't it?"

Imara felt herself wilt with guilt, though she wasn't quite sure why. "Yes. Why?"

Naki bared her teeth and let out a growl. "Oh, don't even get me started on Siluk." She flashed her teeth again, and Imara could tell she was about to go on a tirade. So much for not getting her started. It seemed she was already on her way.

"He's been helping me," Imara said, trying to lessen whatever anger Naki had.

Naki rolled her eyes, but she gritted her teeth before she spoke. "You think I haven't noticed? He seems awfully eager to be there for you now that your boyfriend is gone. You *just* found out Abe died. And now you're already letting someone swoop in and have his spot."

Anger burned inside Imara, which actually came as a surprise. She had forced her feelings out so effectively it was strange to feel anything at all. Her anger grew even higher, making her ears heat up. Crossing her arms over her chest, she said, "That's what *you* would do. You never take a break between boyfriends."

"Exactly." Naki spoke so loud Imara nearly jumped. "You're the better sister; you always have been. The fact that you're acting like me should be the biggest clue that you're wrong."

In an instant, clarity sliced through Imara's anger. Clarity she'd been lacking for several days. She blinked while sentences formed in her mind. They were supposed to be fighting about boys, but all she could hear were Naki's last words.

"I'm not better than you," Imara said.

Naki sniffed and turned away until she had her back to the couch. "Yes, you are. You're brave and selfless. And a truth seer. Who would ever want me when they could have you? I have to get rid of my boyfriends before they realize I'm the worse sister."

Imara jumped from the couch so quickly, Naki blinked in surprise. Imara pressed her lips into a thin line, trying to look as serious as she felt. She couldn't think what to say. She felt more emotion in the last three minutes than she had in the last week, and she didn't know what to do with it.

"Don't…" She bit her lip, trying to find the right words, but none would come. Exasperated, she threw her hands into the air. "Don't talk about my sister like that."

Naki stared with her mouth open before she let out a little giggle. "You mean don't talk about *myself* like that?"

Imara sat down beside Naki and wrapped her uninjured arm around her. "You are amazing, Naki. You are so smart and friendly. Everyone who meets you falls in love with you. You're passionate and fierce, but you're also quick to forgive. Maybe we're as different as two people could be, but I'm not better than you."

She pulled her arms away and slouched next to Naki on the floor. She took a deep breath before she said, "I always wished

I could be more like you. You make friends wherever you go and for so long, I had no one."

Naki's eyes were all different now. She looked like she was seeing her sister for the first time. With the tiniest hint of a smile, she asked, "You really wished you could be like me?"

Imara nodded.

Naki straightened her back. Rather than say more about it, she started cleaning Imara's wound. "Abe would be much better at this than me," she finally admitted.

Now that Imara's feelings were out of their neat little box, pain came right up the surface. Her stomach twisted in knots as she remembered Abe's hands against her skin. So many times he had cleaned her wounds.

For once, the thought didn't make her angry. She was still sad. Sadder than she'd ever been. But this time the pain felt good because this time she accepted it.

It was going to hurt, but maybe, just maybe, she could get through it. That's what he would have wanted.

When Naki finished, she grabbed one of her tiny braids and twisted it around her finger. "I'm sorry I said all that about Siluk. I know the two of you have had a weird sort of thing for years. If you have real feelings for him, I'd never tell you to stop pursuing him." She shrugged. "But he's always been into you more than you've been into him. And it just seems like he's taking advantage of you because you're vulnerable right now." She looked down. "And you're letting him."

Just as Naki slapped a bandage over Imara's wounds, she stood up with her mouth hanging open slightly. Peach-pink wisps of curiosity danced around her, again filled with canary yellow fizzing bubbles of excitement.

"I have an idea," Naki said. She started toward the door without another word.

"What is it?"

But Naki didn't seem to hear. She kept walking and was out of the apartment without a word about where she was going or who she had to see.

TWENTY-THREE

IMARA WENT OVER THE WORDS IN HER MIND again, for possibly the millionth time. Taking advantage because she was vulnerable. Was Siluk really doing that? He did seem to be at her side more often. At every possible opportunity, in fact. He was always there with a hug when she needed it… and sometimes when she didn't.

But.

He was the first to insist Abe was dead. Even when they saw his power signal, Siluk kept saying it would go away. He claimed Abe was gone, and she needed to move on. But did he mean move on so she could be with him?

His presence had been comforting over the last few days. Not just physically, but emotionally too. For some things, she went to him before even thinking of going to Naki. It felt right since he also lost someone important to him.

Was she only going to him because she was vulnerable? *Was* he taking advantage?

She picked at her bandage one more time. Naki had put it on in such a hurry, it wasn't sticking right. As she picked at it, Siluk entered the apartment with a handful of herbs and a small glass bottle. He knelt at her side, setting his things on the ground. She watched his emotions carefully, trying to decide if he was taking advantage of her.

She saw tiny cherry red puffs of love. She'd noticed those a few days ago but managed to convince herself that Siluk only loved her as a friend. It seemed so silly now. She noticed a single, scarlet thread of romantic desire flipping out and she decided to look away.

Her hila was powerful, but it wasn't perfect. She could see negative emotions when she looked for them, and she could see love when she looked for that. Maybe she wasn't objective enough to read emotions right now. Even if Siluk did have feelings for her, she felt certain he wouldn't take advantage of her.

Just then, he cupped his hand over her cheek and gazed into her eyes. Despite her best intentions, the look brought a fluttering of butterflies to her stomach.

"I bought witch hazel," he said. "It will help clean the wound. Can I take off this bandage?"

She nodded and forced herself to look away. He touched her so easily, so intimately, without even a thought. It frightened her how comfortable it felt. When had she let him into her life like that? When had she started allowing such things?

Did she want him, or did she just want *someone* because she was so broken with grief?

He seemed to sense her thoughts were on him. He stopped fiddling with the herbs and looked into her eyes again. When she looked away, he tucked his hand under her chin and turned her head back toward him. His lips were so close she could practically taste them.

If she had any doubt in her mind before, it all fell away now. Siluk wanted one thing right now and that one thing was her. She didn't know if she wanted him or if she just wanted comfort, but his lips were too close to be thinking clearly. Dangerously close.

He leaned in closer and her heart raced so fast she thought she might have a heart attack.

This was it. He was going to kiss her, and she would let him. But as his face came closer, she caught a sniff of a milky, musky scent that immediately reminded her of Abe.

Abe.

Barely a second before their lips met, she asked, "Could you get me some water?"

His eyes never lost their intensity as they stared back at her. For a moment, she thought he'd kiss her anyway. But then, he nodded and disappeared into the kitchen. She knew he'd try again when he got back. He wouldn't give her a chance to back out next time.

Now that he was far enough away, she could breathe properly.

Think properly.

She did appreciate Siluk's presence over the last week, but did she like him like that?

She didn't know what to think or feel. She still wanted Abe. That she knew for certain. She still wanted to cry and never stop.

Her thoughts buzzed around in her head the way they normally did. Everything during the last few days had seemed to happen inside her body instead of outside it. She was usually more aware of her actions, but now she only seemed to be aware of her thoughts.

Her ring buzzed with a phone call, and she quickly tapped her ring to see an anonymous caller. Normally, she never answered anonymous phone calls, but in this case, it may have been one of the tagged. She had promised she would always answer their calls.

As soon as she tapped it, she had the terrifying thought that maybe Santini had somehow gotten one of her taggers to call her. The terror expounded when she saw thin eyes staring back at her. But less than a second later, that terror flapped right out the window when she noticed amber hair cut into a bob.

"Keiko!" Imara exclaimed with a smile. But then her head reeled as if rolling down a hill. "Wait. How are you calling me from Egypt? The forcefield around Nairobi makes communication impossible in or out of the city."

"We don't have much time," Keiko said. "It's a long story, but basically be glad I'm so good at hacking."

Imara opened her mouth to say more, but Keiko raised a hand to interrupt. "Listen to me. This conversation has to take less than five minutes or else Santini will be able to track us and sever the connection. Five minutes, okay?"

Imara tried to nod, but curiosity froze her motions.

"By the way," Keiko said. "I'm not in Egypt. I'm in Kenya and we're just outside Nairobi right now."

"But," Imara turned her head to the side, "has air travel been fixed? How did you get from Egypt to Kenya? It's only been a week."

"I flew here in a jet, a week ago. We crashed and had to walk here. I've spent the last few days trying to figure out how to get past the forcefield."

The words hadn't fully sunk in before she saw his face on the screen. Keiko turned her hologram screen so it would record a larger area. Sitting next to her was the one face Imara wanted to see more than anyone. His copper skin looked darker, maybe from traveling. His hair looked messier too. His eyes sent a shock through her body that made her clap her hands right over her mouth. Tears filled her eyes before the thought of speaking could even begin to form.

"Hi," Abe said.

Tears streamed down her cheeks in droves. Joy spread through her, but surprisingly, it wasn't the dominant emotion. Instead, the grief she'd been avoiding now hit her like a ton of bricks because now she could actually deal with it. "I thought you were dead."

She didn't mean for it to sound like an accusation. She was so happy she could barely breathe. Her legs ached with the desire to jump for joy. But her mouth seemed to have a mind of its own and it made the words sound harsh out of her lips.

"I know," he said. "I'm sorry."

"Look what happened to my arm," she said, peeling the bandage away. She didn't know why it seemed like the perfect moment to bring up her injury. It hadn't been bothering her, but she needed to feel Abe's presence. She needed to tell him something that only he could understand in his own special way.

"Did you put ointment on it? You have a tub of my painkiller ointment, right?"

"Do either of you have any idea how short five minutes is?" Keiko said, leaning in front of Abe. "I know you guys miss each other, and you're desperately in love and all that, but if you can't focus on the conversation, I swear I'll make Abe go into the other room."

"I can focus," Imara said with complete and utter belief that she could.

But then Abe mouthed *I love you* and her whole stomach turned to mush and she was smiling the dopiest smile she had ever made in her entire life.

"Pathetic," Keiko said with an eye roll. But Imara saw silver gems of delight tumbling off Keiko's skin as she spoke.

"We have a plan," Abe said. His face had turned professional. "Keiko can get us into the city, even with the forcefield. She can also bring the forcefield down, but to do it, we have to blow up the glass dome."

Imara bit her lip, her brain immediately serious. "All the council members are there. We're working on a way to get them out, but we haven't figured out how to get past the taggers who are guarding the halls."

Keiko's face fell. Abe's matched it for a moment, but then swirls of hope flew out of him—and she knew it was cheesy, but she couldn't think of a time he looked more attractive than then. "Do you think you can figure out by tomorrow? If we blow up the glass dome, the council members can get the vote canceled for good."

Imara reached for the hair on the back of her neck, stroking and tugging as she thought. "I don't know. Naki had an idea earlier, but she left without telling me anything about it. I think we might have a chance."

"How are the tagged?" Abe asked.

All at once, a wave of guilt smothered her from the inside out. She covered her face with both hands and let out a groan. "I haven't been helping them like I should be. I was, but then

Mali got captured and I focused on stopping the vote. I was supposed to do both, save the tagged and stop the vote, but the vote has taken so much time." She hung her head. The guilt crept up her spine until it seized her muscles. "I'm supposed to keep people from dying, but I've been too busy worrying about the vote to do that. What kind of a person does that make me now? I'm only a good person because I save people's lives."

"No." Abe's answer was so sure and so simple it caught her by surprise. She looked up and found him staring back at her carefully. "You save people's lives *because* you're a good person. It's not the other way around. There are lots of other things that make you a good person."

A tiny smile started growing at the side of her mouth. She wanted to wrap up the way he was looking at her and package it for use when she was feeling down. Abe always had a way of making her feel better than she really was.

"Have you been practicing with the mirror?" he asked.

She let out a laugh. "Uh, no."

"Do it today."

She looked up at him, worry seeming to fill every space in her brain. "I can't, Abe. Not without you."

"You can. And you need to. You have to see that saving people isn't the only good thing about you."

She wanted to grab his face and kiss him right through the hologram screen. Before she could entertain that thought too far, she sensed Siluk's presence less than a meter away. He'd positioned himself so he could see her screen, but so he stayed out of sight.

The memory of their almost-kiss gripped her by the throat. This time, she actually had to cough it out before she could speak. "Where's Darius?" she managed.

"Well," said a familiar voice. Darius's golden curls appeared on the screen just before his hazel eyes did. "Glad to know you remembered me eventually."

Siluk let out a breath of relief but didn't move any nearer to the screen.

"Time's up," Keiko said suddenly. "We'll call you tomorrow if we can."

With that, the phone call ended, and Imara was left with a crushing guilt that only grew as she thought about facing Siluk. She glanced toward him carefully.

He wore a strange mixture of emotions on his face, but they were nothing compared to the emotions coming off his skin. She expected the canary yellow fizzing bubbles of excitement. The maroon mounds of frustration surprised her. She didn't like seeing the cobalt blue drops of sadness pelting off him. But worst of all, his scarlet red threads of desire reached for her with even more purpose than they had before. The sight of it twisted her stomach in ways she didn't expect.

"They're alive, huh?" Siluk said. Was that *disappointment* in his voice?

"Isn't it wonderful?" she asked, jumping up from the couch.

Siluk pushed a glass of water into her hands. She tried to take it without letting their fingers touch, but Siluk seemed intent on having the opposite happen. His skin felt hot against hers. She turned away from him as she drank.

"How did they call through the forcefield?"

"I don't know." She took another sip from the cup.

185

"Why did Abe's power signal die?"

"I don't know," she said again. "Keiko didn't have time to explain." She plucked the bottle of witch hazel from the ground and poured a few drops onto the towel she had dropped earlier.

"They want us to focus all our energy on trying to get the council members out of the glass dome? What about the tagged? Are we supposed to just ignore them?"

The hint of disgust in his voice was unmistakable now. She wanted to tell herself that he cared about the tagged and that's why he was so angry, but she knew that wasn't true. Things had changed now, and Siluk wasn't happy about it. Maybe he was happy about Darius, but not about Abe.

She decided to ignore it. Maybe if she didn't acknowledge his feelings, he wouldn't admit to them. She dabbed the witch hazel onto her cut, reveling in the stinging sensation it provided. Anything to get her mind off this conversation. "We have to focus on stopping the vote now."

"And what do we do after that?" Siluk stepped closer to her. Close enough that he could reach out for her hand if he wanted to. But she didn't want that. More than anything, she was scared he'd take the chance.

She threw the towel to the ground and didn't bother to re-bandage the cut on her arm. It wasn't bleeding anymore anyway. Running toward the door, she said, "We have to find Naki. She has an idea."

TWENTY-FOUR

THEY CAUGHT UP TO NAKI ONLY A FEW minutes later. She still had tears of joy in her eye from hearing about Abe when Imara finally asked, "What's the idea you had earlier? To get the council members out of the glass dome?"

Naki's face went rigid and she turned away. "Oh, it's nothing. It would never work. Don't you two have any ideas? Siluk?"

"It's not possible," Siluk said, a vein popping in his jaw as it flexed.

"What if you made some fire balls like you did at Takara's mansion," Imara suggested. "That tricked the taggers in Egypt."

Siluk rolled his eyes, which only made the dark circles under them more prominent. "That won't work on Santini. She's too smart."

"It worked in Egypt," Imara said with a shrug. "Why wouldn't it work here?"

Siluk all but glared back at her. "It's obvious, isn't it? Takara didn't know us. She only cared about Marco and the Egyptian Council. Santini knows us. She taught us. She knows you best of all, and anything she doesn't know she learns from truth seeing. Besides that, I used a smell against those taggers when they captured Mali. If the taggers smell fire without detecting any other sign of fire, she'll tell them to ignore it. She knows to ignore smells."

"What if it's a smell they can't..." Naki trailed off, her confidence seeming to drop off a cliff. "Never mind. I'm sure you're right."

"What?" Imara asked. "What's your idea? Just tell us."

Just as a smidgeon of confidence seemed to bloom around Naki, Siluk said, "It won't work. There's no point in trying."

The smidgeon of confidence in Naki's eyes plummeted until she had nothing but emptiness inside them.

Imara wanted to smack Siluk across the head. "Tell me your idea. Please."

"Oh, it's nothing," Naki said, wringing her hands. "It won't work. It's like Siluk said, Santini knows us too well."

Imara settled herself in front of Naki, trying to make the most encouraging face she could. "Tell me."

A single smoky swirl of hope danced away from Naki as she showed a tiny smile. She tapped her hologram screen and brought up design plans for a strange-looking gun. "Do you remember that fog gun? I tried to use my hila to make one. It was a huge failure even though I know a lot about water and air and mist because, surprise, I actually know nothing about technology."

Imara wanted to laugh, but she wasn't sure if Naki would laugh with her or if she would be offended. A weird grunt came out of her mouth instead. It sounded strange, but nobody said anything.

Naki continued. "So, then I was thinking I should just use my strength and focus on the weather taster stuff and let someone else figure out the technology stuff and…"

Imara nodded, urging her to continue.

"Well, then I thought, why stop at fog? Why not use a gas that will knock people out?"

"Naki, this is brilliant. I can't believe you haven't told us until now."

With that, Naki stood a little taller. "I'm not finished yet. So, then I was thinking it would be a little inconvenient, not to mention conspicuous, to have a bunch of bodies lying around. I realized there might be an even better way. At my work, we developed a drug that makes people super agreeable. It's kind of like laughing gas. We can't force anyone to do anything, but the drug will make them loopy enough that they won't ask too many questions. And they won't be able to hurt us."

"That sounds illegal," Siluk said, giving her a sideways glance.

Naki rolled her eyes. "Of course it's illegal, Siluk, but we're in the middle of a war. The taggers aren't fighting fair, which means fighting dirty is our only option. It's not like I suggested we go in there and kill them all. We're just going to make them agreeable so we can get the council members out of the glass dome in time."

"Does the drug use pheromones?" Siluk asked.

"No, but…" Naki smiled. "If you add some pheromones, it will make the drug work even better. We'd basically be unstoppable."

Before she could get too excited, Imara asked, "How will we deliver the drug?"

"In a mist gun," Naki said, confidence growing more each minute.

Imara narrowed her eyes. "But you said, you couldn't figure out how to make the gun."

Naki grinned. "Oh, I just called up an ex-boyfriend who happens to be a weapons and technology expert. I have no idea if my gun is anything like Santini's was, but it will do the job nicely."

Imara started to smile. She never thought she be so grateful for Naki's many ex-boyfriends.

"Well," Naki said as her eyes drooped. "There is one other thing that's a problem."

"You don't have access to the drug, do you?" Siluk asked.

"No," Naki said with a frown. "It *is* illegal. We made it too strong, so we had to put it under heavy security. Without police around, we aren't in danger of getting arrested, but…"

"No one else is in danger of getting arrested either," Siluk finished.

"We need to scout the location first," Imara said, grateful for her time in Egypt to know that much at least. "We'll go in, check out the security, then figure out how to get past it."

Naki bit her lip as a tangerine glow of pride came off her skin. "Do you really think this will work?"

"I do," Imara said with a smile. "You should trust yourself more."

☙☙ଊଊ

Imara stared at the warehouse attached to Naki's work. A heavily muscled man paced in front of it carrying a huge gun that did not look legal. How the city of Nairobi had gone from peaceful to violent so fast, she would never understand. Apparently, that's what happened when a crazy woman took over and all the police disappeared.

Trailing behind the muscled man were a few lackeys carrying their own guns. Not as impressive as the big one, but still deadly. Too many to fight with only one stun gun. If it was just one or two, they'd be fine, but with that many, they didn't have a chance.

Imara took a step back into the alley where they all hid. Before she could explain about the guards, another man entered the alley. Without thinking, Imara raised a fist to knock him out.

"No!" Naki whispered, pulling her hand back. "That's Basara."

Imara's eyes widened as she faced Naki. "Basara?" she asked. "The guy you were dating while I worked in Cairo. That's the ex-boyfriend you called?" She turned back just to give him a sneer.

Naki folded her arms over her chest. "You can't say anything bad about him. I didn't say anything bad about Abe while he was being a jerk."

"Uh. Yes, you did," Imara said. "Repeatedly."

Naki shrugged. "Okay, fine I did, but he deserved it. Anyway, Basara is just helping us save the city. We aren't dating, and he's not in love with me anymore."

The cherry red puffs of love coming off Basara's skin seemed to say otherwise, but Imara decided not to share that piece of information.

"I don't think you should be involved in the extraction," Basara said as he looked longingly at the braids trailing down Naki's back.

She pushed him in the arm and rolled her eyes. "I'm brave now, Basara. I can handle it." She had pushed him away and rolled her eyes, but did she too have red puffs of love coming off her skin?

Imara could barely believe it.

She shook the thought away and tried to hide the smile forming on her lips. She wanted to be angry at Basara, but somehow, she couldn't be. "Okay," she said. "This shouldn't be too difficult, actually. There are ten guards out front. We just need to create a big enough distraction to get most of them to leave. Once they're gone, we'll use a stun gun on the rest of them. Then, we get inside the building, grab the drugs, and get out of there as fast as we can." She turned the corner of her mouth up into a smile. "Abe calls it a distract and grab."

"Uh," Basara said turning to her. "We have a slight problem. Naki said it will take some time to get past the security protocols protecting the drug. How long does someone stay passed out after getting hit with a stun gun?"

Imara shrugged. "It depends on age, height, weight, things like that. It can last eleven to twenty-three minutes depending on the person. But we can shoot them with the stun gun as many times as we need to if they start to wake up."

Basara nodded and turned to Naki. His eyes lit up. "I think you should have the stun gun. You'll be safer that way and then I can get the drug."

"What about the distraction?" Siluk asked. "I can get at least some of the guards to go investigate with a certain smell, but they won't be gone for long."

"You're right," Imara said.

Siluk blinked as if surprised she'd agreed with him. He took the opportunity to lean closer to her, and she started regretting it.

"We need more time to figure this out," she said. "Let's get back to the apartment to make a plan and we'll come back later tonight."

"Good," Naki said. She wore a serious face that looked more like she was playing the part of a hero than actually being one.

Basara stared at Naki until he realized everyone in the group had stopped talking. He cleared his throat. "I think I need your help with some calculations, Naki. I'm working on the trigger for the gun so it releases more mist depending on how far you push in the trigger. Could you come back to my lab for a little bit to help me?"

"Yes," Naki said. Her face looked strangely professional, but Imara noticed red in her ears. Just like Imara, Naki's ears seemed to be the only part of her dark skin that managed to betray a blush.

"Great," Siluk said, grabbing Imara's upper arm. "Then we'll see you back at the apartment later."

Naki's muscles went rigid when she saw Siluk's hand on Imara. She opened her mouth to say something, but Imara immediately raised a hand, silencing them all.

Around the corner from their alley hiding place, two women pushed a hover cart that had a huge storage container on top of it. Imara pulled everyone behind her and said, "Never mind, we have to do it now. We won't get another chance like this."

TWENTY-FIVE

IMARA RAN HER HAND OVER THE SHAVED hair on her the sides and back of her head. Then she trailed a few fingers through the curls on top of her head. She ambled toward the hover cart with the biggest smile she could possibly manage.

Think persuasive thoughts she said to herself as she walked. This plan hinged on getting these people to do what she wanted, so she had to be as persuasive as possible.

"Hello," Imara said with a wave. The two women stopped pushing their hover cart to stare at her. They didn't look eager to help. In fact, they looked annoyed.

Imara put on her sweetest smile and spoke in a soothing voice. "I was wondering if you two could help me with something. I'm really, really desperate."

Imara made sure to put an edge in her voice that would make her seem more pathetic. Hopefully the women would be more willing to help that way.

"I know you," one of the women said.

Imara wanted to smile, but she wasn't sure if the woman knew good things or bad things. Anxiety threaded through her as she waited to find out.

The woman turned to her companion. "This is the girl who's been helping the tagged."

The other woman stared blankly for a moment, but then her face lit up. "You're the one who's been tagged *hero?*"

Imara's gut twisted into a knot, and she wasn't sure whether to puke or smile. "I... Yes. Yes, I am, but I didn't ask for it. I'm not working with Santini."

"Oh, we know," the first woman said. "You've been helping the tagged. They've been talking about you on the news nonstop. They say you've done more to help Nairobi than anyone else in this city. They said your tag is the only one that's true."

Another wave of anxiety punched through Imara's body. The urge to vomit got even stronger. She didn't know what to make of this knowledge, but she didn't really have time to consider it. Instead, she pushed it to the back of her mind and tried to focus on her most recent problem.

"Can you help me?" she asked. "I need to borrow your storage container and hover cart."

They pushed it over to her without question, and she didn't know whether to laugh or cry at their willingness. When had the news started talking about her? She'd been so busy the last week, she hadn't even thought to check the news.

"Good luck," the second woman said as Imara pushed the hover cart back toward the others. "Just bring it back around that corner when you're done. We'll be waiting."

The hope in their eyes seemed to pierce through her confidence. It made her realize just how much there was riding on this plan. If it didn't work, there would be no backup. There wouldn't be anyone else that could come and make things right. If they couldn't blow up the glass dome, Santini would take over the world. They only had one shot at this, which meant they had to get things right.

When she got back to the alley, Siluk pulled small spray bottles out of his pocket and started spritzing them around the alley. Imara opened the storage container and let the doors stay wide open while she stood in the back of it. Siluk joined her in the container and sprayed twice the amount inside as he had outside.

When Siluk nodded, Imara left the storage container to let Naki and Basara know they were ready. When she crept outside, neither of them seemed to notice her presence.

"Do you really think so?" Naki asked, looking right into Basara's eyes. "Even with this nasty cut on the side of my face?"

Imara froze with her foot hanging in the air.

"You are the most beautiful person I've ever seen. The most." He sounded sincere when he said it, and his skin glowed more than Imara had ever seen, indicating his words were truthful. Not just truthful, but the most truthful.

Naki seemed to sense his sincerity too. She let out a soft giggle and leaned closer to him.

And now they were both staring into each other's eyes.

Imara thought about retreating into the storage container. They needed to enact their plan sooner than later, but still.

She quickly shook the thought out of her mind. They had less than a day to get the council members out of the glass dome. She didn't have time to worry about intruding on awkward conversations. Instead of retreating, she did the next best thing she could think of and cleared her throat loudly.

Naki's ears went bright red, but Basara merely grinned, looking pleased with himself. "We're ready," Imara said. "Siluk created a trail of smells leading to the box. It shouldn't be long before a few of the guards come to investigate."

Naki nodded with a timid smile. "I guess it's time to be brave."

Basara reached for Naki's forearm. "When we go into the building, stay behind me. I'll be able to watch out for you that way. And Naki," he looked straight into her eyes. "Promise me, if something happens, you'll let me get hurt instead of you."

Naki basically melted on the spot. Bursts of rose gold light came off her skin. Imara knew in an instant that they represented elation.

Naki waved away Basara's concern, trying to pretend it meant nothing to her. "Don't be ridiculous. If I have to get hurt in order for us to get the drug, then so be it. The drug is the highest priority."

"Not to me," Basara said under his breath. Yet, he still said it loud enough for all of them to hear.

Imara nearly gagged, but Naki beamed.

"All right, time to hide," Imara said. "Get behind the storage container. I'll let you know once it's safe to move."

Imara waved Siluk out of the storage container, and they both hid behind it, waiting. "Are you sure this will work?" she asked, biting her lip.

"This smell is guaranteed to get some of those guards to investigate. I wish we had more than one stun gun, but once we separate them, I think we have a chance."

She noted how Siluk stepped closer to her as he spoke, but she didn't react to it. She tried to push it out of her mind as soon as she saw it. She wished they had more than one stun gun too. And she wished Abe was here. He probably would have come up with a better plan than she had.

But at least he was alive. That was enough for now.

A few moments later, five guards marched into the storage container. Before they could realize it was a trap, Imara and Siluk slammed the door closed behind them and secured the door with a lock.

"I only counted five," Siluk said. "That means there are still five guards in front of the building."

"Five?" Naki's voice trembled as she said it.

Imara lifted her chin in the air. "I'll be fine. I've taken down lots more than five people before. You and Basara wait here until I have things under control. Then, get inside the building at the first chance you get."

Hopefully no one noticed the trembling in her own voice. She *had* taken out more than five people before, but never alone. She'd only done it in a big crowd with lots of confusion, and several more people on her side. Not to mention, each of those guards had a gun, and she only had one stun gun.

"Do you need me to come with you?" Siluk asked.

She bristled at the words. "No. You need to stay here and watch the storage container. I'll be fine, I promise."

She tried to walk with an air of confidence that hid her worries. As she moved, she realized what she needed. Confusion. That was the last piece of the puzzle. If she created some amount of chaos, it would be that much easier to take out the remaining five guards.

Before she rounded the corner, she tapped her ring and found a video she took at one of the riots. Several people were screaming on the video. If she increased the volume enough, it could give the confusion she needed.

The moment she hit play, all five guards widened their eyes. Wine-colored fear spikes came off their skin, each covered in a raven black rash of anxiety.

She plucked a stray rock from the ground and threw it at the guard whose fear spikes were longer than anyone else's. He nearly jumped out of his shoes as he looked up and down the street. "I'm out of here," he said as he took off down the road.

Before he even made it to the nearest alley, another guard was right behind him.

Imara smiled. Just three left.

She grabbed another rock but couldn't decide who to throw it at. The remaining three guards all showed equal amounts of fear, and unfortunately, it wasn't much. She threw a few more rocks, but the guards maintained their positions without a single hint of wavering.

With a deep breath, she went on to the next step. She clutched the stun gun as she aimed. This time, instead of targeting the weakest guard, she targeted the strongest. The one with the largest weapon. She knew if she missed, they might all die. Even Naki.

Since Abe had miraculously lived through a jet explosion, she didn't have time to think about whether or not she would take the chance. She had to live because she had to see him again. So, she would make the shot, no matter what it took.

When she finally pulled the trigger, a strange calm overcame her.

Just as the man crumpled to the ground, a putrid smell filled the air, and her stomach churned. One of the remaining guards doubled over as vomit spewed from his mouth. Imara aimed at him, taking advantage of his distraction.

The shot was good, but soon she was vomiting as well. Shaking her head, she ripped the bottom few inches of her shirt off and wrapped it around her head so it covered her nose.

Siluk could have warned her he was going to make such a disgusting smell with his sprays. He must have sprayed more since they were back at the hover cart. If she'd been prepared, she might have been able to take out both of the last two guards. Unfortunately, she hadn't been warned, and she lost valuable time dealing with the smell.

Now that she had shot the stun gun twice, the last guard knew her position. Imara waved Naki over to her side and whispered, "There's only one guard left. I'll go to the left and distract him. You two go to the right and get inside the building as soon as you can."

Naki shook her head so hard, her braids whipped around her. "What if he shoots you?"

Imara didn't answer. She had no time to consider things like that.

After peeking around the corner, Imara jumped out and waved her arms. The last guard started shooting right away. She ran to the left in a bob and weave pattern. The man kept shooting, but her constant movement made her a difficult target. She threw her last rock over her shoulder and into his face. The shooting stopped for only a moment before he regained focus.

She glanced back long enough to see him aiming. A shot that probably wouldn't miss. She ducked and felt the bullet slice through her clothing, burning her skin.

For a moment, the world seemed to stop as her body processed what happened next. The bullet hadn't broken her skin, but it grazed through something worse.

Her temperature-controlled underclothes.

The underclothes had a mechanism to prevent them from shorting out, but rare freak accidents had been reported. Usually when a bullet grazed across the underclothes instead of going through it. Exactly like now.

A buzz shot through the underclothes as they shorted out. It shook her until her legs gave out under her.

Feebly, she tried to reach for the stun gun that had fallen millimeters from her face. Another shock went through her, and every breath seemed to leave her body.

The guard laughed at her effort.

At least Naki and Basara had made it inside the building. Hopefully they could get the drug and make it out safely because she didn't know how she'd get out of this one.

Her fingers were too weak to reach for the stun gun, let alone squeeze the trigger.

The final guard let out a laugh as he stepped forward. "I've heard of temperature-controlled underclothes killing by electrocution, but I've never seen it in person. It's very rare."

The man raised a hand and brought his finger to the trigger. *Finger.*

Her fingers were too weak to squeeze the trigger of the stun gun, but maybe she didn't have to use her fingers. Maybe she could use something else.

As the man took aim, Imara did her best to distract him. "How many people have you killed?" she asked. "Do you remember them all? Their names?"

His arm faltered for a moment before he sneered at her. The brief hesitation gave her just enough time to move her head closer to the stun gun. She dropped her mouth over it.

"Is your brain already fried?" the guard asked, gawking at her. "Are you trying to eat that gun?" He shook his head and finished under his breath, "Idiot."

While he spent his time insulting her, she used her chin to arrange the stun gun into position. Then, she used her tongue to squeeze the trigger.

He finally realized what she was doing a second too late. The blast from the stun gun shot across the ground toward his foot. He jumped to miss. The shot caught his foot, but it only seemed to reach his shoe because he remained unaffected.

Imara heaved and forced herself to a sitting position. As the man watched her, the fear spikes surrounding him grew. She grabbed the stun gun, but when she tried the trigger, her finger was still too weak. She brought the stun gun to her mouth instead.

Just as she pressed her tongue against the trigger, Siluk appeared and slammed a fist into the guard's head. At the same moment, the blast from the stun gun hit the guard squarely in the chest. He dropped to the ground in a crumpled mess.

What if the combination of those two hits had killed him?

She shoved that thought far, far away and fell back to the ground, weakened by her few seconds of sitting up.

Siluk dropped to his knees and touched the singed material on her arm. "What was in his gun?" he asked.

"It wasn't his gun. It was my temperature-controlled underclothes. The bullet grazed them, and it made them short out."

Siluk's face went slack. "You got electrocuted?"

She tried to shrug it off, but it was difficult with her injury. When she attempted to stand, her body collapsed from the effort.

Siluk glared at no one in particular while blood red flames of anger burned around him. He was usually so easy going, so carefree. Now he looked ready to kill.

He glared at her and then at the building. "Are they done yet?"

Imara tapped her ring and tried to call Naki, but her body wasn't working right. Nothing was working right. She lowered her head to the ground and felt her curls brush the pebbles on the street. It suddenly seemed like a brilliant idea to curl into a ball and forget the world even existed.

She tried to ignore that this injury was partially her fault. As always, she did everything she could to rescue others and gave no thought for her own life. But this time, she thought about the pain of losing Abe. Even though he wasn't dead, she thought he had been and that hurt more than she could have ever known.

What if he had to deal with her death? Could she do that to him?

As she contemplated that, one of the guards began to fidget. She reached for the stun gun, but the effort was more than she could handle. Instead, she tugged the bottom of Siluk's pants and vaguely pointed toward the guard. Without a word, he plucked the stun gun from the ground and shot the guard before he awakened.

And then they waited. In complete silence.

Several minutes later, Naki and Basara emerged with their hands full of boxes. "We have to get to my apartment quickly," Basara said.

Naki's gasped when she saw Imara on the ground, still wincing in pain. Naki tried pushing her things into Basara's hands as she said, "I'm going with Imara back to our apartment. I'll come to yours later if I can."

To her surprise, Siluk let out a little laugh. "Naki, she's fine. She's just tired, so she sat down to rest. She's totally and completely fine though. You go with Basara. Imara and I will go back to the apartment and we'll meet up with you guys later tonight."

Imara blinked at him, too stunned to speak. She didn't even know what to say. Naki seemed unaware of Imara's surprise and let out a breath of relief. She nodded toward Imara and said, "Be safe on your way back to the apartment. We'll let you know when we make some progress."

Imara knew what Siluk was trying to do, and it wasn't worth the effort to stop him. If he wanted to talk, they could talk. She'd put it off long enough.

Once they were out of earshot, Imara turned to Siluk and narrowed her eyes. Before she could say a word, he dropped the stun gun next to her and said, "I'll release those guards from the storage container. Just stun anyone that tries to get near you before I get back."

"Siluk," she said.

He glared at her while the blood red flames of anger burned around him. "When I do get back, you and I are going back to the apartment, and then we're going to have a little chat. I guess I should be grateful you're injured because this time you won't be able to run away."

"Siluk," she said again, but he ran off, ignoring her protests.

Two of the guards stirred while she waited. She tried to move her legs, but only her toes would wiggle. She figured it was a good sign that at least something was moving, but overall it was still disconcerting. Worst of all, she didn't know whether to be more worried about her legs or about Siluk.

TWENTY-SIX

WHEN SILUK RETURNED, SHE TOLD HIM where to deliver the storage container and hover cart to return to the women. He complied without argument. When he returned a second time, he had a new hover cart with him.

"Where did you get that?" she asked.

He didn't answer. He just scooped her off the ground and set her onto the cart. He pushed it down the road as he ran alongside it. She tried to talk to him, but he couldn't hear while they were moving so fast. Or he was purposefully ignoring her. She was pretty sure it was the latter.

Without nothing else to do, she thought about Naki and Basara. If they could make those guns work, then Abe and Keiko could blow up the glass dome. They could stop Santini. This would work. It had to.

While she thought, her ring buzzed, and she quickly answered an anonymous phone call. Her heart burst with excitement when she answered. Abe's face appeared, and he looked as relieved to see her as she did to see him.

"I forgot to tell you yesterday," he said. "You won't be able to call me even once we make it into the city because I had to take off my ring."

"What?" Imara said, her mouth gaping open. "You did what?"

Abe held up his hands to show that both his hands were empty of rings.

Her eyes widened as she let out a gasp. Nobody took off their rings. Nobody. Not ever.

No wonder his power signal had disappeared. "But," she said, "what about everything you have saved to your ring? What about your personal records? Your DNA? Don't you have financial records and pictures that aren't saved to the cloud? All of that gets deleted if you take off your ring."

"Yep," Abe said nonchalantly. She couldn't believe she was actually hearing these words.

"I sent the most important financial records to my dad. And he also has my DNA and identity records. I lost some pictures and a few other things, but at least I'm not dead." He laughed. "Actually, Keiko thinks the hardest part of all this will be convincing the Egyptian Council that we're not actually dead. My dad's DNA records should help."

Imara shook her head in disbelief. Then she took in a sharp breath as she ducked to avoid a small branch from a bush they passed. When she looked back at Abe, he had one eyebrow raised.

"Where are you?" he asked.

Before she could answer, a more pressing question came to her mind. "Do you know how to heal electrocution? If my legs can't move, does that mean it's permanent?"

The color seemed to drain from his face as his eyes narrowed into tiny slits.

She shrugged. No need to give him something else to stress about. "A bullet grazed my temperature-controlled underclothes, and they shorted out."

"And you can't walk?" Abe asked. His voice was steady with a reassuring tone, but the glints of periwinkle worry coming off his skin told her a different story.

She tried to smile. "I'm guessing that's bad, since you have about a thousand glints of worry coming off you right now."

He gulped and didn't bother answering. "Can you wiggle your toes?"

She nodded and an olive-green sheet of relief billowed off him. "Okay," he said. "I don't have any experience with electrocution. Start by treating any burns and get lots of rest. I'll do some research and be ready to fix you up when we get there tomorrow."

"Thanks," she said.

"Why was someone shooting at you?" Again, his voice sounded calm and collected, but those glints of worry multiplied around him. At least he wasn't scolding her like he had in Egypt. He knew if they wanted to beat Santini, they had to fight. He wasn't asking her not to fight, he was just desperately hoping she wouldn't get hurt too much in the process.

She explained about Naki's guns and their plan to get the council members out of the glass dome. When she finished, he explained he was calling on a black-market ring and how it was going to help them get past the forcefield.

"Keiko thinks the forcefield might be related to the tags. I'll let her explain," Abe said. Imara nodded all through the explanation. At the end, Abe said, "Please take it easy until I get there tomorrow. Your body needs to rest. We have to go now," he added with a frown.

Imara nodded and tried not to think about how much her heart hurt about having to say goodbye. She tried and failed to smile.

He looked at her in the eyes and her heart leapt in her chest. He said, "I know you're doing what you have to do. I know you want to keep people from dying and I promise I'm supportive of that. But please, promise me you'll try to be safe. Please."

"I promise," she said. "And I can't wait to see to see you."

Keiko leaned into the screen. "We love you Imara, but we have to go *now*."

Before Imara could say anything, Keiko was gone. Imara tapped off her ring immediately, afraid that keeping it on would somehow aid Santini in tracking the black-market ring they had used to make the call.

A few minutes later, they arrived at the apartment. Once there, Siluk carried her inside and set her on the couch. A sudden déjà vu hit her from after Siluk found her at Takara's mansion. It hadn't meant anything to her at the time, but now she wondered if Siluk brought her to the safehouse without waiting for the others just so he could be alone with her.

"What did Abe say?" Siluk asked as soon as she adjusted herself on the couch.

"They had to take off their rings."

"No," Siluk said letting out a laugh.

"That was the only way for them to get past the forcefield."

Siluk's face remained blank for several seconds. But then, a smoky, turquoise blue swirl of hope twirled off his skin. "Did Darius take off his too?"

She thought back and finally shrugged. "I don't know. Abe and Keiko did for sure. They have a black-market ring with no identity programmed into it. That's how they've been able to call us through the forcefield."

Siluk nodded, his mind seemed to be working at twice its normal speed. He took this information much differently than she expected. He almost seemed excited by it.

"Abe said I should treat any burns from the electrocution, and then try to get some rest."

Siluk nodded and left the room without a word. He seemed extremely determined about something, which made her even more worried.

He returned with a tub of burn ointment and some scissors. A milky scent surrounded him with a familiar musky undertone. It reminded her of Abe, but without the spicy cinnamon that was so uniquely him. Even without the cinnamon, she found herself sniffing the air more than she should have.

After Siluk cut off her shirt sleeve, he slathered the ointment over her whole arm. She had a feeling there were more burns under the rest of her shirt, but she wasn't about to tell Siluk about them. She'd have Naki apply ointment to them once she got back from Basara's apartment.

Without warning, Siluk took Imara's hand and looked into her eyes. The scent overtook her, giving her the strong desire to lean into Siluk so she could breathe in the delicious smell. If it hadn't smelled so much like Abe, she probably would have.

Instead, she tugged her hand away. That didn't stop Siluk from staring her down. For several seconds, he just stared, and it made her stomach squirm.

Finally, he said, "We need to run away."

She blinked at him. It didn't make any sense. Run? *Away?* The concepts were so foreign, it took her a moment to internalize them. Even when they settled, she still didn't understand. Did he mean run away with the council members? That wasn't a bad idea.

They had to get the council members out to blow up the glass dome. But maybe they should help them hide in another city until the vote had been canceled or at least postponed.

She began to nod and Siluk beamed.

"Yes," she said. "After we get the council members out, we'll run away with them and hide until everything with the vote gets figured out. We can make a refuge and—"

"No," Siluk said. No trace of the beaming remained on his face now. "That's not what I meant."

She stared at him. What *did* he mean then?

He took her hand again and didn't let go when she tried to pull away. "Just you and me. We need to leave Nairobi. I thought about letting Naki come with us, but she's too invested in the vote now. I think Basara will look after her anyway. That dude is more obsessed with her than anyone I've ever seen."

He kept talking like his words made any sense, but they didn't. The longer he talked, the more frustrated Imara got. She sat up in the couch and yanked her hand out of his grip. "What are you talking about? We can't run away. We have to stop Santini. We actually have a chance now."

Siluk let out a huff as he glared. "We have no chance at all. If we do this stupid idea Naki has, we're all going to die—and guess what? I'm not letting you die, no matter how hard you try."

Imara gritted her teeth, seeing now what he was really trying to say. "You don't get to decide what I do."

"Maybe I should," Siluk said with blood red flames of anger shooting out of his skin again. "You're a little crazy sometimes. Maybe you need someone who can talk you down when your ideas go too far."

She folded her arms over her chest. "Where is this coming from?"

Siluk laughed. "Oh, I don't know. Maybe it's because some psychotic woman wants you dead for the second time in a month. Maybe you're willing to sacrifice yourself, but I'm not willing to sacrifice you, so this is done now. If you don't agree to come with me, then I'll force you to do it."

"You'll force me?" she said through her teeth. "I hope you know you would lose. Abe taught me how to fight, and I happen to be a natural."

Siluk rolled his eyes. "Yeah, I would definitely try to fight you. That's a *great* idea. I'll just punch you in the face to knock you out and then you'll be even more hurt." He rolled his eyes again. "Obviously I have a different idea. Why would I fight you when I can use my smells to..." He let out a mischievous chuckle. "Persuade you."

Her mouth dropped while she stared at him. He was actually serious. She wanted to think this was some kind of sick joke, but it wasn't. He wanted her to run away. He actually planned to force her if she wouldn't do it.

213

She clenched her jaw tight, looking Siluk square in the eyes so he would know she was serious. "That won't work, especially if I know it's coming. You said your smells aren't always effective anyway."

"It will work," Siluk said, and unfortunately his skin glowed to indicate his words were true. Or at least he believed they were. "I know it will work because I'm not trying to convince you of something you don't want to do. I'm convincing you of something you've wanted all along but were too afraid to admit to yourself. Once I give you the chance to escape all this craziness and also to be with me, you won't be able to refuse. Your true feelings will take over."

He whipped his head to the side. "Besides, I've never used illegal levels of smells and pheromones before, and I've gotten you to do plenty of stuff. Just think how much more effective it will be once I throw the laws out the window."

The milk and musk dancing into her nose suddenly seemed sinister.

"Then I'll plug my nose," she said while trying to keep her shoulders from shivering. She glared at him, seriously wondering if this was a dream. Or maybe a nightmare. A sick bile came up her throat. What did he mean *I've gotten you to do plenty of stuff*? Had he been manipulating her through the years without her realizing it?

She always felt like he was there at personal times, asking questions like they were the best of friends. Even when she hated everybody, he always acted like they were close. Had he always thought something more would happen someday? Had he been so completely unaware of how much he hurt her? Was he still unaware?

She gulped and felt the bile drop back down. "I'm not going with you. I'm staying here, and I'm going to stop Santini."

He flashed his teeth at her. "Why? Why are you so concerned with saving the world all the sudden?" He kicked at the floor with a glare. "You used to be perfect. You still wanted to rescue people and be a good person, but you didn't feel like it was your responsibility to save the entire world. You didn't even want to fight the taggers back then."

He rolled his eyes back, letting his head dip back as he did. "Then Abe came along and convinced you people are good or whatever stupid crap he said. And now it's suddenly your responsibility to save the world?" He looked her straight in the eye. "I want the old Imara back."

She clenched her jaw tighter and tighter, trying to find some semblance of calm. Before she could grasp any, something else took over. Gritting her teeth together, she spat, "I hated you back then. That's who you want back?"

He reached for her hand and didn't stop when she flinched. "You would have come around eventually. I was just about to break through your defenses before Abe came and ruined everything."

She ripped her hand out of his grip. "Maybe instead of breaking through my defenses, you should have recognized I wasn't interested. I never was. Whatever you think we have, we don't. We never did."

He grabbed her hand again and reached into the pocket that held his sprays. "Yes, we did. I know we did."

With every bit of strength she could muster, she ripped her hand away from him and plugged her nose. She jabbed her finger toward the apartment door and said, "Get out. I don't feel that way about you. And you know I'm in love with Abe. I want to stop this vote because if we don't, Santini will take over the world. You know what I feel for you?"

Siluk stared back with a blank expression.

"I feel like you should have been my friend, but you were so concerned with what you wanted, you never stopped to think about what I wanted."

His jaw flexed, but he didn't speak.

She pinched her nose tighter and glared at him. "I swear I will keep plugging my nose until the end of time if I have to. I want you out of this apartment. Don't you ever come back."

He turned away and kicked the coffee table over. "I'm just worried about you. I don't want you to die. Is it wrong to care about someone?"

"It is when you do it like this," she said.

He didn't have a response to that. He stared for another minute, but when she sat there plugging her nose even harder than before, he finally left. Once he was gone, a panic started to flow through her. Naki had the drug, but she expected to add Siluk's pheromones to the formula. Would it still work without his help? How could everything fall so completely apart when they were so close to the end?

TWENTY-SEVEN

IMARA CURLED HERSELF INTO A BALL WHILE she lay on the couch waiting for Naki to come home. Keeping all those feelings pushed down only made them hit her that much harder now. She had called Naki as soon as Siluk left. Naki had growled and promised to get revenge on him. For now, she was on her way home. Without a bubble car, it would take a while.

Imara's body shook as she lay on the couch alone. She didn't know if it was because of the electrocution or because of her emotions. Or maybe it was just because of stress. She wanted to call Abe.

All she wanted was to keep people from dying. It seemed like such a sensible desire. Now, she had to worry about the stopping the vote, which might not even be possible with Siluk gone. And they still had to get all of the council members out of the glass dome. And they had to blow it up. How had everything gone so wrong?

Naki burst into the apartment fuming and apparently plotting her revenge against Siluk. She helped Imara to her feet and led her back to their room. The only good news was Imara's legs were working a little better now.

"I'm going to punch Siluk in the face if I ever see him again," Naki said, lowering Imara onto the bed. "I'm going to hit him so hard, I'll break his nose."

Imara smiled as she adjusted herself on the blankets. "You don't even know how to punch someone in the face. It hurts more than you think, especially if you don't do it right. You might break your finger before you break his nose."

Naki shrugged, her eyebrows lowered in a glare. "Well, I'm still going to try. That little freaky stupid face deserves it. I knew there was something wrong with him."

Imara had to look away before she could speak again. "You were right. He was taking advantage of me. I shouldn't have let him get close to me like that. What am I supposed to tell Abe? I feel awful."

Naki rolled her eyes. "Don't blame yourself for Siluk's mistake. You were just grieving, and Siluk swooped in and took advantage of you."

"He almost kissed me," Imara said, barely able to recall the memory without bone-crushing guilt. She lowered her voice to a whisper. "I almost let him."

Naki ran her fingers up and down Imara's arm with a touch so comforting, Imara wondered how she had lived without it for so many years. Having a sister on her side was so much better than she ever imagined. "Don't blame yourself, Imara. I won't let you. And I'm still going to punch Siluk if I ever see him again. Or maybe I'll have Basara do it. He's probably strong enough." At the mention of Basara, Naki's eyes lit up, even though she tried to hide it.

"Abe called me again," Imara said.

Naki's eyebrows rose and a branch of butter yellow surprise drifted off her skin. "When?"

"Before Siluk's outburst."

Several sheets of olive-green relief blew over Naki's surprise. "What did he say?"

"They know how to blow up the glass dome, but there might be some complications because other signals are coming out of the glass dome too. Keiko thinks Santini is using some kind of signal to create the tags."

"That's perfect!" Naki said. "That means the tags will disappear once they blow up the glass dome."

"Actually," Imara said, feeling her face fall with the word. "It means the exact opposite. Once the glass dome is destroyed, there might not be a way to remove the tags. Maybe if we can get Santini to cooperate there will be, but that's not likely."

Naki let out a huff as she pouted. She took a chunk of Imara's curls into her hand and started braiding them. "Do you think it's still worth it? To blow up the dome even if it makes the tags permanent?"

Imara sat for a long time before she answered. "Yes, but I think it would be stupid to blow up the glass dome without at least trying to remove the tags first. If I could get my hands on just one of the tagging devices, I bet we could figure out how to remove the tags."

Naki's hands froze mid-braid as she seemed to sense where this was headed. "All the taggers would recognize you. You can't go into the glass dome."

Imara bit her lip, trying to think of an alternative. She promised Abe she would be careful, but this had to be done. "That's where all the tagging devices are. I don't see any other option. Unless *you* want to go into the glass dome."

Naki's face went rigid, which was exactly what Imara expected. Imara shook her head, resigning herself to the inevitable. "Basara would get killed if he even tried looking at the glass dome. No offense, but he wears his heart on his sleeve, and he would look too suspicious. With Siluk gone, I'm the only one who can do it."

Naki started braiding again, but her fingers felt different this time. She didn't pull tighter or too hard, but there was tension that hadn't been there before.

"I know a way in," Naki said quietly. "Mali and I found it before she got captured. There's a window with a blind spot, but you have to get the motion sensor security camera to turn the other way. Once you get inside, there aren't any guards until you go around the corner."

Before Imara could respond, Basara threw open the bedroom door wearing a smile that would put even the happiest man alive to shame. "I did it!" he said.

Naki jumped off the bed and ran straight into his arms. "You figured out the touch-sensitive trigger?" she asked, already hugging him.

He nodded and pulled her closer.

She stepped away and jumped into the air. "Basara, you are the freshest, smartest, *best* boyfriend anyone could ever ask for."

Imara could barely blink, and suddenly they were kissing. Naki had assured everyone that Basara was *not* her boyfriend, but apparently that had been long forgotten. Rather than be annoyed, Imara found herself smiling.

But then they kept kissing.

Imara cleared her throat. "I can leave if you want."

Naki pulled away from Basara and straightened her blouse while her ears burned bright red.

Imara stood up. "I'll just, uh—"

Naki pushed her sister back onto the bed. "Don't be silly. You are suffering from tragic heartbreak for Siluk being the biggest jerk alive. Basara can go. You and I need bonding time."

Basara looked affronted by this suggestion, but Naki gave him a look. Imara didn't see the look, but Basara quickly nodded and left the room without another word.

Naki grabbed the blanket from the floor and curled into the bed next to Imara. The bed wasn't really big enough for both of them, but at the moment, neither of them cared.

Over the next hour, Naki filled the air with happy words about how they would stop Santini and how their plan would work. Occasionally, her voice would drift off.

In those quiet moments, Imara could do nothing but think—and the guilt always came crawling back. So did fear. They had a chance, but it was so small, so tiny, it might not be a chance at all.

And then Naki would jerk back awake and start talking about hila school, and her favorite band, and how she didn't understand why everyone in the world wasn't fascinated with the weather.

Naki's voice remained a constant companion throughout the night. They lay there giggling with each other over all the things that didn't really matter. Things that made them feel like there might be a light at the end of the tunnel.

They did eventually fall asleep, but the last thought Imara had before sleep overtook her was not a pleasant one. She had barely escaped the glass dome last time she was there. If she didn't escape this time, what would Santini do with her?

TWENTY-EIGHT

IMARA PULLED ON HER SHOES AND TOOK THE towel off her head, shaking the last of the water out of her curls. Naki was still fast asleep on the bed with her arms thrown out across the entire length of it. Imara dipped her fingers into a little pot of coconut oil and started running it through her hair.

When she finished, she figured it was time to wake Naki up. Basara had already been by to ask about her twice.

"Naki," Imara said, gently shaking her sister by the shoulders.

Naki's body jolted upright while a look of pure terror covered her face. She let out a strangled word that sounded vaguely like *Imara*. But once Naki saw Imara right in front of her, her whole countenance changed to one of joy.

"Good morning," she said brightly. She skipped out of the room a moment later without another word. Since Basara was already in the kitchen waiting for her, Imara had some time.

She waited another minute before she left the room. She wanted to make sure Naki was fully distracted before trying to slip out of the apartment. They'd gone over the plan several times last night.

Even though Naki had acted supportive, she insisted they break into the glass dome together in order to find a tagging device. Imara had agreed to appease her sister, but never intended to take Naki at all. She had to go alone, and she knew it. Naki would never understand.

An unbridled fear began crawling around in her gut. She wanted to scold it, but only because it seemed like a living entity at this point.

She tiptoed out of the bedroom. Held her breath walking past the kitchen. Waited until a cupboard slammed before she tapped her palm against the door opener.

And then she was outside the apartment.

She didn't stop holding her breath until she'd gone several steps down the path. When she did finally take in a breath, she immediately broke into a run.

Her feet pounded the ground, and she felt fear growing inside her like no fear she had ever known. It was stronger and scarier and annoyingly pricking at her conscience. But she had never felt so sure about what she had to do.

Tagging had caused riots, and even death, in Nairobi in a matter of days. If the tags became permanent, those people would never again be able to live a normal life. They might be murdered just like Marco Santini had been.

She wanted to stop the vote, but she'd never forget her first goal, to keep people from dying. In order to do that, she had to figure out how to erase the tags.

When she arrived at the glass dome, it took her a few minutes to find the window Naki had told her about. Imara ran through the words Naki had said. *Get the motion sensor camera to turn the other way, then sneak in through the window.*

224

Imara plucked a rock from the ground before pressing herself against a wall that was still hidden in shadow. She chucked the rock in front of the security camera, but it remained motionless.

She let out a sigh. It had probably been a huge advance in technology that motion sensors could ignore small objects like rocks or birds, but it did make her job harder at the moment.

She glanced around for anything that might help with the sensor. After going down a few streets, she managed to find a cricket bat and a small hat. If she placed the hat on top of the cricket bat, it might sort of look like a child. At least enough to fool the motion sensor.

She went back to the glass dome and once again, pressed her back against one side of it. While watching the security camera, she tossed the cricket bat and hat through the air just under the camera. This time it worked.

As soon as the security camera moved away from her, she found the hidden window and jumped inside the glass dome. Right away, it felt like she was back in the catacombs. The walls were close around her just like the narrow and winding passageways. The only thing missing was the dark.

She crept down the hall and peeked around a corner. One guard manned the corridor, but he was on his way down another hall. She tiptoed behind him, intending to catch up so she could try to steal his tagging device.

Her plans changed when she nearly walked past a door camouflaged into the wall. Why would a random door be camouflaged?

She reached up for the hair on the back on her neck. The short bristles of her hair caught in the space under her fingernail. After another second of staring through the camouflage, she noticed a nearby keypad hidden with a troxler puzzle.

This door was special.

It had to be. Why else would it be hidden with camouflage and a troxler puzzle that only a truth seer could see past? Abandoning all thought of going after the tagger, she focused in on the puzzle. Now that she knew how a troxler puzzle worked without her hila, seeing past it *with* her hila was easy. And luckily, Santini still had no idea her hila was back.

She recognized the same nine-dot code from the catacombs and had the door open in a flash.

Right away, she knew this room had everything she needed. A bookshelf filled with plastic binders sat in front of her. She found one labeled *tagging devices* right at eye level.

She cursed the inefficiency of paper as she snapped picture after picture, sending them all to Naki as she worked. Ten pages in, she already knew more than Keiko had explained during their last phone call.

If they destroyed the tagging devices, it would erase the tags. If they blew up the glass dome without destroying the devices, it would make the tags permanent like they had guessed. But, she also knew at least three ways to destroy the tagging devices now—and would probably learn more the longer she read.

After a few more pages, she decided it was time to head back to the apartment. Her heart beat wildly, but she had never felt so ready to take on the world. For the first time since she'd seen Santini's face in Cairo, Imara felt like they could stop her.

She was so excited to start working that she forgot to check the hall before leaving the room. Wearing a wide smile, she stepped out of the small room and closed the door with a quiet click. When she turned around, she came face to face with a tagger.

Great.

She slammed a fist into the woman's gut and turned to run without stopping to think. Rushing down a hall, she tried to escape the sound of footsteps behind her. She turned a corner, and her brain turned to mush. Where was that window she'd come in through? If she couldn't find it, maybe she should just look for the front door.

She rounded a corner, and the memory of being there with Safiya came back to her. Safiya. She tried to push past the guilt in order to remember the layout. After a moment, she nodded to herself. *The front door is close.*

Turning the next corner, she slammed right into a pack of taggers.

Great. Again.

She recognized Vikal right as he hit her across the head with something long and hard. *Why does it always have to be him?* Her knees gave out and her ears started ringing. They had her tied up while her head spun in circles.

Her stomach twisted. They forced her down the hallway. There were six of them and she had no weapons. She hadn't even brought the stun gun because she wanted Naki to have it just in case. She cursed herself for that decision now. This wouldn't be easy to get out of.

Maybe she could wrest herself out of the grip of the two taggers holding her arms. Then she'd have time to headbutt the tagger behind her. That only got rid of three of them, which still left three more.

Her mind was busy churning when Vikal pushed open a door. Imara recognized the large room where Safiya had died. Her muscles tensed at the thought. They took her straight to the iron cage, this time locking her inside with a giant padlock. Imara glanced around the room, trying to not feel too defeated.

How on earth will I get out of this?

TWENTY-NINE

SANTINI WALTZED INTO THE ROOM WEARING
a smirk that made Imara even angrier about her situation. They
had had a chance. A real chance. Had everything really been
ruined because of one tiny mistake? An amateur mistake too.
How had she forgotten to check the corridor before entering
it? What would Abe say? Well, he'd probably say she was still
perfect, but he was biased so that didn't count.

"I thought I would have to find you," Santini said, wearing
a smile that grated Imara's nerves. "But then you were kind
enough to come to me. Impeccable timing too. I was just about
to send my taggers."

"You were going to come after me?" Imara asked. Maybe
it wasn't so bad that she'd been caught, then. If the taggers had
come to her apartment, there was no telling what they might
have done to Naki. At least this way Naki stayed safe.

"You can leave now," Santini said, waving her taggers
away. "I need to speak with Imara alone."

They all nodded, but Vikal did it more intensely than any
of them. It was almost a bow rather than a nod. It seemed his
respect for Santini had grown into something more like
obsession.

"What do you want with me?"

229

Santini brought up a chair, still wearing that smirk. "Now, now, Imara, there's no reason to be frustrated. You aren't hurt and none of your friends are either."

Imara gritted her teeth. "What do you want with me?" she asked again.

"I already told you," Santini said. Her eyes narrowed as she said it. She pointed back to the wall hologram behind her, and Imara noticed a little box in the corner that hadn't been there the last time she was here. She didn't have time to inspect it further because Santini brought up blueprints of the glass dome. On it, the air vents had been highlighted yellow like glowing snakes.

Santini ran her fingernail along the yellow lines as she said, "Before the global vote tonight, you are going to give a speech and convince every council member to vote yes, making me judge of the world."

Imara scowled. "They won't vote for you. They have access to the news feeds. They know what you've done to the city. Plus, you're holding them hostage. No one could write a speech persuasive enough for that."

Santini raised a hand to silence her. "I've already done most of the work. I broke plane and bubble car travel worldwide. They know I did it, and they know I can fix it. They also know I won't ever fix it unless they vote for me."

Imara's stomach clenched. "That's blackmail."

Santini gave her a sideways glance before shrugging. "Call it what you will, you can't argue how effective it is."

A shout of protest formed in Imara's mouth, but it stopped when Santini smiled. "Giving them access to the news feeds was part of my plan." Her smile grew. "You should hear what they say about you. They whisper about you when I allow them to talk to each other. They call you *hero*. Just this morning, one of them said, 'If anyone is going to save us, I put my money on the girl. She's the hero we all need.'"

An icy hand seemed to grip Imara's heart—and crushed it into dust.

"You did that on purpose. You tagged me as a hero so…" She couldn't finish. The words stuck in her throat like a fly in honey.

This had been part of her plan all along. Santini tagged her as a hero and let her give refuge to the tagged so people would believe in her. So the council members would believe in her.

Did they trust her enough that one speech would change their mind about the vote?

She slammed a door on that thought and locked it up tight. It didn't matter if that were true because she'd never give a speech like that. Not ever.

As Santini stared at her, Imara knew she was watching the emotions coming off her skin. She hoped Santini would see her resolve to never give the speech.

"Yes," Santini said. "I hand delivered you trust from almost every citizen of Nairobi. That trust has trickled over to the council members within these walls."

Imara stomped one foot, grinding her teeth as she glared. "Do you know how much damage your tags have done? You've only tagged in one city and the place is falling to pieces. Nairobi hasn't had such violence in a hundred years."

Santini rolled her eyes. "As smart as you are, I didn't think you would still be so vehemently against tagging."

"What are you trying to accomplish? Don't you see how much destruction tagging has brought? When has tagging ever helped anyone?"

Surprisingly, Santini sat back in her chair and looked at Imara with all new eyes. She tapped her chin and said, "That is a good question. My taggers know the story, but you don't. I suppose it's a good time for you to hear it."

Imara wanted to protest this. She didn't think it was a good time to hear a story. She had to get out of here. But if Santini was talking, she wasn't plotting. So, maybe it was worth it to keep her busy.

Santini sat back in her chair with an air of importance, as if she was about to tell the most enthralling story that had ever been told. "When I grew up in Italy, my parents taught me that nothing is more important than family. Now, I loved my parents more than life itself; I always have. When they taught us the importance of family, I trusted their conviction. Imagine my surprise when I noticed my father's wandering eye toward a woman in our neighborhood. At the time, I was new at truth seeing, so I assumed I interpreted the emotions wrong. There was no way my father could fall in love with another woman. Not *my* father. Not the one who had taught me the importance of families. But the signs were there, and I finally decided not to ignore them. I forced myself to look past the consequences, and I told the truth. I told my mother and my father what I saw. Do you know what happened?"

Imara felt a pit in her gut. It made sense that Santini would have some tragic backstory to explain her actions, but it still hurt hearing it. She had ached for her former teacher over and over and did it once again after hearing this story. She didn't want to be sympathetic, but she couldn't help it.

Looking down, Imara said, "Your dad left your mom and crippled your perfect family?"

To her surprise, Santini grinned. "No. The truth was exactly what they needed. My parents admitted to the problems they were having because I had forced them out. They were forced to accept how bad things had gotten and then, because family is everything, they did all they could to fix it. Within a year, all thoughts of the other woman had vanished from my father's mind, and my parents' marriage was stronger than ever. The truth saved them. It can save you too if you let it."

Imara blinked back, not sure how to respond. In a way, Santini was right. The truth *had* saved her family. It had. But Imara knew just as surely that tagging was wrong. But then, why had it been right for Santini's parents and not for the world?

Santini smirked again. She seemed to see the dilemma in Imara's mind. Imara wondered what emotions Santini could see. Whatever they were, they were making Santini feel even more sure of her plan. She was starting to understand Santini in a way she never had before. And truthfully, it scared her.

Santini clapped her hands together. "Now that we have that out of the way, we can discuss the real reason you're here. You are going to write and deliver a speech to the council members tonight. You will explain to them why the world needs tagging and why I, as the most powerful truth seer in the world, will be the perfect judge to do that."

"I'm not going to do it," Imara said quietly. Maybe she hadn't figured out how Santini's past could be right but tagging

233

could be wrong, but it didn't matter. She wasn't about to destroy the world.

"You will do it."

"I won't!" Imara shouted. She remembered the tiny old woman on the Egyptian Council that had stood up to Takara. She wanted to be brave like her. Determined like her. Resolute.

Santini's face remained impassive. For a moment, she hesitated. Several drops of cobalt blue sadness pelted off her skin, which reminded Imara that Santini still cared about her.

When Santini opened her mouth to speak, Imara knew the words wouldn't be good, especially if Santini was sad to say them.

"Do you see these yellow lines?" Santini asked, pointing to the blueprints.

"The air vents," Imara said.

Santini nodded. "Yes, the air vents. The bedroom air vents are separate from the air vents in the rest of the dome. Do you know what that means?"

Imara looked away. "Safiya said you'd be able to cut off air supply to the bedrooms and murder all the council members, but every other place in the glass dome would be safe."

"Exactly," Santini said. "Not only can I cut off oxygen, but I can also suck it out of the bedrooms." She pointed to a button on the wall hologram; a frown pulled her lips down. "If I press this button, every council member will be dead within thirteen minutes."

Imara's body froze. She held her breath, waiting. Wondering. All at once, the wondering stopped, and the plan became clear. After gulping over the lump in her throat, she said, "If I don't give the speech, you'll kill all the council members."

"Yes, I'm glad you're keeping up. With the council members dead, the world will be in mass confusion. I assure you that I'll still become judge eventually, but it will take longer and be deadlier than if the global vote passes. I prefer to become judge through the vote, but I promise, I will do whatever I must to become judge. If you don't write the speech, I'll kill them all."

Her skin glowed to indicate truth, and Imara wished she could sit down and cry. "You killed Headmaster Bello and Safiya. How many more people will you kill? You're a murderer."

This time, Imara knew she'd hit a sore spot.

She saw cerulean chunks of regret spattering off Santini's skin so fast, they almost looked like a blur. Some part of her, however deep, did regret all the terrible things she'd done.

Santini gave a tiny shake of her head, and the regret vanished in an instant. She set her face into a determined stare and looked away. "History is written by the winners. No one will accuse me of murder once they see the good I can do."

There was no point arguing now. It was too late for Santini. Nothing Imara said would make any difference at all.

Santini tipped her chin up as she continued to speak. "You should have listened to me in the catacombs. I told you saving people was your greatest strength, but it would be your greatest weakness too. I know you would never let those council members die. You always, always have to save people."

Imara's chest heaved as she sucked in deep breaths. Santini was right. She couldn't let those people die, not if she could do something to help them. But she couldn't give the speech. If she did, she'd condemn the world to the same fate Nairobi had lived the past few weeks.

She couldn't do that either.

"I'll give you whatever you want," Santini said. "I'll let you disappear forever. I'll let you take your friends, family, anyone. Or, if you want power, I'll give you that too. If you give the speech, I'll give you anything."

Imara weighed the options over in her mind, trying to decide which scenario was better. Let hundreds of people die, but save the world? Or save the world, and watch hundreds of people die?

Neither. Neither option was acceptable.

"I almost forgot," Santini said. "I hacked this footage from a security camera last night. I got a little tip from Siluk."

Imara's ears pricked up, a flush of anger spreading through her.

Santini merely chuckled. "He was trying to bargain for your life. He didn't mean to give anything away, but since I'm a truth seer, I learned more than he wanted. He regretted it, by the way. Coming to me. I don't know if that makes any difference to you or not, and frankly, I don't care. But there it is anyway."

When the footage appeared on the wall hologram a moment later, Imara's stomach dropped. Naki's nimble frame came into view as she stole drugs from a secure vault inside her workplace. Imara gulped. With video evidence like that, Naki could be jailed for years.

Tears pricked at Imara's eyes while the weight of her decision only increased.

"I thought that might change things," Santini said. "If you don't write a speech to convince the council members to vote for me, then I'll kill them all. I'll also release this video of Naki, and she'll be jailed for life. If you give the speech, I'll destroy this video, and no one else will ever know it existed."

Imara stood. All she could think about were the people she had to save. No more deaths. There had been too many already.

Santini removed the padlock from the iron cage and dropped it to the ground. "You can go now. I expect you back in three hours so I can look over your speech before you give it."

Imara blinked at the unlocked door of the iron cage. "You're letting me go?"

"Of course. You have a speech to write. I'm sure you'll write better at your apartment than you could here."

Imara blinked. This had to be a trap. It had to be. "I could run away," Imara said. "I know how to get past the forcefield. I could run away so I don't have to give the speech."

Santini let out a snort so crude, Imara couldn't believe it came from her former teacher's nose. Santini's voice tittered with laughter as she said, "Don't you understand? I'm a truth seer. I don't have to guess what you're going to do, I already know what you're going to do. I have no reason to keep you trapped when I know you'll do what I want."

Santini turned away to look at the wall hologram. She laughed again and muttered, "*Run away*? I'm surprised you managed to force those words out of your mouth. You'd *never* run away."

She laughed to herself again while Imara stared at the open cage. She had no reason to stay except her certainty that this was a trap. But for what? What could Santini do now that she hadn't already done?

Imara thought back to the last time she was here. She had barely escaped.

Or had she?

Maybe Santini let her go that time too. Maybe Imara ran away and never realized that no one chased after her or bothered to stop her.

She glanced back at Santini and actually, physically shuddered.

And then she ran.

THIRTY

IMARA TAPPED HER RING FOR THE thousandth time in the last ten minutes. She kept willing Abe to call her, but he didn't. He was supposed to get through the forcefield today, but she didn't know when. If he got back before the vote, they still had a chance.

If he didn't...

But he knew when the vote was scheduled. Of course he'd be back in time.

"Why can't we just do what we've been planning all along?" Naki asked when Imara got back to the apartment and explained what had happened. "Basara's almost done with the guns. We'll sneak in, get the council members out, then hide until Keiko blows up the glass dome."

"I've thought about that," Imara said. "She let me go, but I'm pretty sure she's having me followed. If I don't do what she wants, I think she'll kill me. She'll kill you too. And Mom and Dad. And Abe. She's unhinged. She'll stop at nothing to get what she wants."

"There has to be another way," Naki said, throwing her hands into the air. The floor had started to wear from Naki's constant pacing.

"Do you have any suggestions?" Imara asked hopefully.

Naki frowned and went back to pacing. No, not pacing. Marching. Basara hadn't contributed to the conversation at all since Imara got back. He did bring out little snacks for them. As if that would help.

Imara shoved her palms into her eyes, trying to squeeze out an idea. Anything.

It was an impossible dilemma, and the only real way out of it was giving that speech. But then she'd be letting Santini take over the world.

But if she didn't give the speech, Santini would kill the council members, and her, and still become the judge anyway.

"You have to destroy that video of Naki," Basara said from behind a mug.

Imara gulped.

To her surprise, Naki rounded on him with a glare. "Don't pressure her like that. She already has enough to deal with. Trust me, Imara would do anything to save me if she could. She's already risked her life for me multiple times."

Basara shrank back with a nod, but Naki suddenly burst into tears. "Who knew Santini was this sadistic all along? Who knew she had so much lust for power?"

"At least we know how to erase the tags," Imara said. "Maybe we could still rescue the council members and blow up the glass dome and everything. Santini will kill us, but at least the rest of the world will have a chance. Although…"

"What?" Basara asked when Imara stopped.

She looked down. "Santini has had every step planned all along. She probably has a backup plan for her backup plan's backup plan."

"Maybe we can convince the council members to call a revote," Naki said. "You give the speech like Santini wants, but afterward, in a week or so, talk to them again and convince them to do another global vote to kick Santini out."

Imara shook her head so hard the curls grazed her forehead. "That will never work. Santini will put laws in place that give her absolute power. Once she's voted in, it's all over."

Naki jumped in front of Imara. She scooped her hands up, looking into her sister's eyes while a turquoise swirl of hope drifted out of her skin. "What's that thing you always say? 'When faced with two options, one bad, the other worse, choose a third option.' We just have to find the third option."

"Not this time," Imara said, dropping her head to her chest. "This time, there isn't one."

೮೮೮೮

Imara had perched herself on the end of Naki's bed. She was running out of time before she had to go back to the glass dome. Before she left, she had one last thing to do.

Her shoulders shook as she slid open the desk drawer. She pulled out the pewter mirror with opals embedded into the handle and bit her lip. She had promised Abe she would try again. As much as she didn't want to, there had never been a time she needed to see good in herself more than this moment.

Closing her eyes, she moved the mirror into position in front of her face. With one last deep breath, she opened her eyes. She flinched before she could stop herself. Blood, mint, and rust rippled off her skin. Anger, distrust, and doubt. Slicing through each emotion were thick wine-colored fear spikes.

241

Her eyes fluttered shut as she sucked in a breath.

She could do this. She just had to find one good thing about herself. Just one.

Peeking through one eyelid, she begged herself to see past the smattering of negative emotions pelting off her skin. She pried the other eyelid open and forced herself to look. Really look.

It hurt.

She gripped the mirror by the handle and swallowed as doubt and fear overtook her senses. She allowed them control for a brief moment, and then she dove through the emotions she saw. They were true, but they weren't the only true things she felt. Deep down, there had to be something good.

After several minutes, a pearlescent glow glinted from behind a blood red flame. Imara focused in on it until the glint became solid. It started taking shape until it moved from behind the flame to the front of it. A rope. A pearl-white rope fluttering as if it had a purpose.

As she stared, more pearl ropes appeared all around her skin. Each one fluttered with a steady rhythm. Consistent. Determined.

No.

As she had learned to do with so many emotions, Imara soon grasped the meaning of this one. Resolute.

Her heart thrummed in her chest as the emotion filled her. Resolute.

The longer she stared, the more certain she became. This emotion had been a part of her all her life. It defined her as much as hope defined Abe. She'd made mistakes in her life, but she'd always been resolute. Strong. Determined.

She thanked Abe in her head for making her promise to try again. It hurt to look in that mirror, but now that she saw her fluttering ropes of pearl-white resolution, she hoped the emotion could sustain her. She needed it to sustain her.

Because she knew what she had to do now. And it wouldn't be easy.

THIRTY-ONE

ABE WATCHED AS KEIKO CALCULATED THE final measurements on her ring. "Are you sure this will actually work?" he asked.

The forcefield didn't look very inviting. It fizzled with electricity. He thought some of it could be for show, but he wasn't too keen to find out.

"Can't we call Imara before we try?" He didn't want to admit it, but he was slightly afraid that attempting to get through this forcefield would kill them all. He wanted to at least say goodbye one last time. Their last conversation had been cut so short.

Keiko rolled her eyes with a scoff. "I already told you. We're too close to the glass dome. Santini will be able to track our ring and make the forcefield block it just like all the other rings."

"But what about once we're inside the forcefield?"

"Santini will still be able to track the ring, and an anonymous identity will be suspicious. We have to wait until we get to her apartment."

Abe huffed and started tapping his toe. They'd been waiting for days to get inside the city and now he had to sit here and wait some more. He was getting sick of it.

Darius pushed his blond curls out of his face, which only made Abe miss Imara more. He wanted to run his fingers through *her* curls, not be stuck with Darius's.

"I hope you appreciate how much I've sacrificed to come with you guys," Darius said.

Abe shared a look with Keiko who rolled her eyes back dramatically.

"I took off my ring for this. Do you have any idea how much information I lost because of that?"

"You are such a baby," Keiko said. "We both took our rings off too. Can't you be fresh for once and just help without complaining?"

Darius huffed.

As much as he complained, Darius had helped them a lot. He was always willing to use his hila, his strength, or anything else to make sure they could get to Nairobi in time. He just couldn't seem to do it without a slew of complaints.

"Ready," Keiko said. "Now remember, this is still going to hurt like a mother and there's no guarantee we'll actually survive."

"Yet another sacrifice I'm making," Darius mumbled.

Keiko ignored him and continued. "The forcefield will feel like walking through thick mud, but the ring is what actually prevents people from passing through. Since we aren't wearing our rings, we just have to deal with a little electrocution. Or a lot. I'm pretty sure it's a low enough voltage that we'll survive, but we won't know for sure until we try."

245

"Let's get this over with," Abe said. He walked to the edge of the forcefield, trying not to imagine the feeling of cutting knives that was about to go through him.

He looked to Keiko, who nodded, and then he started walking.

Thick mud wasn't really a proper description. It was more like quicksand. In the middle of a rushing ocean current. And it was all on fire.

Stinging knives of pain cut through him as he forced his feet forward. Each second, it got a little bit worse.

He used his shoulder to edge himself in farther. He pushed and pushed and for a second it felt like he couldn't go any farther. The pain was too great.

It only took one thought of Imara to regain his resolve and he pushed through and suddenly the forcefield spat him out on the other side.

He fell to the ground in a heap and had the strong desire to stay there forever. Instead, he got to his feet and checked on the others. They were still pushing through.

He reached for Keiko's arm. Once his fingers touched the forcefield, the electricity shot through him again. He ignored it as he grabbed Keiko's elbow and pulled her inside the city. With their combined strength, Keiko made it through the forcefield seconds later.

They went to Darius next, each of them grabbing one of his elbows before pulling him inside.

Darius whimpered as he whipped the hair out of his face. "I don't know if I'll ever be the same after this. That was worse than Napoleon's defeat at Waterloo."

Keiko snickered, but Abe ignored them both. Now that he was inside the city, he only cared about one thing. Imara.

ᎷᎷᏟᏟ

After too much running, Abe only had one block until he reached Imara's apartment. They passed a large crowd of people gathering around a wall hologram. Abe heard someone say, "It's her. It's the hero."

With mild curiosity, he glanced at the hologram screen only to see Imara's bright face looking back at him. Except, her face didn't look bright at all. It looked...

He searched for a word to describe it but couldn't find one. It just looked different. Her dark brown skin was as rich as ever, but the youth in it seemed to have vanished.

Her voice stayed calm and steady as she spoke, but that didn't seem possible considering the words coming out of her mouth.

"Again, I urge all council members to vote yes in the global vote. We need Carlotta Santini as judge. After reviewing everything, I am positive this is the right thing to do. The people of the world need you to vote yes. Please, council members, we're all counting on you."

In almost an instant, the people around the hologram screen changed from a crowd to a mob. "Follow me," he said, pushing Darius and Keiko away from the people. "Imara's apartment is close by."

It took some time to get away from the mob, but they managed eventually.

"She betrayed us," Darius said as soon as they were free.

Abe glanced at him with an eyebrow raised, but even Keiko looked worried.

"She didn't betray us," he said.

Darius snarled. "We had a way to stop Santini, and she just threw it out the window. Now all the council members are going to vote for Santini, and everything is lost. We took off our rings for her, and she betrayed us."

Abe shook his head aggressively. "No, something else has to be going on."

Darius rolled his eyes. "You can tell yourself that, but it isn't true."

When they reached her apartment, Abe pounded on the door as hard as he could.

"I'm coming!" he heard Naki yell through the door.

When she opened it a moment later, she let out a sigh of relief. "Finally!" she said. "Took you long enough. Now get inside so I can—"

Her voice cut off, and Abe wasn't sure why until he heard Darius take off from behind him. Now Darius was going to run?

Abe turned back with his hands balled into fists—but they relaxed when he saw who Darius was running to. Siluk. They clapped each other on the back, which made Abe happy. But now he was ready for his own reunion.

He walked into the apartment and noticed a young man standing there who looked familiar. Darius pulled Siluk inside the apartment while Abe tried to remember where he had seen the young man before.

"I'm Basara," the young man said. At once, Abe remembered where he had seen him before. Naki's boyfriend.

Or, at least, he was her boyfriend when Imara got kidnapped by Takara. But hadn't Naki broken up with him?

He shook his head. That didn't matter right now.

He whirled himself around long enough to see that Imara was nowhere inside the apartment. He didn't really expect it since they had just seen her on the hologram screen giving a speech to the council members. Apparently, part of him had been hoping it was a recording of some sort.

He let out a sigh and turned toward the others. "It's good to see you, Siluk. And Naki."

But Naki was glaring at Siluk harder than he'd ever seen her glare at anyone. Even harder than she had glared at him after Imara broke up with him.

"What do you know about Imara's speech?" Keiko asked Naki.

Naki ignored her and glared even harder at Siluk while simultaneously pulling her hand into a fist. "What are you doing here?" she asked him.

Abe had no idea what was going on but seeing Naki angry at Siluk brought up all of the emotions he had been ignoring for months. He suddenly had the very strong urge to hit Siluk as hard as he could.

Siluk merely stared at the ground. "I was waiting for Darius. I knew they were supposed to get here soon."

Naki let out a hiss as her nostrils flared.

"And I saw Imara's speech," he said, raising his hands in defense. "I figured if she was saying stuff like that, Santini must have done something horrible to her."

"Seriously?" Darius asked, shaking his head. "You're on her side too?"

Darius looked ready to continue, but Abe pushed him to the side. The desire to punch Siluk was growing. He looked Siluk in the eyes and asked, "Why does Naki hate you?"

Naki gritted her teeth, making no attempt to hide the fist she was making. "Yeah, Siluk. Why *do* I hate you? Tell him."

Siluk swallowed and took a step back until he almost walked into the wall. He swallowed again as he looked down but didn't supply any words.

"Go on," Naki said, seething.

Siluk quickly glanced at Darius, maybe for support, but Darius just looked at him and shrugged. It's not like Darius had any idea what was going on anyway. And now, Abe was losing his patience.

Apparently Naki was losing her patience too. "No?" she said. "You won't tell him?" She flipped her head back so her braids flew through the air. "Then I will."

Naki folded her arms across her chest and turned to Abe as she spoke. Pointing her head toward Siluk she said, "He made a pass at Imara while you were gone. Multiple times. He kept at it even after she said no. Then he got mad when she said she wanted you and not with him. And then he RAN AWAY EVEN THOUGH WE NEEDED HIM."

Siluk kept his eyes firmly on the ground. "She didn't say no the first time."

"You idiot!" Naki said, throwing her hands into the air. "She thought Abe was dead and you took advantage of her in a moment of weakness."

At those words, something inside of Abe snapped completely in half. He didn't even realize he was moving until he had Siluk's shirt collar gripped in his fist. He held his arm across Siluk's shoulder, pinning him to the wall.

"What did you do to her?" he said through his teeth.

"Nothing!" Siluk shouted back at him.

He pushed Siluk further back into the wall, making him cough to regain his air.

Naki moved next to Abe. She looked very pleased with the situation. She flipped her braids over her shoulder and said, "I was planning to punch you in the face if I ever saw you again, but honestly, I think this is better."

Siluk flashed his teeth at her. "Would you tell Abe I didn't do anything before he kills me?"

Naki let out a huff and turned her back on Siluk. "I guess you can let him go. They technically only hugged."

Those words brought Abe a wave of relief along with a crushing tumble of jealousy all at the same time. He loosened his grip but didn't let go. Instead, he stared at Siluk until Siluk had to avert his eyes.

"I'm sorry," he said.

Now Abe let go, but he made sure the murder in his stare didn't let up one bit.

"She definitely wants you and not me, okay? You don't have to rub it in." Siluk's voice sounded so much smaller than usual.

Naki rolled her eyes.

"Uh, *hello*," Darius said with his usual level of impatience. "A crazy woman is about to take over the world, remember? Don't we have more important things to discuss than Imara's love life?"

Naki jumped onto her tiptoes. "Oh, I almost forgot." She grabbed Basara and left the room without another word.

Abe ran a hand over his face, suddenly feeling a thousand times more anxious.

"We can still blow up the glass dome," Keiko said.

Abe shook his head. "No, not anymore. All those council members are still inside."

"And Imara," Siluk said.

Abe's stomach turned over, and he thought about punching Siluk anyway. Just for spite.

They sat in silence until Siluk said, "We could kill Santini. This whole vote is to make her the judge, but if she's dead, they'll have to cancel the vote."

Abe looked at Siluk, trying to decide if he was serious or not. "You want us to murder someone?"

"Doesn't she deserve to die after everything she's done?" Siluk asked. "How many people have already died because of her? How many more will? A few of the tagged have already been murdered, and that was with Imara and me trying to rescue as many people as we could."

Abe tried not to think about Imara and Siluk doing anything together but didn't succeed.

"I'll do it," Keiko said.

"What?" Abe asked, forgetting for a moment what they had been talking about.

"Kill Santini. I'm under eighteen. My punishment won't be as bad if I get caught."

Abe glared at Siluk, hoping it made his insides writhe. "You're not killing anyone, Keiko. Maybe we can get the police to arrest Santini before the vote goes through."

"The police are all captured," Siluk said. "They have been since the forcefield went up. There's no one here that can help us."

Abe groaned at these words, but Naki suddenly burst back into the apartment. "We're ready. We only have an hour, so hurry."

THIRTY-TWO

IMARA STOOD IN FRONT OF SANTINI WANTING to wipe the taste of the speech out of her mouth. Santini stared back with pride while the grass green threads of desire whipped around her in such great numbers, they seemed to be suffocating her.

Imara sat, not in the iron cage, but on a chair next to the wall hologram.

"All the votes are in," Vikal said, leaning toward Santini as he spoke.

Santini gave him and three other taggers instructions on how to deliver the results of the vote. They would have to leave the city by foot since the bubble cars were down. Their rings would allow them to pass through the forcefield unharmed. Once they left the city, all four at different points, they would send the results to all governments around the world and every possible news station. Once the vote was recorded, Santini would lower the forcefield and allow the council members to go home.

She hadn't said what she intended to do with the police yet.

While Santini gave instructions, Imara was more interested in the colors coming off the taggers. Vikal had cherry red puffs of love along with scarlet threads of desire that twisted tight around Santini. She'd been right about his obsession.

The emotions coming off the other taggers were more intriguing. Two of them showed canary yellow fizzing bubbles of excitement. The last one had grass green threads of desire that whipped around just like Santini's did. Imara now recognized it easily as lust for power. One that might be even stronger than Santini's.

When the taggers left the room, they all seemed certain that everything was going the way it should.

Santini turned to Imara with a confident smile. "Did you see how excited they were?" She stopped and shook her head. "Oh, of course you didn't see. You don't have your hila anymore."

"They're hungry for power," Imara said. "That's the only reason they're excited."

Santini scoffed and went back to the wall hologram. She brought up security camera footage in order to watch the taggers leave the city.

"With that much lust for power, I'm actually surprised you aren't worried."

Santini scoffed again. "None of them cares about power. The taggers are loyal to me because they believe in our cause."

Imara sat back in her chair, letting herself get comfortable. "Vikal? Yes. He worships you. But the woman who was here? She only wants power. She might be the next Takara."

Santini flinched at the mention of her former tagger. Her shoulders bunched up, but then her face suddenly calmed, and she spoke in her soothing voice. "Don't be ridiculous."

"The most intriguing person was that tall man. He's starting to question you. He's wondering if the lengths you've gone to might be too far."

A flame of blood red anger burst out of Santini's skin before she could compose herself. "You don't have your hila anymore. You can't possibly know that." Her voice sounded sure, but Imara watched a rust-colored string of doubt fall away from her skin.

Imara looked at her old teacher, careful to make direct eye contact. "You only see what you want to see. You taught me to do the same thing, by the way. I used to only see negative emotions. You would be a better truth seer if you learned to see all emotions and didn't interpret them immediately."

A raven black rash of anxiety erupted from Santini's skin. Imara knew better than to interpret it right away. It could have been from anything. Most likely, Santini just wanted to be judge, and she was stressed that the results were still being delivered. But maybe she was losing her nerve.

"How dare you presume to teach me how to use my hila," Santini said, every trace of her soothing voice gone. "There is one reason I taught at the best hila school in the world, and it's because I am, by far, the most powerful truth seer the world has ever known."

"You don't see truth; you change it. You take what you see and mold it to fit the story you want to tell."

"What?" Santini said with a scowl. "What are you talking about?"

Imara glanced at the corner of the hologram screen, then let herself relax before she spoke again. "You create fanciful lies, but you package them with just enough truth that they seem logical. But just because it's partially logical, doesn't mean it's right."

Santini let out a condescending sigh. "Truth is truth. If logic proves it, then it's right."

Imara stood from the chair and swept over to Santini with her chin held high. She stood to her full height before her teacher. She'd never noticed until this moment, but she was actually taller than Santini.

"I said partially logical, not actually logical. That's the difference."

Santini turned away while even more rashes of anxiety came off her skin. She started wringing her hands together. "You are talking in circles, and it makes no sense. Name one example of when I used partial logic to make something wrong seem right."

"When you saved your parents' marriage." The words came to Imara so easily, Santini actually turned around in surprise.

Santini shook her head and waved a hand as if the words were not important. "I did save my parents' marriage."

"I agree," Imara said. Again, Santini turned to her in surprise. "But tagging wouldn't have."

Santini scowled, but Imara never once lost her conviction. Santini had forced her to deliver a speech that would change the course of history. Now Imara would force her to listen.

"You told your parents the truth about what you saw, and it *did* save their marriage."

"Yes, I'm aware. I'm the one who told you the story. What does this have to do with partial logic?"

Imara let out a smile and went back to her chair. "You told your mom and dad about what you saw, but you didn't tell anyone else. You didn't tell the neighbors or the man at the grocery store. You didn't tell your mom or dad's coworkers. You only told the people who needed to know. Your mom and your dad. Tagging tells the world of a person's mistakes. It brands them with something they might have tried to fix. If you cared about rehabilitating instead of tagging, I might be on your side. But you don't. You don't want to help people; you want to take away their chance to become better."

Santini wrinkled her nose as if the room had been filled with a foul stench. Erasing the look, she put on a saccharine smile. "If a woman goes into a jewelry shop, steals a necklace, and later gets caught and goes to jail for a few years, don't you think a jewelry shop owner has the right to know her past mistakes? Especially if she's applying for a job in retail. If she has a history of stealing, wouldn't it be best for her to not be allowed a job with such a great temptation?"

"Yes," Imara said. "Yes, that's exactly my point. In that scenario, I think it's extremely important for the employer to know the past. But again, only the employer has to know. When you tell the people who should know, that's important. But that kind of information can be discovered during a background check. If the woman has done her time in jail, she shouldn't have to be reminded of her crime every time she interacts with another person for the rest of her life."

"Stop it." Santini stood up, throwing her arms into the air. "Just stop it. Tagging is right. You're the one who has it wrong."

Imara frowned, looking carefully at the woman. "It's not too late for you. The voting may be over, but you don't have to let the results get delivered. You can end all of this now."

Santini pulled her hands into fists. "I've worked too hard for this. If you don't stop arguing—" She stopped midsentence when her ring buzzed with a phone call. When she answered the call, it came up on the wall hologram.

Vikal appeared on screen for only a moment before a familiar brown hand covered his mouth.

Basara tackled Vikal to the ground while Naki stepped in front of him to face the camera. "Oh, hello, Santini," Naki said in a glittery voice. "I'll make this simple. Let Imara go and we'll let your people go."

Santini's mouth hung open for several seconds before she managed to speak. "What do you mean *people*?"

"Oh, I was hoping you'd ask," Naki said, a hint of laughter tracing her words. She pulled up her own hologram screen and held it out for Santini to see. The other three taggers that had been sent to deliver the votes were each shown in a video on Naki's screen. The taggers were all tied up, gagged, and sitting on the ground. Siluk, Darius, and Keiko stood at their sides.

Santini growled at the sight and turned off her ring before Naki could say another word. Santini threw a chair across the room while blood red flames of anger burned around her. So much for her perfect calm.

"You stupid, stupid girl. You think this changes anything?"

Imara stood from her chair, feeling herself emit the calm Santini usually held.

Santini flashed her teeth. "I have taggers all over the city. I can send backup to those others within minutes. Even if you caught all of them too, I can take down the forcefield and send the vote results myself."

"The council members will try to rescind the vote once they see what you've done to the city."

Santini let out a forced laugh. "Let them try. Let them—" Her voice cut off for a moment while a terrifying combination of emotions erupted out of her. Blood red flames of anger, magenta curls of determination, and worst of all, jagged shadows of graphite recklessness. All at the same time.

A crooked smile etched onto Santini's face. "You didn't keep your end of the bargain. You were supposed to help the vote go through."

"You only said I had to give the speech."

"Well, I *implied* the vote had to go through. Just the speech wasn't enough. By stopping the taggers from delivering the vote, you didn't hold up your end of the bargain."

Imara gulped. She knew what was coming next.

Santini paced as her smile grew more crazed by the second. "I have to kill the council members now. Don't you see? This is your fault, not mine. You're the murderer."

Imara cringed as Santini stepped toward the wall hologram. "I'll tap this button and the council members will lose their air. They'll be dead in thirteen minutes. When they are dead and I am judge, I'll give myself power to choose new council members for every territory. I'll fill every council in the world with my taggers."

Her smile got more deranged as she reached for the button.

"Don't!" Imara screamed. Every bit of her calm had vanished now. "Please, Santini. Carlotta. *Please* don't do it."

Santini ignored her and kept reaching.

Imara dropped to her knees, physically begging. "You don't have to be this person. You're about to kill hundreds of people. Think about that. They have families, friends."

"I am willing to do whatever it takes to make this world a better place. *That* is what makes me a great leader."

As Santini tapped the button, Imara hung her head. She let the reality wash over her and only wished it didn't have to hurt so much. Santini wanted to prevent people from changing for the better, but maybe she was holding herself back most of all.

"Abe healed my hila," Imara said as a tear fell from her nose.

"What?" Santini asked, glancing over with mild interest.

As she knelt on the ground, Imara watched her teacher's emotions. She knew Santini was surprised that Imara hadn't tried to fight harder when she pushed the button. But it didn't matter now. Imara finally accepted that it was too late.

Too late.

As Imara got to her feet, she watched Santini's emotions more pointedly. She knew her teacher would recognize where her eyes were looking. At the skin and just around it.

"Abe is mashimo," Santini said while wearing a snarl. "Just like Itafe."

"That's what he thought at first, but he was wrong. Abe is a healer."

Santini froze in place, taking careful breaths as she watched her former student. Imara's calm seemed to unnerve her.

Finally, Santini rolled her eyes, an expression so foreign, Imara gawked at it.

"Wonderful," she said sarcastically. "I still won. In a few minutes, the council members will all be dead. I'll lower the

261

forcefield and deliver the results of the vote. But it's just *fresh* that you can see my emotions."

"I can also see this," Imara said, pointing to the corner of the hologram screen. A troxler puzzle concealed both the location of the Kenyan police and the code to release them.

Santini sucked in a sharp breath while Imara tapped the hologram screen. The information behind the troxler puzzler immediately disappeared.

Imara looked back at Santini with the calmest expression she could manage. "I messaged Naki when I first got here, while you were reading over my speech. She's had plenty of time to free the police."

Santini opened and closed her mouth several times before attempting to answer. "I don't believe you," she finally said.

Imara shrugged. "That doesn't change anything."

Santini continued to scowl at her, but the surety in her face wavered. She tapped the wall hologram to make a phone call, but it rang and rang with no answer.

Santini swallowed while large rashes of raven black anxiety grew away from her skin. She pulled up the feed for a security camera. It showed the building where the police had been held. Both doors hung wide open.

"They're probably still making a plan and gathering weapons, but I imagine they'll be here soon."

Imara turned toward a whooshing noise and didn't realize it was Santini's hand until the back of it collided with her cheek. Stinging ran through her skin, and bright spots appeared in her eyes.

Santini struck again while Imara blinked, unable to believe this was real. Santini shoved her to the ground and dug the heel of her shoe into Imara's chest.

"You always save people. You can't stand by and let them die. But what about the council members?" Santini gave a satisfied smirk. "You didn't save them."

"No," Imara said attempting to stay calm. She gripped Santini's shoe, trying to prevent it from digging into her chest. She let out a cough, feeling her air escape. "This time I realized it was more important to keep you distracted. This time, I let someone else do the saving."

"Saving?" Santini laughed as she dug her heel further into Imara's chest. "There was no saving. They're dead by now"

When Imara didn't answer, a fear spike as long as the room shot of out Santini's skin. She shoved her heel deeper into Imara's chest, and then stomped over to the wall hologram.

Imara grabbed her chest, noting a drop of blood and a bruise shaped like a heel. She forced herself to her feet as Santini brought up the security camera feed from one of the council member's rooms. As Imara expected, the room was empty.

Santini let out tiny gasp. She checked another room.

Empty.

And another.

Empty.

She checked another and another and another, but they were all as empty as the first. Santini started screaming as she checked. She checked one last room and every semblance of her control seemed to snap.

She pulled a gun from her pocket just as a gray strand of hair escaped from her bun.

"They also destroyed the tagging devices," Imara said, hoping to distract her.

"No," Santini said in a hush. "How did you … No! It's not possible."

Imara tapped her ring, turning the hologram screen so Santini could see it. Blinking back at them, Imara's name read, *Imara Zawadi Kalu*. Her tag was gone.

Santini whirled the gun precariously in her hands. With a horrible chuckle she said, "I can still take down the forcefield and send the results of the vote. Did you have some miraculous way to stop that?"

Imara almost protested but realized Santini would recognize the lie.

Even keeping the words inside her mouth, Santini had still seen it in her emotions. With a devious smile, Santini reached for the wall hologram. This time, Imara lunged at her.

Santini's hand was still reaching when Imara's body slammed into hers. She pushed her to the ground and forced them into a roll. The roll made the impact less painful, but it also brought Santini that much farther from the button.

Santini tried to fight back, but she didn't have the training Imara had. Or the strength.

But she did have the advantage of being very, very angry. Santini grabbed a handful of Imara's curls and yanked. The hair ripped out of her skull, leaving a stinging feeling much worse than the slap.

It may have been bleeding too. Was that possible? Could the scalp bleed from having hair ripped out?

Santini tore one of her stilettos off her foot and aimed the heel at Imara's neck. Imara jumped to her feet and took a step backward. Santini lunged forward, and Imara let the stiletto heel graze her skin.

She needed Santini to think she had a chance in the fight. In reality, Imara jumped and dodged in just the right directions to get them out of the large room and toward the exit of the glass dome. The police should be here soon. She only had to last until then.

When Santini lunged at her again, Imara made sure to fully feel the terror and anger that went along with the moment. This wasn't a time to stay calm. This was a time for theatrics.

She wouldn't twist the truth, but she would let Santini see exactly what she wanted to see. She'd let herself feel every emotion and let Santini think she had a chance. With the police on their way, all she really needed was time. She'd keep Santini distracted no matter what the physical cost to herself.

It would all be over soon.

They moved into a hallway and Imara threw a punch. The familiar feeling of muscle and bone crunching felt more brutal when there was this much emotion attached. Santini lifted a leg and caught Imara off guard with a swift kick in the stomach.

Imara had to bend over and catch her breath. That gave Santini more time to attack. She lifted her high heel and aimed for the neck again. After the recent hit to the stomach, Imara wasn't as quick to avoid the hit as she had been the first time. The heel hit its target and a warm trickle of blood started running down her neck. Her brain went fuzzy. She tried to shake the feeling away.

Santini lunged at Imara, now wielding a knife she had pulled from a deep pocket. Imara jumped back toward a wall to avoid the weapon. Inadvertently, she jumped into an open doorway.

Imara whirled around on her heel, trying to get her bearings. Too late, she realized she stood in one of the council members' bedrooms. Santini slammed the door shut. Imara gulped when she heard a lock click.

She tried to open the door right away, but it was no use. It could only be opened from the outside. She took a deep breath, but it felt shallow.

The air vents.

The room had already been emptied of oxygen. It probably only had a little air now because Santini had opened the door. But that tiny amount of oxygen would be used up in no time.

Imara told herself not to panic. She grabbed the hair on the back of her neck, grateful that that hair hadn't been lost. She could get out of this, she just had to think.

Black spots appeared in her vision, and panic took over again. She slammed her body against the door, but the door barely moved. She backed up farther and did it again, hoping the greater distance would give her more power.

The door did shake this time, but it wasn't enough.

She backed up again all the way against the back wall and ran with the most strength she could manage. Even with the greater distance, this hit was less powerful than the others. Her air was running out, and her body was growing weaker. Maybe she could break the door down with sheer force if she had enough time, but she didn't.

She sucked in a tiny breath, but it didn't feel like she could breathe at all. She slammed her shoulder against the door. It shuddered again, but weakly. She dug her fingernails in between the door and the wall, trying to force it open, but of course it did nothing.

She closed her eyes as the black in her vision grew. For some reason, she didn't like the idea of seeing herself go unconscious. It seemed better to have closed eyes through it. She dug her fingernails into the space between the door again, but it only broke a nail.

She felt herself drift away as her body crumpled to the ground.

THIRTY-THREE

IMARA SAT IN A CRUMPLED MESS ON THE
ground when the door slid open. Someone pulled her to her
feet and called her name. The words sounded so far away, like
a single leaf drifting in the midst of a tornado.

But the arms around her gave her a sense of peace. And
peace gave her courage. She sucked in a breath while her lungs
clung to the new oxygen inside her.

"Imara," the voice said again. Now she placed the owner
of the voice.

"Abe," she said, sinking deeper into his arms. "I think you
just saved my life."

He had been touching the bald spot in her hair, but his
hands froze. Looking into her eyes, he said, "Really?"

She nodded, feeling more strength return with every
breath.

"Finally," he said, with a victorious grin. "I finally did it."

She chuckled until her head snapped up with a start.
"Santini was going to lower the forcefield and send the results
of the vote herself. She might have done it already. She got
away."

Abe pulled her back into his arms. "The forcefield is still up. The police caught Santini before she did anything. She won't tell them how to lower the forcefield. They need us to evacuate so Keiko can blow up the glass dome."

"They caught her?" The words seemed unbelievable. Impossible.

Abe kissed her forehead. And then her lips. Then he seemed to forget everything as he hugged her even tighter to his body.

He came up for a bit of air and said, "I missed you."

She nodded, her brain feeling a bit fuzzy again, but it had nothing to do with oxygen this time. "When do they need us to evacuate?"

He blinked and turned away from her as if trying to break the spell her presence had cast on him. "Oh yeah. Right now. They're waiting for us." He shook his head and trailed a finger down her neck until it found the drips of blood coming from the bruise in her chest.

"The bruise on your face is superficial, but I don't like the bald spot in your hair. I need to take care of that immediately. And this bruise is even more concerning. What did she hit you with? A stick?"

"It was her high heel. She dug it into my chest while she stood on me."

He cringed, but nothing could take away her good mood now. He was here, and the police were free, and the council members were alive, and Santini had been caught.

She tried to step forward, but with her body in its weakened state, it was difficult. Without a word, Abe lifted her into his arms and trailed down the hallway.

When they left the glass dome, the air felt fresher than ever. Abe helped her to her feet with his hand on her back to steady her.

Just when Imara was certain her mood couldn't improve, Naki jumped in front of her and wrapped her into a hug. "I did it, Imara. I got all the council members out of the glass dome and I didn't panic once." She squeezed Imara even harder. "Basara helped, of course. I couldn't have done it without him, but still. He couldn't have done it without me either, and we actually did it."

Naki pulled away and did a little jump in the air. "We did it!"

"Mali," Imara said when she noticed the contortionist standing nearby.

Soon Naki had all three of them in a group hug.

"You're alive," Naki said. "I was so worried when you got caught, but you're here and it's over."

Mali extricated herself from the hug, but she had a hint of a smile on her lips. "Yeah," she said. "The city definitely turned to crap without me, but you didn't let Santini take over the world, so there is that."

Naki chuckled and went back to Basara. Imara noticed Siluk trying to hide behind Basara's tall frame.

Abe had somehow acquired a bag of medical supplies and started working on Imara's wounds. As always, the pain seemed to disappear with impossible speed. When Imara noticed Siluk again, a lump of guilt settled into her throat.

Before she could do anything about it, another police officer came up to her and said, "The council members would very much like to know what is going on. They're confused about your speech and seem to think you're the only one who can give them answers."

Imara nodded and started walking even though Abe was in the middle of dabbing one of her wounds with ointment.

"Do they need to know right this second?" he asked as he continued to dab, trying to keep up with her.

"They've been locked up for weeks. This is the first time they've been out. I think they've waited long enough."

Abe grumbled under his breath, but he didn't try to stop Imara as she kept walking. He didn't stop tending to her wounds either. It probably looked funny with them walking down the street while he dabbed at her head and chest with ointment and bandages.

By the time they reached the council members, the butterflies in Imara's stomach had decided fluttering was insufficient. They were jumbling now. It made her brain and nerves a mess.

In the back of her mind, she had known this was coming. Since she gave the speech, she knew she'd have to explain it. Now that the time had come, she didn't want to do it.

The police officer directed her to a short platform. She fiddled with her ring, taking her time to find the microphone app. Abe had stopped tending to her wounds, at least. He gave her an encouraging nod. He ended with a quick wink.

For some reason, remembering that she still had to tell Abe about the pearl-white resolution she had seen in the mirror made it that much easier to stand tall. She took in a deep breath. "Earlier today I told you to vote for Santini. I made it sound like she was worthy to be the global judge. That was a lie. I'm sorry for lying, but I did it to protect you. If I hadn't, she would have killed you all."

The entire front row of council members had a mass of fear spikes grow out from their skin. She recognized distrust in their eyes as well. Why wouldn't they be afraid to trust her? She just admitted to lying.

But the more she talked, the more they warmed to her words. Their emotions showed trust, but it was more than that. Their faces looked brighter. They understood that this nightmare was finally over now.

When she stepped off the platform, they all cheered. She felt her cheeks flush and hoped they wouldn't notice the red in her ears. Abe started tugging her away from the crowds toward an empty alley nearby. Her heart leapt in her chest at the thought. They hadn't been alone together in so long.

Before they could reach the alley, the chief of police himself stepped in front of Imara. He grabbed her hand, shaking it maniacally. "You're hired," he said. "We would love to have you work for the Kenyan police. We don't even care if you're still a fugitive in Egypt. Mali told us all about you and your skills. We'd love to have you work for us."

Imara opened her mouth to speak, but no words came out. Her brain didn't even supply thoughts. Even her emotions seemed unable to react.

Weeks ago, her only goal had been to keep people from dying. Now, her goal had changed. She didn't just want to save people's lives, she wanted to save their souls. As noble as being a police officer was, it probably couldn't help her with that goal.

She managed to squeeze out a quiet thanks, but her heart wasn't in it. The chief of police didn't hide his disappointment at her lack of response, but Abe saved her yet again.

"If you don't mind, Imara needs a moment to relax. She's had a lot of stress, especially in the last few hours. Maybe you can catch up with her later."

"Of course," he said. "I completely understand. But Imara, do let us know once you've had a chance to rest."

She barely had time to nod before Abe snuck her away. Somehow, they made it to the alley without anyone else bothering them. The moment they rounded the corner, his eyes locked onto hers with wave of desire. Her body responded to the look, leaning into him as if magnetized. But deep in her navel, something held her back.

Just as Abe reached her, she turned away. "While you were gone, I …" She couldn't bring herself to say the words.

"Siluk," Abe said.

She glanced up at him while guilt sliced through her. How did he know?

Guessing her question, he said, "Naki told me."

Imara let out a sigh, grateful she didn't have to be the one to say it. But still, how much did Naki say? Naki would have made the whole thing look like Siluk's fault. It mostly was, but Imara knew she wasn't completely innocent.

She rubbed her arm as she turned away from Abe, afraid to face him. "At first he just comforted me. We thought you and Darius were dead. I checked your power signal and it was there, but then it was gone. I was devastated. We both were."

Abe gently took her arm and pulled her back toward him. "It's fine," he said. "I don't care what you did."

273

"You don't care?" she asked, raising an eyebrow.

He huffed and loosened his hand on her slightly. "Okay, yes, I do care. Of course, I care. I keep having an image in my head of him holding you, and it makes me want to punch something. At least all you did was hug."

Her hand flew to the back of her neck. She stared at the ground as she tugged on the short strands.

She heard him gulp before he asked, "Is that all that happened? That's what Naki said, but—"

"He almost kissed me."

Abe let out a sigh of relief and took her hand. "You thought I was dead. Even if you had kissed him, I can't blame you. I'm glad you didn't, but either way, you shouldn't feel guilty about it."

He leaned in closer now, his hands getting hungrier as they slipped around her waist.

"I didn't kiss him, but I thought about it. I should have stayed away from him, especially because you were worried about him and me. I thought you were dead, but still. Do you think I'm awful?"

He pulled her so close, his knees bumped into her thighs. "I think we've been away from each other for too long."

Just before their lips met, she asked, "You're not mad?"

"Imara."

The hint of impatience in his voice did more to soothe her guilt than anything else had. She let out a tiny chuckle and finally let him have what he wanted. What they both wanted. He pushed her right up against the wall and kissed her with a fire that warmed her straight through.

THIRTY-FOUR

THE NEXT DAY, NAIROBI WAS STILL IN CHAOS, but things had started to calm down. Imara stood in front of a pile of glass and steel rubble. This was all that remained of the glass dome. She stared at it, still trying to believe everything was over now.

Her dad appeared and scooped her into a hug for no reason at all. "Your mom and I still can't believe everything you and Naki did. You told us you were staying out of trouble."

"We did stay out of it," Imara said. "Well, we *got* out of it. Eventually."

Abe came to her side carrying one of the broken tagging devices. Her dad didn't even flinch at the sight of him. Apparently, saving her life was all Abe had to do to make her parents love him.

"They finally figured out how they work," Abe said, staring at the device. "Mostly because of Keiko. They were able to get the asterisk off my name. You know how I had an asterisk that Santini put there during the graduation party?"

"Oh good," her dad said. "Did they get Naki's off too? She got an asterisk that night as well."

Imara grinned as they talked. No distrust or anger lingered between them at all. Nothing about this day could possibly get any better. Just then, Mr. Nazari cleared his throat from behind them.

She turned while her stomach twisted in knots. Maybe Abe had won her parents over, but she was far from doing the same with Abe's dad. When their eyes met, Mr. Nazari smiled. It was such a rare expression; she didn't know what to think of it. After greeting his son, Mr. Nazari turned to Imara and said, "I'm glad you're okay. Thank you for saving the world."

Imara blinked, unable to find any words to follow a statement like that. Finally, she managed. "Thank you, Mr. Nazari."

He laughed. "Please, call me Itafe."

Itafe? she thought as she stared at him. How could she call him Itafe? That would take more effort than it took to stop calling Santini *Professor*.

He seemed amused by her internal turmoil, letting his mouth show the tiniest smile. "You'll get used to it," he said.

Imara didn't know what to say as Mr. Nazari disappeared back into the crowd.

Imara's mom and Keiko arrived at her side a moment later. "Maybe you should move here," her mom said to Keiko. "I have a few friends in the symphony. I'm sure they could find someone to give you violin lessons at a discount."

Keiko held back a chuckle. "You're just like Imara, always trying to help people."

For some reason, Imara's mom beamed like that was the greatest compliment anyone could bestow. Before they could keep heaping unnecessary praise onto Imara, she spoke.

"Do you think this will be enough chairs?" she asked.

Imara's mom popped up at the sound of her daughter's voice. She didn't pull her into a hug right away like her dad had, but she did squeeze her hand before looking out at the chairs. "I think it's incredible that you've touched so many lives."

A few minutes later, Imara sat on the front row of chairs next to Abe. He gave her hand a little squeeze just as a member of the Kenyan Council stood at the podium in front of them.

The Kenyan Council member began a speech detailing the events of the last month. She talked about the global vote, the state of Nairobi, and how Santini was safely locked away from the world.

And then it was time for awards.

Imara didn't think they were necessary, but Naki was so excited to receive hers, it made the whole experience worth it.

After Naki, the others all received awards as well. Basara, Siluk, Keiko, Darius, Mali, and finally Abe. He grinned at the award as if it was a joke.

Each of them gave a short acceptance speech, but they saved Imara for last. She stood on the podium, not feeling happy exactly, but grateful this was all over. "Thank you for this honor," she said. "I cannot forget the police officers and their bravery. I cannot help but be astounded by the council members and their steadfastness. We saved many people yesterday and that deserves to be celebrated. But now, I want to talk about some other people. Those who didn't survive. Many people were hurt or killed because of Carlotta Santini. Many people suffered at her and the taggers' hands. Those people deserve recognition."

She pointed toward a large mound of flowers in front of her. "Please take one flower for any person you wish to honor. Then, place the flower on the rubble, and we will burn them in order to say goodbye."

The crowd started moving without a sound, choosing flowers with an air of solemnity. When Imara reached the mound of flowers, an even greater hush came over the crowd. She had so many flowers to choose. Too many.

One for Safiya. One for Aida. One for Rajesh and one for Marco Santini. One for all the people in the prisons that Takara killed with her drones. One for Headmaster Bello. The longer she thought, the more people she remembered. She held back a sniffle as she took one more.

That one was for Abe. His was the death that never was, but the one that had hurt her the most.

With her arms now full, she wandered over to the rubble. A few other people had arms almost as full as hers. Her heart caught in her throat as she lowered the flowers down. Somehow, she held back the tears.

Abe dropped his flowers right beside hers and then wrapped his arm around her shoulders. Several minutes went by and more people added their flowers to the rubble. When everyone had finished, the pile of rubble had been transformed into a garden.

And then the garden turned to flame as the flowers were lit. A reminder that something beautiful had been destroyed when each of those people died. So many people gone, and nothing could ever bring them back.

The fire burned for over an hour. Imara stayed long after everyone else had gone. Abe stood with her, a steady presence at her side. When she the last of the flames had turned to embers, she walked with him to the empty alley where they had kissed the day before.

They stood without talking for a long time. No words seemed appropriate to match the thoughts in her head. She didn't try to ignore or push away the emotion like she had after Abe's jet crashed. Now she let herself feel it, each thought pricking her insides in a different way. While the grief started to settle, a new emotion stirred within her.

Santini was gone. The taggers were gone. They'd all been arrested and locked away. Defeating them had cost Nairobi greatly, but a better future lay ahead. She held onto that thought. It was one emotion that had taken her too long to feel. Hope.

Abe seemed to sense she was ready for conversation. "Do you want to work for the Kenyan police?" he asked.

She bit her lip and looked away. "I don't know. I wanted to join the police force because I wanted to make the world a better place. But now it doesn't seem like enough. Just throwing people in jail doesn't help them. I kind of want something bigger than that now. I don't want to only stop people from doing bad things, I want to help them change. I want to give them a reason to start doing good things."

With a grin and a huge burst of hope swirls, he said, "I was hoping you'd say that." He grinned even wider. "I was talking to the Kenyan Council about..." He paused, staring at her with that grin. When she leaned toward him expectantly, he finally said, "A rehabilitation center."

Her eyebrows rose as she began considering the possibility. Rehabilitation. Like a refuge, but with the power to change.

Abe started talking fast, looking at his hands as he went, as if unsure how she would take the news. "With my entrepreneur skills and your passion, I think it could be successful. They offered me a grant, which means they'll work with us, but I'll still own the business. We'll get money through donations. You can use your hila to help people understand their emotions and confront their mistakes."

"It sounds like you've thought about this a lot," she said, feeling her cheeks tighten with a smile.

He looked up from his hands and into her eyes. "I didn't want to say anything until I knew it would work, but I think it will. At least business-wise. And well... if you do it with me, I think we can change people's lives."

She chuckled to herself. "When we first met, I didn't even care about stopping the taggers. Now I want to change the world."

He popped a curl down over her forehead and gave her that look that always made her heart flutter. "You wanted it all along, you just didn't think it was possible."

"You're right," she said. "I thought saving the world was all about grand, dramatic gestures, but it's not. Saving the world is more intimate than that. It's all about people. Grand dramatic things might *cause* change over time, but it will happen because we focus on people. One at a time."

Want more from Kay L Moody?

Join her email list for exclusive news and updates. You'll also get *Gift of Glass* for free. *Lyra can crack and shatter glass, but the only people who call it a gift are the ones who don't have it.* Grab your copy with this link:
www.kaylmoody.com/gift

Author Bio

Kay L Moody is proud to be a young adult fantasy author. Her books feature exciting plots with a few magical elements. They have lots of adventure, compelling characters, and sweet romantic sub-plots. Most of her books have a dystopian flair. They include a variety of technology levels and lots of diversity in characters.

Kay lives in the western United States with her husband and four sons. She enjoys summertime, learning new things, and doing her nails. Visit her website to learn more.

www.KayLMoody.com

Author's Note

First and always foremost, thank you, reader for finishing this trilogy. These books have taken me on such a journey and it's incredible to think that I'm finally at the end of it.

I hope you enjoyed seeing more of these characters and learning how everything wrapped up. Thank you so much for sticking with me to the end.

As much as I loved writing this series, I am even more excited about my next series, The Elements of Kamdaria. This new series features a girl who can manipulate the elements. Her goals seem very straightforward, but life has a way of changing her plans.

If you enjoyed the Truth Seer Trilogy, I would be honored if you tried out my next series too.

Acknowledgements

As I sit here, I'm still in awe that I even got this far. The list of people to thank is so long and my heart is so full.

First, thank you to Kristy. You are the best beta reader and cheerleader anyone could ask for. You have been a constant even when I wasn't sure this book would make it.

Second, thank you to my wonderful writers group: Alaura, Catherine, Emily, Jamie, Marissa, Nicole, and Stephanie. You have been instrumental in getting me through all the inner turmoil I experienced while writing this book. Thank you for being there for me.

Finally, thank you most of all to my husband, Mark. Thank you for pushing me to be a better person even when it's hard. And thank you for supporting me in exactly the right ways. I still think I got the better deal.

Kay L Moody

Read on for a short story preview of Kay L Moody's next series, The Elements of Kamdaria.

THE ELEMENTS OF
KAMDARIA

ICE
AND
FIRE

A SHORT STORY BY
KAY L MOODY

ICE AND FIRE

ICE THROUGH THE FINGERS, FIRE IN THE veins.

Talise closed her eyes as she pushed the mantra through her mind, willing it to become reality within her. Controlling the element of water was easy, but ice was a whole different story. Ice required freezing temperatures and freezing caused hypothermia.

Creating a fire inside her combatted the cold but manipulating two elements at once required a level of concentration most Shapers never achieved.

Talise stared at the porcelain bowl of water sitting on the desk in front of her.

Ice and Fire.

She could do this.

With a sharp intake of breath, she used her skills as a Shaper to levitate the water from the bowl. Holding her palm upward, she moved her fingers through the air as if twisting an invisible ball.

The puddle floating water slowly started spinning. Round and around until air appeared in the center and it resembled a spinning donut. Her fingers twisted faster and soon the water shape went from donut to a thin circle of water just big enough to fit on the crown of a head.

She continued spinning the water, taking several deep breaths to prepare herself for what came next. Biting her lip, she let her fingers freeze both literally and figuratively. As the water stopped spinning, tiny ice crystals appeared around the bottom edge, freezing the water.

Talise stood her fingers straight up, willing the water to grow tines and slowly froze the tines as they grew. As the ice crown took shape, her heart thumped in her chest, reminding her of the cold.

Momentarily ignoring the crown, she breathed a fire through her veins until her heart stopped its complaining. When both the crown and the heat were just right, she used her fingers to levitate the crown through the air until it landed on her head.

After exactly five seconds, she levitated the crown off her head and dropped it back into the bowl. She melted the ice as it moved through the air, so it was nothing more than a puddle of water by the time it hit the porcelain.

A victorious smile spread on her lips as she stared back at the water. She had this competition in the bag.

"Elements in their containers please," Mrs. Dew said. She clapped her hands together, pressing her lips into a thin line. "We leave for the palace in a few minutes. Remember, the Emperor of Kamdaria will only choose one of you as Master Shaper. Whoever is chosen will receive a permanent place at the palace with the other Master Shapers. But even more importantly, that person will receive great honor that will be passed down for three generations."

In the seat to her left, she noticed Aaden mockingly opening and closing his hand while mouthing *blah blah blah*. He rolled his eyes and whispered to whoever would listen, "She says this like it's the first time we've heard it. As if this wasn't what we've been preparing for all our lives at the academy."

Talise pinned him with one of her most wicked glares, hoping he would squirm in his seat. The entire point of this competition was to win honor. If Aaden mocked his elder so openly, he had no business winning anything at all. Unfortunately, her glare did nothing but make Aaden chuckle and run a hand through his hair coolly.

"You're just afraid I'll win. Maybe you can manipulate ice, but my fire sculptures are more detailed than anything the emperor has ever seen."

She grumbled to herself the whole way to the train because like it or not, Aaden was right. In their class of twenty, she and Aaden were the only ones with any real chance of winning.

As the last person on the train, she didn't have the chance to sit anywhere except the seat in the very back. Right next to her least favorite person. Aaden didn't bother to acknowledge her existence as the train rolled away.

Instead, he held his palms out in front of him and narrowed his eyes until flames appeared above his hands. The flames quickly formed into trees, the branches growing out of the burning trunk just like real branches.

It took Talise far too much concentration to not be mesmerized as the flame trees grew in Aaden's palms. Soon, little blossoms popped out from the branches, perfectly mirroring the cherry blossoms that covered each of the trees surrounding the palace.

Forgetting her anger, Talise leaned forward to get a closer look. Aaden's detail had always been exquisite, but this surpassed anything she'd ever seen him do before.

Without warning, a few branches grew out of control until one licked her face. "Hey," she said, putting a hand to her cheek. "You burned me."

The flame trees vanished, and Aaden turned to her with a sneer. "Then use your ice shaping to heal it." He turned away from her without a trace of guilt.

Her jaw flexed as she clenched her teeth together. She had pushed ice through her fingers and against her cheek already, but what if he'd been sitting by anybody else? He should have been more careful. And besides, they weren't supposed to practice on the train anyway. Mrs. Dew had been telling them for weeks.

Just as Talise prepared to give him the lecture of the century, sharp footsteps brought her gaze to the train aisle.

"Aaden," Mrs. Dew said with no small amount of contempt. "Were you shaping on the train?"

"No," Aaden said, looking straight into Mrs. Dew's eyes.

Talise let out a huff. "You compete for honor, yet you lie to your elder like it's nothing? You don't deserve to win, no matter how detailed your fire sculptures are."

Aaden held his chin high wearing a face that declared *she* was lying, not him.

"Was he shaping, Talise?" Mrs. Dew asked her.

For a moment, her breath stilled. If he admitted to lying, he would be punished. But if he said nothing and she told the truth for him, his punishment would be much more severe. She stayed silent for a few breaths, giving him the chance to come clean. Still, he said nothing.

Clenching her jaw, she shot him with another glare. Today was too important to protect someone like Aaden. She needed to win the competition. Years spent living in the outer ring had taught her how much one good mark could change a life. She *needed* to be chosen as Master Shaper.

"He was," Talise said with her eyes to the ground.

"Aaden," Mrs. Dew said through an exasperated breath. "I told you no one was allowed to practice on the train, and you did it anyway?"

He said nothing as he stared back, never once breaking eye contact.

"Nothing?" Mrs. Dew said. "No explanation?" She did a tiny shake of the head as she turned around. Over her shoulder she said, "Then, you will be disqualified from the competition today."

"What?" Aaden said in a whisper. When Mrs. Dew kept walking, he stood up and shouted the same question. "What?"

With no response still, Aaden shouted, "You can't do that! I've been training all my life for this."

"We're here," Mrs. Dew said, now at the front of the train. "Everyone file out in an orderly fashion."

Talise's jaw had dropped, which she only noticed when she realized she'd been holding her breath. Disqualified? Aaden deserved punishment, but this?

Every ounce of sympathy drained out of her when Aaden gripped her by the shoulder. "You," he said. He didn't speak another word, but he didn't have to. Another pair of flames burned out of him, this time not from his hands, but around his irises. As his eyes burned, they said one thing as they glared at her.

Revenge.

Talise gulped and jumped from her seat, eager to put as much distance between them as possible.

* * *

Talise stood at the end of the line of students that hugged the throne room's wall. Aaden was still arguing with Mrs. Dew when the demonstrations began. She maintained that he wouldn't be able to participate.

Guilt crawled through Talise's shoulders, settling into a knot at the base of her neck. It wasn't her fault that Aaden broke the rules. She did accuse him of it, but she accused fairly. He deserved to be punished. It was his own fault for breaking the rules. But no matter how she justified it, she was partially responsible for the punishment he now bore.

Tearing her thoughts away from Aaden, Talise turned to face the emperor. Another student, Gale dropped a bundle of scarves and ribbons on the ground in front of the throne. With a timid smile, Gale used his wind shaping to lift the scarves in swirling dances around him. It wasn't the most original demonstration for a wind Shaper, but the effect was nice.

After Gale, Terra plodded over to her spot in front of the emperor. One of the imperial guards handed her a small box of dirt. She arranged several clay bowls around the dirt before she began separating the different minerals from the soil. Muscovite in one bowl, olivine in another, feldspar in a third.

While this skill was certainly practical, the demonstration wasn't as flashy as the others had been.

Terra finished with a glum expression, apparently realizing too late that she had missed out on the flash. When her bowls were cleared away, she came to join Talise at the end of the line.

"That was great," Talise whispered to her friend.

Terra's lips folded into a frown. "Don't patronize me. I know it looked stupid."

Hooking her elbow around Terra's, Talise said with a grin, "At least it's over."

"True, and I was never going to win anyway. I can't wait to see your demonstration. It's sure to win."

Talise rubbed a hand up and down her arm as the first bite of anxiety stung her.

"Oh, don't make that face. Even the emperor can't shape ice. I know he can manipulate all the elements, and he's amazing at shaping water, but ice is beyond even his abilities. He's sure to be impressed."

Talise bit her lip as she watched another student shaping a huge puddle of water into a fountain and then into a dragon. Shaping ice *would* be impressive. That was the entire reason she chose ice in the first place. But it came with risks. If she didn't get the temperature in her body just right, she could get hypothermia or frost bite. And if she warmed her body too much, even for a split second, her crown would fall apart.

Two fire shapers went next, one after the other. The first one created a circular fire that cooked two fish to perfection. The second student did fire sculptures shaped like the palace, but hers lacked the detail and control that Aaden's sculptures always showed.

Talise glanced back at him, feeling another surge of sympathy. He glared at the fire sculptures as if they were personally responsible for destroying his entire family and everything he had ever loved.

Finally, it was her turn. Talise stood tall, remembering her presentation of self was just has important as her presentation of shaping. She wore a light smile that spoke of confidence but not arrogance.

In front of the throne, she bowed deeply to the emperor until her nose brushed the ground. When she stood, he wore an expression that was difficult to decipher. His lips twitched at the corner of his mouth, almost as if they wanted to smile. But maybe only because he was laughing at her on the inside. His brows were knit close together, giving his eyes a hardened stare.

He looked… disappointed? But how could he be disappointed when she hadn't even started yet?

A thrum of fear rippled through her muscles, but she did her best to ignore it. A guard brought her a bowl of water. Before he even placed the bowl on the ground, she had the water in the air.

Her heart was beating faster than usual, which was usually an indication that her body temperature was off. In this case, it was all thanks to her nerves. She breathed in deeply as she spun the water into a thin circle.

If she couldn't rely on her heart to tell her if her internal temperature was right, then this would be even more difficult than normal. A quick smile and an even faster spin of the water made it seem like she had everything under control. Or, she hoped it looked that way, at least.

When she stiffened her fingers and brought ice through them, she breathed a fire through her arm, careful to keep it far from her wrist.

This time, as she stretched her fingers through the air, she made sure the tines growing up from the circle of water weren't just any tines. With narrowed eyes, she shaped the crown to look exactly the same as the one the emperor wore in his most famous portrait.

Three quarters of the way through its creation, the emperor recognized the crown. The crease between his eyebrows disappeared as his eyes widened. Talise wore another smile, but this one was genuine.

She felt a slice of cold through her forearm but tempered it with fire almost as quickly. When the ice crown was finished, she levitated it higher. It wouldn't land on her head this time. She had to place it on the emperor's head so he could feel that it was truly ice.

As the crown flew toward the emperor, a smile curved onto his mouth.

Now she had impressed him. The crown was inches from his head now. Close enough that he could feel how cold it was. She'd just leave it on his head for three seconds before bringing it back to the bowl.

Just as she was lowering her creation onto his head, the crown melted. With her fingers working to levitate ice, the change to water caused her to lose control. Just for a split second, but it was enough. Too much.

The water splashed all over the king, soaking his hair and shoulders. The crease reappeared between his eyebrows, even deeper than before.

Everyone in the room gasped. Though they were whispers, she still heard the comments from onlookers. "How embarrassing." "She'll never be chosen now." "What a shame. She was so much better than the others."

Talise tightened her hand into a fist. What happened? She had control. Everything was going perfectly. She ran her thumb across the tips of her fingers. Just as she suspected, they were as cold as they should have been. Colder even. She hadn't done anything that would make the crown melt.

But if it wasn't her…

While the guards hurried to supply the emperor with towels, Talise scanned the students along the wall until she found who she was looking for. Aaden held his palms out in front of him, so they were directly facing the emperor. Even more incriminating, he wore a smirk and stared back at her with fire in his eyes.

He had done this. He sabotaged her demonstration by sending a wave of heat that must have melted her ice. She wanted to burn him and freeze him all at once, but a tiny part of her couldn't help be impressed by his skill. He must have sent the world's smallest and most direct heat wave in order to do what he did.

Still, no matter how skillful, what he did was wrong. She wasn't about to let him get away with it.

Just as Talise opened her mouth to accuse him, Mrs. Dew appeared in front of her, giving a short bow to the emperor. "Your imperial highness," she said. "I have one more student who is very skilled, but he was disqualified from participation because of an incident on the train."

"Who?" Emperor Ruemon asked. Even with his wet hair slicked back, he looked regal and unperturbed.

Mrs. Dew pointed out Aaden who had somehow arranged his face to look submissive and innocent. It was a stupid act, but annoyingly convincing.

Talise wanted to scream.

The emperor snapped at one of his nearby guards and pointed at Aaden and then at her. "Take these two to the antechamber while I make my decision. Everyone else will wait in the library."

Talise barely had time to register the hand around her elbow before it began yanking her away. "Wait," Talise called out in desperation. It was bold to defy the emperor's orders, but she was desperate. "I can't leave yet. I have something to…"

Her voice trailed off as her eyes met with the emperor's. He didn't shape fire over his eyes like Aaden had, but rage burned through his facial features with even greater passion. With a steady voice, he said, "You will leave my presence without another word."

She gulped as the arm at her elbow yanked her away again. This time, she let herself be pulled away. Through a side door, they entered a small corridor that was empty but for a few servants. The corridor seemed to go on forever and only had one door in the middle of it.

The door was red with a silver moon painted on it. The imperial crest. With four heavily armed guards standing in front of the door, Talise knew the door was important. It must have led to the emperor's personal living quarters.

A few moments after passing the door, the guard pushed her into a small room that looked more like a waiting area. "Wait," Talise said, before the guard could leave. "I didn't melt the crown. It wasn't my fault. You have to tell the emperor."

The guard brushed her hand away while a look of disgust fell over his face. "You dare address your elder with such fire in your tone?"

She shrank away from him, biting her bottom lip.

"What makes you think you can disrespect me like that? Aren't you from the outer ring? You're nothing more than filth."

The door slammed shut as he left the room. A moment later, they heard the lock click. "Please," she said, slamming a fist against the wooden door. "Somebody has to listen."

"Disrespecting your elders now, are you?" Aaden said. He leaned against the stone wall with one shoulder, still wearing his ridiculous smirk. "Welcome to the dark side."

"How could you?" she said, grabbing his shoulders and slamming them against the wall before he could stop her. "Do you have any idea what you've done?"

He used one finger to push her away. "What *I* did?" he asked, raising an eyebrow. "What about what *you* did?"

She growled at him in response.

Folding his arms over his chest, he leaned toward her until his face came dangerously close to hers. "I deserved a chance to win just as much as you did. I needed this." Without warning, he turned away from her and punched the wall so hard, the stone seemed to crack on the inside. "I really needed this."

"So did I," she said. But it seemed weak compared to his argument. His whole body was alive with passion. It came out as rage, but there was something deeper to it she could just barely discern. His whole body rocked as if he had just lost the only thing that had ever really mattered.

They stared at each other for a few seconds as understanding seemed to ignite between them. Both of them had lives so much deeper than the other person knew. They'd gone to the academy together for years, but they'd never really known each other at all. In this one moment, their souls seemed to communicate to each other how important this competition really was.

"Why?" Talise asked. Maybe it was because he was so exhausted, but he opened his mouth on her command.

"My dad made a huge mistake when I was only five years old. My record is black because of him. Winning the competition meant I could erase the black. For three generations! But now?" He shook his head. "Now my future children will have a fate even worse than me all because of my dad's mistake."

His head hung. He stared at the ground while all the muscles in his face slackened. She'd never seen him look so... defeated.

"I need to live at the palace," she said. "I can't go back to where I used to live. I *can't.*"

When he looked up, he wore an expression she had never seen on him before. "Are you really from the outer ring? I know the guard said that, but I thought people in the outer ring couldn't shape."

She rubbed her hand over her arm, faster and faster, as if that would make the words seem less horrifying. "They have the biological ability to shape all four elements, just like anyone. But you're right. Most of them can't do it."

He leaned closer to her, his face softening with each of her words. "Is it really as bad as they say it is?" he whispered.

"Worse."

He gulped, and the last inkling of bravado slipped away from his face. His usual arrogance was replaced by an expression of such genuine concern, she didn't know what to think.

Turning away from him, she said, "Most people in the outer ring are malnourished. It makes their bodies weak and incapable of shaping. Not to mention, they'd have no time to perfect the skills even if they had them. They're too busy worrying about survival."

"Then how did you get to the academy? How are you so good at shaping?"

"It's a long story," she said with a sigh.

He stared back at her, waiting for more of an answer. When she didn't give one, he said, "Just tell me. We could be in here all day; it doesn't matter if it takes a long time."

Raising one eyebrow, she asked, "Are you going to tell me the huge mistake your dad made?"

"Uh, no."

"Then don't expect to hear my story either."

"Fair enough," he said with a nod. He glanced at her, but then quickly looked away. And then he did it again a second time while the tips of his ears turned red. "I'm sorry," he said. Then he reached out to her and brushed his thumb over her forearm.

Her body jolted as she instinctively pulled away. "Your skin is hot."

"Yeah." He ran his fingers through his hair with a lopsided smile. "Fire does that." His spine straightened as he looked her in the eye. "It didn't burn you, did it?"

She shook her head quickly from side to side, since she had apparently lost the ability to form words. Her skin bristled where he had touched her. On the inside, sparks went through her unlike any kind of fire she had felt before. This flame had nothing to do with elements and everything to do with touch. *His* touch. She tried to shake that thought away as he tucked his hands into his pockets.

"Aaden."

His eyes lifted at the sound of her voice. A trance seemed to come over him as he stared back at her. He seemed less interested in her eyes and more interested in her lips where his name had escaped.

"Tell them what you did," she said. "Tell them you melted my crown, and then I'll be able to leave the outer ring and live at the palace."

The trance lifted as Aaden took a step back. "No," he said. He turned away from her and said it more forcefully. "No, I'm sorry, but I can't do that. I have to defend myself to the emperor. If I defend you, you'll become Master Shaper and I'll be sent to the outer ring. I know it's bad for you, but if I help you, I'll be resigning myself and my future family to that same fate. I can't do that. I won't. I have to fight for myself."

Her body steeled as another fire surged through her, but this one felt more like rage. She clenched both of her hands into fists and immediately started pacing the floor. Of course he wouldn't help. *Of course* he wouldn't. She'd been stupid to think he ever would.

Now they would have to wait here until the emperor decided to deal with them. She just hoped when he did get there, he would be willing to listen. The longer she thought about that, the more ridiculous it seemed. Aaden wouldn't change and neither would the emperor.

In fact, maybe he didn't intend to meet with them at all. Maybe he just planned to send one of his guards to deal with them.

She paced the floor until her feet ached. There had to be a way out of this. The emperor needed good shapers. That was the whole reason for the competition in the first place. And she and Aaden were better shapers than any of the other students in their class.

All they really needed was another chance to prove themselves. Just one little chance to show the emperor what they were capable of. But if the emperor never saw them again, they'd never have that chance.

A spark of an idea took hold inside her. She bit her lip as the idea grew. It would require skilled shaping with no mistakes. That she could handle. But it also required one other thing that she really wished she could eliminate. No matter how she played through the scenarios in her head, she still needed the one thing she didn't want to use. Aaden.

Letting out a huff, she resigned herself to the inevitable. She crossed her arms over her chest and said, "I have an idea, but in order to do it, we have to work together."

Aaden looked her over from head to toe. His nose seemed to be caught mid-wrinkle, as if he was trying to decide whether or not to trust her.

Rolling her eyes, she said, "We don't have time for this. Are you in or not?"

"What's your plan?" he asked, still reluctant to commit.

He agreed to everything once he heard her idea, but he made sure to scowl as they worked. "Are you sure this is a good idea?" he asked. "They locked us in here. Don't you think we'll get in trouble for breaking out?"

"Seriously?" she said as she pulled water from the air and added it to the puddle levitating above her palm. "You care about breaking the rules now? If you were so worried about rules, you shouldn't have practiced shaping on the train."

His jaw flexed as he gave her a sideways glance. "Yeah, yeah, no need to rub that in." He narrowed his eyes at the air as he also pulled water from it. Since fire was his primary element, he had a much harder time with the process than Talise.

It took several more minutes, but eventually they had a big enough water puddle. When Talise nodded, Aaden got on his knees in front of the door and lit a fire above his palms. It took some time, but soon he had lit the bottom of the wooden door on fire.

She stood over him carefully, strategically dousing the wood with water so the smoke wouldn't get out of control.

When the smoke was eliminated, Aaden would re-light the door.

At first, the wood turned to blackened, but perfectly strong wood. After more fire and more water, it began to weaken. Eventually, some of it turned to ash. It turned out, the puddle of water wasn't big enough and they both had to stop and pull more water from the air before they could proceed.

Aaden continued lighting the door on fire, and finally, finally, they had an opening big enough for them to crawl through. He went first and helped her to her feet after she had gone through.

Her skin prickled with heat where his hand had touched her. She wished very much that she could remove the feeling and all memory of it from her body. But another part of her wished it would never go away.

She clenched her jaw at that thought. Aaden was a competitor and nothing more.

As they drew closer to the guarded door of the emperor's living quarters, Talise began pulling more water from the air. She needed a big enough puddle that would make a loud sound when she turned it to ice and smashed it against the stone wall. The distraction had to be big enough that all four guards would come running to investigate.

While she worked, Aaden stared at the fist sized piece of wood he had taken from the door. He blew embers into the wood but kept them low so it didn't smoke too much.

Finally, Talise nodded to Aaden and he blew on the wood until it glowed from the embers inside. On cue, they both threw their objects down the corridor, far from where they stood. Talise levitated the ball of ice against the wall as hard as she could. Aaden threw a fireball at the piece of wood as it flew in order to increase the smoke level.

Just as they had intended, the ice smashed against the wall just as the smoke started billowing. The effect made it sound and smell like an explosive rather than a piece of ice and a piece of wood.

They both hugged the walls as the four guards came crashing down the corridor toward the sound. The guards didn't notice them as they ran, which gave them the chance to sneak up to the red door without any interference.

"Wait," Aaden whispered as they reached the door. "Are we just going to walk in?"

Talise's patience had ended long before this moment. She glared at him and said, "It's a little late to get cold feet."

Aaden tapped his teeth together wearing fear in his eyes. "Yeah, but we're just going to waltz into the emperor's bedroom and expect him to listen to us?"

"It doesn't lead to his bedroom; it leads to his living quarters."

"How do you know that?"

Talise grabbed the door handle. Through her teeth, she said, "Are you coming or not?"

He nodded and didn't say another word as she opened the door. They entered a sitting room with a desk and a few cushy chairs. To the right, a long hallway led to several different doors.

"Don't you think it's a little weird the door wasn't locked?" he asked as he shut the door behind him.

Considering his question, she locked the door, then nodded. "If we lock it, they won't know we got in."

Aaden rolled his shoulders back and closed his eyes as moved his head side to side to stretch his neck. All his fear seemed to have been forgotten as he stretched and moved. After a moment, he opened his eyes and cracked his knuckles. "We should practice. How long do you think we have before the emperor comes in here?"

She shrugged. "I have no idea, but you're right. We do need to practice. We have to make this bigger and better than anything the emperor has ever seen, or he'll never listen to us."

Without a word, they both raised their hands and started shaping. As they had previously decided, they both grew trees out of their palms with little cherry blossoms growing out of the branches. Aaden's trees were fire and Talise's were ice.

When they had both grown their trees, they moved their palms closer together and let the trees sit directly beside each other. The flames licked at the ice, forcing Talise to push even more cold through her fingers than usual. She had to compensate it with fire that went right up to her wrists.

With a deep breath, they began the next stage. This would be the most difficult shaping either of them had ever attempted. Aaden let a one flame branch move through the ice tree until it seemed that the flame was coming off the ice trunk, not the fire trunk.

Then, Talise moved one ice branch, careful to keep the ice tree in tact while also levitating the one ice branch until it looked like it was coming off the flame trunk. When she had moved it into position, both she and Aaden let out a breath of relief. But this was just the beginning.

Beads of sweat lined Talise's brow as she added more heat to compensate for the added freezing temperature in her hands. She and Aaden took turns moving their branches from one tree to the next. Each one became more difficult as her need to compensate for the heat was constantly counteracted by the need to keep her body a reasonable temperature.

When they each only had one branch left to move, she was vaguely aware of a noise coming from nearby. The cause of it remained a mystery as her need to concentrate overtook all her other senses.

At last, they had moved all their branches so the ice trunk had only flame branches growing out of it and the flame trunk wore ice branches.

She and Aaden both heaved a sigh, but their relief was short lived. From the doorway, a familiar voice said, "How did you manage—"

Both Talise and Aaden dropped their hands in alarm. Water splashed around their ankles as they turned to face Emperor Ruemon. He *did* seem to be impressed by their shaping, but more than that he seemed angry. Much too angry.

Dropping his head into his palm, the emperor said, "What are you doing here?"

"We had to show you our abilities," Aaden said, finding his voice much faster than Talise. She was still busy watching that crease between the emperor's eyebrows grow deeper by the second.

"What did you think would happen?" the emperor asked with a frown. "Did you think you'd sneak into my private quarters, the most secure part of the palace, and then I'd suddenly be interested in your shaping?" He snapped and two guards appeared at his side.

"You deserve three black marks for what you've done. Maybe a life in the dungeon as well." He squeezed the bridge of his nose and let out a sigh. "One of you has to be punished for this, and one of you has to become my next Master Shaper because the rest of your class was pathetic compared to you two."

Talise gulped, feeling the color drain from her face. The emperor eyed them both for a moment and time seemed to stand still.

Finally, he pointed to Aaden and said, "Lock him up. And use the fire gloves so he can't escape again."

That meant she had gotten Master Shaper after all. Except.

Aaden would be punished and thrown in the dungeon. A lump hardened in her throat as the guards put him chains. They dropped red gloves over his hands while a sense of finality washed over her.

She stared, but swallow after swallow did nothing to help. He had to fight for himself and she had to fight for herself. That's what they decided. They would only work together to show the emperor their abilities, but whatever happened, they didn't owe the other person anything.

But she never imagined this.

As the guards forced Aaden to his feet, a strangled cry left her lips. "No. Please, your highness. Breaking out of the room was my idea. Aaden didn't want to do it, but I convinced him." With a sniff, she forced the final words out of her mouth. "If you're going to punish somebody, punish me. Not him."

She glanced up to see the emperor staring at her with a contemplative look. But it was nothing to the look Aaden wore. His jaw had dropped. He stared at her like he had never really seen her in his entire life.

"Fine," Emperor Ruemon said, his voice steady. "Then you will be punished and sent to the dungeon instead. Aaden will be my newest Master Shaper."

He snapped and the guards moved so fast, she barely had time to blink before shackles were clapped over her wrists. They fitted blue gloves over her hands and started pushing her through the door before three seconds had passed.

"Wait," Aaden said, blinking furiously. The moment the guards removed his shackles, he ran both hands through his hair. The blinking never stopped as he looked side to side. His words failed him.

The emperor stood patiently for only a few seconds. Then he snapped at his guards and they started pulling her out the door.

"No, stop!" Aaden shouted. "I…" He gulped and pulled his hands into fists. "I melted her crown. In the throne room, it was my fault you got all wet. I wanted revenge because I got disqualified from the competition. But this was my fault. All of it."

"I see," the emperor said. He stared at them while all the hardness in his face drifted away. "It seems you both possess honor, which is the greatest trait of all. Since you are also two of the greatest shapers I've even seen, I think no one will complain if I choose two Master Shapers this year."

Talise narrowed her eyes as the guards removed the shackles from her wrists. Her brain worked double speed, trying to make sense of everything that had just happened.

"This was a test?" she asked. "You threatened to send one of us to the dungeon as a test?"

"Are you questioning my methods?" the emperor said with an eyebrow raised.

"Of course not, your highness."

Emperor Ruemon waved to one of his guards. "Take them back to the antechamber, but this time leave the door unlocked." He looked at Talise and Aaden now. "You will have to help fix that door, but that should be punishment enough. Someone will be by in a bit to show you to your new living quarters."

He snapped, and the guards led them out of the room before they could say another word. Once they were back in the antechamber, Talise paced around the room with wild excitement. "I can't believe this. I never expected us both to become Master Shapers. This is better than I could have ever dreamed. Now we both win. Now—"

She stopped mid-step when Aaden suddenly appeared in front of her. His eyes were soft now and his breath warm. "Talise," he said, reaching out until his fingers wrapped over her hand.

Everything inside her seemed to freeze all at once, but in a delightfully heated way.

Aaden gulped before he spoke again. He kept his eyes away from her face, staring at their hands instead. "Thank you for…"

He squeezed her hand and the heat seeped through her skin so fast, she worried it would burn her insides. Except, she had never appreciated heat more than she did in this moment.

"I'll never forget what you did for me today," he said. Finally, he looked into her eyes and a thousand sparks seemed to ignite within her. She had a feeling that neither of them would forget. Not ever.

If you enjoyed this short story, don't miss Ice Crown (The Elements of Kamdaria Book 1)!